Amy Myers was born in Kent, where she lives near the North Downs. For many years a director of a London publishing company, she is now a full-time writer. Married to an American, she lived for some years in Paris, where, surrounded by food, she first dreamed up her Victorian chef detective series starring Auguste Didier. He was followed by two contemporary series, before she returned to the Victorian age with her chimney sweep Tom Wasp novels. She is also currently writing a 1920s series featuring another chef Nell Drury, and is the author of historical romance and suspense novels. Tom Wasp and her other sleuths also appear in short stories.

PRAISE FOR THE TOM WASP SERIES:

'Tom Wasp is one of the most engaging characters I've encountered in years' – Ellen Keith, *Historical Novels Review*

PRAISE FOR AMY MYERS:

'Myers always turns out a polished tale' – *Library Journal*

Also By Amy Myers

TOM WASP AND THE SEVEN DEADLY SINS

AMY MYERS

ENDEAVOURQUILL

AN ENDEAVOUR QUILL PAPERBACK

First published by Endeavour Quill in 2019

Endeavour Quill is an imprint of Endeavour Media Ltd
Endeavour Media, 85-87 Borough High Street,
London, SE1 1NH

ISBN 978-1-911445-69-2

Typeset using Atomik ePublisher from Easypress Technologies

Printed and bound in Great Britain by
Clays Ltd, Elcograf S.p.A.

www.endeavourmedia.co.uk

Table of Contents

Author's Note

Tom Wasp relates his own story in this novel, and as he's a chimney sweep in London's east end in the reign of Queen Victoria, his use of English is sometimes idiosyncratic. Luckily, as a climbing boy during his childhood, he mistakenly landed in the hearth of Lady Beazer, while sweeping her chimneys one day. Taking an interest in him, she paid for his schooling.

As his scribe, I thank my agent, Sara Keane of Keane Kataria Literary Agency, for her invaluable help and all the time and effort she has poured into Tom Wasp's story. A professional chimney brush can sweep away countless specks of soot where these have gathered unnoticed, so thank you, Sara. My thanks are also due to the wonderful team at Endeavour Quill and the late Dorothy Lumley, who seized on my idea of a chimney sweep sleuth and encouraged me to write about him.

At the end of this novel, Tom Wasp has provided 'A Literary Journey', adding details to the journey that he took in this novel as the plot unfolded, and I have added a historical note to differentiate fact from fiction.

CHAPTER ONE

A Grim Discovery

'I won't go there, guvnor.' Ned was looking at me defiantly, swinging his soot bag over his shoulder. I could see him trembling, though.

'It's only a boy carved out of stone, Ned,' I said gently.

I'm Tom Wasp, master chimney sweep, and Ned's my chummy, that meaning my apprentice; he's twelve or so — I've never known his true age. He's a lad who can face with confidence the boozed-up matelots in east London's docklands and tell 'em what he thinks of them.

I can't be sure why he's wary of the Boy of Panyer Alley, as he's known, but I can guess. The Boy isn't doing any harm, just sitting on a basket of bread — but Ned believes he's astride a rooftop, looking at his foot burnt by the chimney he's just climbed up. Ned was a climbing boy before I rescued him from that fate and he finds it hard to face up to anything that reminds him of those days. I was once a climbing boy too, and my bowed legs haven't forgotten what it feels like to wriggle up a narrow chimney that's sometimes as little as ten inches wide.

'Stir your stumps, Ned. We won't go down the alley if you don't fancy it.'

Our first job of the day should have been in Newgate Street at the far end of the alley, but instead we'd go straight to Dolly's, the famous chophouse just off Paternoster Row near St Paul's Cathedral in London City. In addition to sweeping their chimneys, I had another, more private, mission there today.

On a cold Thursday morning in April at the first signs of dawn, when we chimney sweeps have already been hard at work for an hour or two, Her Majesty Queen Victoria's London can be a fearsome place or a beautiful one, in this year of 1864, depending on how you look at this grand old lady of cities. St Paul's Churchyard, which we had just left, gives its name not only to the yard itself but also to the noisy, busy streets that encircle its railings. It was already packed with workers marching to their posts for the day and carriages clattering over the granite stones with such urgency you'd think old London was afire again. It's a time of day I love, there being a sense of purpose as the wheels of the city whirl into action.

With the great cathedral of St Paul's towering behind us and streaks of gold creeping into the grey sky, I was inclined to count my blessings, but Ned is young and fixed in his ways. And today his way wasn't going to be past the Boy in Panyer Alley.

As we made our way along Paternoster Row to Dolly's, workers were already hurrying along together with most of the horses and delivery vans in London. The Row, now flourishing with booksellers and publishers, was well known for its silken cloth in the old days, when the diarist Mr Pepys was a customer, but that was before the Great Fire of 1666. His Majesty King Charles himself came to help extinguish that, but he arrived too late to stop much of the Row and St Paul's itself from being burnt down, including an old tavern called The Castle. That's where Dolly's Chop House now stands.

'I'll see about a pie for you once we've done our job at Dolly's,' I reassured Ned and his face brightened.

Dolly's, famous for its mutton chops and steaks, is in Queen's Head Passage, which like Panyer Alley, runs from the Row through to Newgate Street. The Queen of this passage isn't our own Queen Victoria, but Queen Anne, whose picture is in one of the chophouse windows. Dolly's has been there for a great many years, first as Dolly's Tavern, then Dolly's Coffee House, and for as long as I can recall, as a chophouse and hotel.

We trundled our handcart under the arch in the passage and past Dolly's main entrance. All was silent, and the dawn chill still struck at our bodies. At the far end of the building is the open gateway to Dolly's small yard with outhouses, three stables and room for several diners' carriages. In daytime it's a bustling, lively area, but before Dolly's has come to life it looks dismal and unwelcoming.

But it wasn't so now. In the still greyish light as we entered the yard I saw something ahead that made me look twice — and then again. The nearest outhouse to us was the log store. Its door stood partly open, but protruding beyond it I saw what looked like a foot. An old shoe? No. The wrong angle for that. A gentleman of the road still sleeping it off?

'You stay here, Ned,' I said sharply.

But he'd seen it too and, being a curious lad, he left the handcart and ran forward, with me hobbling after him. My legs make running hard.

'It's a bloke. Looks like he's kicked the bucket,' he called out to me matter-of-factly.

Despite his strange dislike of the Boy in the alley, Ned has no fear of the dead, living as we do between London's docklands and the old rookery of the Nichol where I was born. Poverty and brawling there bring many a man to an early grave — and their women, too.

As I reached the log store, I saw the man lying, half in the store and half sprawled in the doorway, eyes staring sightlessly, blood on his face, tongue protruding from his mouth and rope around his now purple neck. He'd been garrotted. Even Ned was wincing at the sight and, as for me, I was torn with revulsion, pity and shock.

This was no tipsy matelot wandered in here by mistake, no tramp. The dress coat lay open, a silk top hat had either rolled or been thrown away. Such was the fearful state of his face that at first I did not recognise him. This was a gentleman of quality, who had probably dined here last night, and he was as dead and cold as the dawn he had never seen.

Worse, it was someone I soon recognised.

'Ned,' I said, 'we passed a peeler in the Row. You fetch him.'

Off he ran, which left me time to look more carefully at this poor man. I would have to break the news at Dolly's. No one seemed to be stirring yet, although kitchen maids at least must be around. Most on my mind was how to tell Mrs Clara Pomfret, who is by way of being a friend of mine and is the licensee and hotelier of Dolly's.

Clara is what I would call a comfortable lady and not just in size. She's comfortable to be with, to talk to, to rely on. Being a sweep, I don't have lady friends unless they are sweeps themselves — (only one or two of them in the whole of London) — or sweeps' families. Apart from our smell being a deterrent, I don't seek ladies' company out of respect for my own good woman, who died these ten years back. But Clara is different. The sort you can put your arms around for comfort, for support, or for the sheer joy of life.

She's about my age — which I think is about thirty-seven or eight — and has one of those faces that lights up like a sunbeam when she smiles, which is nearly all the time. How would she take this news, however?

The dead man was Mr Arnold Harcourt. I'd once seen him here at Dolly's, where the Tarlton Ordinary Club meets once a month for

4

supper on a Wednesday evening. He could have been attending that last night — was he robbed as he left?

Even as that thought passed through my mind, my eye fell on his elegant albert chain and fob; the bulge in the pocket suggested the watch still lay within. Robbed? No thief would overlook *them*, nor the silk top hat, which was also worth a shilling or two.

I've seen death before many times and he never comes alone. Hidden from our sight are all the mourning faces, all the tears that the rest of the world never sees as it goes about its daily business. In the shadows sob the wives, the children, the friends — and all the rest of us mortals who listen for the tolling bell of death. Sometimes even our Lord must weep when he sees what we're doing to ourselves down on this earth. He meant it to be clean and beautiful like Victoria Park on a summer afternoon, and it's our job to keep it as best we can for Him like the chimneys that Ned and I sweep so hard.

In the dawning light, I heard the eerie sound of the peeler's rattle. Ned had found him and the City of London Police would soon be with us.

Not one but two peelers very shortly arrived, looking most officious in their City of London Police blue coats and red and white cap bands. I stood there while they cast a brief look at the victim, and then concentrated suspiciously on me.

'What you doing here?'

'Appointment to sweep the chimneys.' Having some experience of this sort of situation, I knew I had to speak quickly. 'Will the Scotland Yard Detective Department be taking this case?'

They looked puzzled. 'What for?' said one of them. 'We've nabbed you already, sweepie.'

Me? My heart sank to the bottom of my old boots. I had feared this, from past experience. 'On what charge?' I enquired.

'Robbery and murder.'

Ned looked at me nervously, so I gave him an encouraging smile.

'Why would we stay here and report the crime if we did it?' I tried to ask reasonably. 'I'd have taken this.' I pointed to the albert and its watch.

This puzzled them even more. Then one of them came up with the answer: 'You ain't yet snatched it off him.'

I saw Ned fidgeting, and he might say something I would regret, so I said even more firmly, 'Ask for Sergeant Williamson or Constable Peters of the Metropolitan Police Detective Department. They'll know me.'

They chortled. 'You an old lag then, sweepie?'

Nevertheless, doubt began to creep into their faces. 'This,' I said, 'is a gentleman of importance. You don't want to do nothing wrong where he's concerned. Your sergeant wouldn't care for that.'

They immediately saw my point, and while they waited for this sergeant to come, I requested permission to break the news to Dolly's, where there were now clearly people stirring. It was refused, but Ned took it upon himself to go into the hotel in my place. Ned has seen too many dramas at the penny gaffs for him to miss this chance of taking part in one, and from the shrieks I heard from the kitchen it was clear he was in fine form. That worried me, because of Clara — I'd like to have broken the news myself.

As it was, she came rushing out after a few minutes, a shawl thrown hastily over her black bombazine working dress and her hair askew.

'What's going on here, Tom? Ned's shouting about a murder.' Then she took in the presence of the peelers, who had fortunately had the thought of throwing two sacks over Mr Harcourt's body and were on guard standing by it.

'You knew him, Clara,' I said quietly, hoping they wouldn't hear our conversation. 'It's Mr Harcourt.'

Mr Harcourt had run Harcourt's Antiquarian Bookstore, not far from Dolly's and further westwards along the Row, and he had lived in the rooms above it. I'd cleaned the chimneys there once; I didn't take to him, but I can't afford to turn work down. I need my six or seven chimneys a day if I'm to feed and house Ned and myself.

'Him?' she exclaimed in horror. 'Lawks a mussy, Tom, what happened? He was here last night. The Ordinaries were up in the coffee room having their usual high jinks. Could one of them —' She broke off, but it was clear what she had been going to say.

'We'll hope not, Clara.'

'What am I going to do about opening up, Tom?' she moaned. 'We're usually open at seven and it's nearly six now.'

I had no answer to that, as I saw the sergeant arrive, and behind him more peelers. Now it was beginning: the questions, the step by step digging into the darkness to unravel the mysteries of the murder of Mr Harcourt — who had been the subject of my private mission here today.

*

I waited in Clara's 'greeting room', her name for the ground floor room that serves as her office. It is quite unlike any office I've ever seen. Comfortable armchairs and tea are what I associate with that room. Even today, while we waited to be summoned yet again by the sergeant, it had a peaceful feel about it, an island in the middle of a stormy sea. It had been ten o'clock before the sergeant gave Clara his permission to open Dolly's; by that time the body had been removed, and I had been questioned several times as to the reason for my presence (which I gave only as chimney sweeping) and my movements on arrival at Dolly's. Ned had been comforted with pies and muffins, and Clara had been interrogated too. That had not been easy for her.

7

She had completed her toilette and changed into a plum red dress swept back in a bustle that made her look so imposing that she rivalled the Queen herself. She knew she looked a stunner, so that had helped her through the sergeant's inquisition.

'Mr Harcourt was here last night, Tom. I had to tell the sergeant that.'

And I had to tell her about my private mission. 'Clara, I was asked only yesterday morning to warn you about Mr Harcourt.'

She looked at me sharply. 'Who by?'

She hadn't asked me *what about*, I noticed.

'Mr Phineas Snook, the dancing clown.' I call Phineas a clown but he's more one of these old-time fools I've seen in pictures. Singing, dancing and playing the pipe are what he's best at, though he jests as well. 'He's by way of being a friend of mine,' I explained, 'and being at his trade entertaining all day, he couldn't come himself.'

Clara looked at me gravely. 'I know Phineas Snook, Tom. What did he want to warn me about?'

'He's sweet on Hetty, Clara, and she was the subject of attentions from Mr Harcourt —' *careful, Tom*, I told myself — 'which she is too shy to resist.' Shy did not describe Hetty, who is Clara's daughter and one of the three lady waiters at Dolly's; she's a pretty lass and innocent at heart but aware of her own charms. I had to tread as carefully as if I was edging along a chimney flat.

'Arnold Harcourt,' Clara said heavily, 'was a lecher, but Hetty didn't see that. What's she going to say now? She thinks I was jealous, wanting him for myself, me being a widow.'

That shocked me. 'You wouldn't, Clara. Not you.'

'No. I had my Simon. He was enough for me, though he's been gone these ten years.'

She hesitated. 'You don't think *he* did it, do you?'

I knew what she was thinking. 'Phineas? He wouldn't know which end of the knife to use for such a deed. He's one for life is Phineas, not death. He's a dreamer not a doer.'

'Remember Harcourt was here last night, Tom, dining with the Tarlton Ordinaries. He didn't hide his liking for Hetty. William knew about that.'

William White, head waiter here, is sweet on Hetty like Phineas, although not as humble as Phineas over his chances of winning her heart. William is a pleasant lad, but ambitious. Being a waiter at Dolly's is a prized job, and the price Clara charges these waiters for the privilege of the job (as is the usual arrangement) proves it. The waiters pay her this fee and live on their tips; they have to work hard for them so chops and steaks flash off the gridiron and on to the tables quicker than a pie disappears down Ned's throat.

'How many Ordinaries were here last night, Clara?' She had explained to me that this group, composed of local booksellers and publishers, met in memory of an old English clown called Richard Tarlton who lived in the reign of the great Queen Elizabeth.

'Eight. They're a weird bunch, Tom. All so merry with each other when they're here, and yet I wouldn't put anything past any of them if it didn't suit their purpose.'

'Sounds of discord last night?'

'I couldn't say. William was better placed than I was. I wasn't there except when Maria Fortescue arrived. I couldn't stop her from running up the stairs to burst in on them.'

The Ordinaries were privileged in having the grand coffee room upstairs kept for their visits. In that room writers like Mr Goldsmith and Dr Johnson ate and drank, and a splendid portrait of the original Dolly herself hangs over the fireplace, painted by Mr Gainsborough many years ago.

'I could hear them though,' Clara continued, 'roaring out all the old chants as they always do. *He that will an alehouse keep* is their regular one,' she added scathingly. 'Let them try, say I. It's not all porter and songs. Anyway, there they were with pipes and tabors as usual, before they begin what they call the *proceedings*. When Maria pushed her way in, I knew there'd be trouble. A mere woman interrupting them!'

I had to laugh at that. 'I've met more mere women who run businesses like you do, Clara, than I've seen men at a dog fight.'

She accepted the compliment and beamed. 'Maria insisted on joining them. I couldn't stop her. But for Mr Harcourt to end like that. Garrotted. She couldn't have done that herself.'

I knew of Mrs Maria Fortescue. I'd met her once and felt sorry for her. She was an anxious sort of lady. A proper Miss Twitchy, nose into everything. She was Mr Harcourt's clerk in his bookstore, and it's said more than that. The Tarlton Ordinary Club is for gentlemen only of course, so no women would be permitted to join them, except for service — and then it has to be Hetty.

'That caused a to-do all right,' Clara continued. 'When they threw Maria out, I said she could wait in my parlour till Mr Harcourt left.' She hesitated. 'I shouldn't say this, Tom, but we both know there's talk of her being Mr Harcourt's bit of fluff. A week or two ago he gave her the boot from his bed. She went on working in the bookstore but then yesterday he gave her the boot on that score too. That was why she was so upset.'

'Mr Harcourt was a busy man where the ladies are concerned.'

'Indeed he was. And there's worse. We don't see her in the Row, but I heard only yesterday that there's a Mrs Harcourt very much alive, whereas he let Maria think he was a widower. Mrs Harcourt doesn't live here in London, for they have a home in Essex.'

I began to feel Mr Harcourt was even less likeable than Phineas' warning had suggested. I hardly dared ask this question therefore: 'Did Mrs Fortescue leave Dolly's with him?'

'Yes, but not alone,' she answered, to my relief. 'The Ordinaries were the last customers here. Only William was left of the waiting staff, apart from Hetty. And Jericho in the kitchen. He likes to make sure all's tidy ready for the morning before he leaves. All the Ordinaries left through the front entrance about midnight. Four of them seemed in a group which went out first and close behind them were the other three; Mr Harcourt was supported by Mr Splendour and Mr Manley, with Mr Timpson behind them. I don't know what happened to them then, except that when Maria heard them leaving, she was out of the parlour and down the stairs as quick as a glass of gin on a bad day.'

Last winter I'd heard the Tarlton Ordinaries' songs. I'd listened to them as the sounds floated across the still of Queen's Head Passage. The background noise from the nearby busy streets was quiet that evening, and for once the voices filled the air not with raucous chants but with sweet song. *Come away, come away Death*, I remember, which was a melancholy tune that touched the heartstrings. And now death had struck again.

I did not know the three gentlemen Clara had mentioned, but she went on to explain. 'Mr Algernon Splendour — now there's a nice polite gentleman for you, for all that he and Mr Harcourt must have been at each other' throats, both trading in old books and their bookstores being opposite each other in the Row. They must all be rivals, although they pretend they're friends. Mr Manley is eager for new books to publish; he's expecting another Sir Walter Scott to come along. Mr Timpson — well, he publishes anything that makes him a penny or two, from Bible tracts to three volume novels. All these books around now — who in the world has time to read them all? The Tarlton Ordinaries don't talk about the penny dreadfuls though, only about finding another William Shakespeare and making their fortunes.'

'What reason might any of them have to kill Mr Harcourt, Clara?' It seemed to me that Clara had even more to worry about than the Tarlton Ordinaries being suspects; what if any of Dolly's staff had cause to want him dead?

'You never know with those who deal with books, especially old ones,' Clara said darkly. 'People get very upset over them, particularly where money's involved.'

'It seems to me that of the seven deadly sins, greed for money is one of those committed most often.'

'What about lechery, Tom? Arnold Harcourt knew about *that* all right. William complained to me about how he behaved to Hetty and as a result he insisted on serving the Ordinaries last night. It's normally Hetty. William told me that Mr Harcourt was boasting that like Richard Tarlton, lechery was his favourite sin.'

It's hard to go through life and not fall into the pit of one of those seven sins, but to my mind the trick is how far you fall and how quickly you pull yourself out of it.

'Even so, would one of the Ordinaries rush after Mr Harcourt last night and kill him?'

'There's Flint's mob,' she answered me soberly. 'He might have run up against one of them.'

That was a chilling thought. Flint's mob operates both east of London City and in the west of it. It is no ordinary gang. Flint himself is the putter up, the organiser, the brains, and his mob falls into two parts. The first is a swell mob, whose members dress in a style that won't make them stand out in fashionable areas. This is run by Flint's deputy Lairy John, who is as cocksure as his name suggests. The second part is the one that does the dirty work, run by his other deputy, Slugger Joe. A nastier man you could never meet.

Both Slugger and Lairy are known faces, however. Flint is not. No one, save his two deputies, knows who he is. Murder and violence are tools of Flint's trade. He prides himself on the quality of his victims and those who stand in the way of his obtaining a rich prize are likely to find themselves removed with the assistance of Slugger and his pals.

'You mean one of them might have hired Flint's services,' I said. That was the way it worked with Flint.

It was at this point that Ned came rushing into the room, pie crumbs round his mouth. 'The big pigman's here,' he cried breathlessly, 'pigmen' being the less than polite word for policemen used round our way. 'Asking for you, guvnor.'

'Here we go,' Clara said sombrely, rising to her feet to greet the new arrivals. She is not a lady to be scared of the police, but this murder on her very own premises had been a great shock.

I could hear the tread of boots along the passageway. And then they were with us. I could see from his uniform that the high ranking one was a senior divisional inspector. The City of London police does its own detection work and values highly its independence from the Metropolitan Police, protecting the square mile of the City into which St Paul's and Paternoster Row fall. Although I knew something of the Detective Department at Scotland Yard, the City of London Police were new to me.

Inspector Harvey, as his sergeant announced him, was a small man in height for a policeman, but with eyes that darted everywhere. They didn't even blink as they passed over me, a chimney sweep, but travelled around the room like one of my machine brushes around the chimney gathering up specks of soot. I wondered what soot the inspector was collecting about the death of Arnold Harcourt.

'You're the sweep that found the body?' the inspector asked me pleasantly enough, and when I agreed he added: 'Hairbrine Court is some way from here. It's Metropolitan Police territory. What are you doing here?'

'Earning an honest sixpence,' I said, impressed that he knew where Hairbrine Court was. When I'd given my address to the sergeant earlier, he'd looked as puzzled as a mudlark in a desert. The inspector gave a sort of harrumph, asked me a few more questions, and observed that no ordinary robber would have left the chain and watch behind.

I waited for him to accuse me of wanting to steal them, but after informing me that he might want to talk to me again, he turned to Clara. 'Mrs Pomfret, I'm told by his wife that Mr Harcourt dined here last night.'

'His wife is in London?' Clara asked in surprise.

'Her husband had asked Mrs Harcourt to come up from the country this morning and she arrived an hour or two ago.'

'Yes, he lived nearby and was a member of the Tarlton Ordinaries Club that meets here regularly,' she replied. She went on to explain this gathering to the inspector who listened intently, but then switched his approach.

'Do you know a Phineas Snook?'

*

That troubled me, as Ned and I made our way home, since the inspector had said no more about why my friend Phineas was of interest. How could he have anything to do with this affair? The inspector had informed

14

me that I could take my leave and I had, unwillingly, taken it. Apart from telling him about Phineas, would Clara reveal her knowledge about Mr Harcourt's lady friends and his behaviour towards Hetty?

I was anxious to give Phineas the news about Mr Harcourt's murder before he learned it from the evening newspaper editions, but Ned and I took the handcart back to Hairbrine Court before I set off to find Phineas. Our home, tucked away in the crowded and poor area behind the Tower of London, is a fair way to walk from the Row, and by now I would have expected Ned to be champing at the bit to tell the world about the murder.

'I reckon that Boy knows something about it,' he said at last, as we rounded the last corner into Blue Anchor Yard.

I didn't pick up his meaning at first, and then I realised what still worried him. 'He's a carving on stone, Ned. How can he have anything to do with Mr Harcourt's death?'

He didn't reply, and as we went through the entry into Hairbrine Court I had something else to think about. Our rooms are up a flight of stairs inside the house to the right of the court, and there was a young peeler waiting by our door. It was Constable Peters from the Detective Department at Scotland Yard. It was brave of him to come here, for peelers aren't a welcome sight, especially for the villainous part of the population of the East End, which can sense his line of work from his general bearing. Even if he's not in uniform — and he wasn't today — his trade makes him stick out. Unlike most peelers, though, Constable Peters has a cherubic face, all pink and usually smiling. He's clever too. My word, he is.

His face brightened. 'Good afternoon, Mr Wasp.'

The constable met his wife partly thanks to me and I appreciate his resulting goodwill greatly. He is tall and slim and looks like a gawky schoolboy, but it's a mistake to think of him that way.

'I wanted to see you,' he added awkwardly. That was already clear to me, as no one would wander into Hairbrine Court if they didn't have to.

'How's Mrs Peters?' I asked.

He grinned. 'Well, thank you, Mr Wasp. As is young Master Bertie Peters.'

Now that was a delight to hear. I had no idea that his family had grown and talking about Master Bertie's teething problems quite took my mind off why his proud father might be here.

'Would it be the murder at Dolly's brings you this way?' I asked at last, not thinking it could be, since it was out of the Metropolitan's jurisdiction.

'No. What's that about?' he asked, looking most interested as I told him.

'I wish I had been there for that,' he then said. He looked rather wistful as he likes interesting cases. 'But it's the Flint mob, Mr Wasp. Any ideas on where it's operating at present? One of our narks tells us the mob's got something big on.'

'I haven't heard.' I hesitated, as I was about to tread on delicate ground. 'Can't the Rats help?'

Mrs Jemima Peters was the daughter of the former Rat mob leader, who is thought to be in retirement, his reputation having suffered through having a peeler as a son-in-law. Despite this, his mob is still active, although it goes underground if Flint's in town. We're not all criminals this side of Bow Bells of course. Crime's like soot. The harder we sweep the chimney, the more soot comes down, but light a fire or two and up it springs again. There's one difference with crime, though. Once we've sieved it, I can sell my soot to the nightsoil men who sell it on to smallholders outside the city who bring their produce back to feed the hungry of London, so it all works out for the good. Crime isn't like that.

The constable shook his head and I had a thought. 'If Flint is mixed up with the chophouse murder,' I suggested, 'might that be your big job?'

His face brightened. 'It's possible. Don't see gents like those book-sellers dirtying themselves with physical blood on their hands. Tell me more about it.'

I suggested he come up to our rooms for a chat, assuring him that he would be in no danger from our fellow tenants. Fortunately, Ned and I are known to have associated with peelers in the past, so our unusual behaviour in this respect is occasionally tolerated by our neighbours.

The first thing that Constable Peters said as he entered our rooms was: 'Do you know someone called Phineas Snook?'

CHAPTER TWO

Enter Phineas Snook

It was well into the afternoon by the time I was able to look for Phineas Snook. As Ned and I have to earn our daily bread, I'm grateful for regular jobs and have one in nearby Dock Street with two chimneys that have no fires burning at this time of day. I kept thinking of Phineas though, as the patterers would be shouting out the news of Mr Harcourt's death by tomorrow morning at the latest and more likely this evening. I needed to speak to him before that.

Constable Peters had unwittingly given me troubling news. He had told me that the City of London Police had asked Scotland Yard if they knew Phineas — he was wanted in connection with a case of theirs. Mr Harcourt's murder, as I had feared. I had to find Phineas and be quick about it.

On a bright spring day such as this, he might be still a-dancing but I decided to try his home first, as that's close to Dock Street. Phineas sings, plays and dances wherever he pleases and he lodges with his mother, the Widow Snook. She lives the far side of Wellclose Square — not in one of the smart houses, but one hanging on their coat-tails in a yard off Pell Street.

Phineas had told me that his father died of drink two years back. Widows have a hard time of it in this part of the world, most of them forced to take in laundry or some other ill-paid tasks until, worn out with labour, they die themselves. The Widow Snook was no exception, although to my mind the laundry she takes in is likely to come out as dirty as it reaches her. She has a smile for everyone who brings her business, but that seldom means there's one inside as well. Life is a battle and one she wages grimly. It was from his father that Phineas inherited his dancing skills. The day Widow Snook dances I'll eat my topper.

'Well now,' she greeted me, her black skirt rustling with disapproval at the sight of my sooty face. No smile, as I brought no laundry with me. She's a large lady and her sturdy figure filled the doorway. English is an obliging language with its twists and turns. I'd call Clara *plump* but Mrs Snook *sturdy*, yet they're both about the same size. It's a matter of yielding. Clara's figure invites you forward, Mrs Snook's, smile or not, suggests you stay right where you are. It did so today. 'If it ain't Mr Wasp,' she continued. 'Run out of chimneys, have you? No use coming here.'

'I'm seeking Phineas, Mrs Snook,' I said peaceably.

The smile disappeared. 'That rascal? He's gorn. Lives at Mrs Tutman's.'

Mrs Tutman runs a lodging house in John's Hill, which is near the docks down off the Ratcliffe Highway — or St George's Street, as it's now been named in the hope of people forgetting its past murderous history. To us who live here it stays the same old Highway, close to which several murders of innocent householders had taken place within less than two weeks. For all it was over fifty years ago, it's still talked about round here, even though there has been many a killing here since.

'Phineas being so fond of you I'm surprised to hear that, Mrs Snook.'

The scowl deepened. 'He's no good that one. Now he's flush, he's no time for his old mother. I heard he took an evening job at the gaff.'

By that she would mean the penny gaff along the Highway near Paddy's Goose, the notorious pub Shadwell way that sees more crime than the Old Bailey. Penny gaffs are the poor man's theatres, where actors stride the stage as nobly as in London's Haymarket, save that they get through more plays more quickly. Why, you can see four performances including a whole play by Mr William Shakespeare and be in and out of there in half an hour. It's true that many of the young audience have other things in mind than watching plays, but nevertheless a job there is good for a street clown like Phineas. It's not enough for him to be rolling in riches though.

'Always after a tanner is Phineas,' his mother continued, sniffing. 'We were grand folk once until his father came down in the world. Phineas' granddad played with Grimaldi, but Phineas won't get nowhere. The gaff most likely threw him out — the poor dear,' she added belatedly.

That concluded her views on her son and she was about to slam the door on me when a roar came from inside the house. 'Who's that, Martha? Come 'ere, whoever you are.'

Mrs Snook treated this interruption as though it was an invitation from Her Majesty the Queen herself. 'That's Phineas' Uncle Joe popped round today, Mr Wasp. Chimney sweep, you dollop,' she yelled back into the depths of her house.

Uncle Joe promptly appeared in the form of a menacing dark shape behind her, glaring out at me. I swallowed hard, because I recognised him at once. Only I didn't know him as Uncle Joe. To me, the police and the whole of the London underworld he was Slugger Joe, Flint's right-hand man.

If he was either living here or a frequent visitor, no wonder Phineas had moved from his home. What was Slugger's interest here? I wondered. Was he enamoured of the Widow Snook, or was he here in a working capacity? If so, what was that? I didn't like this situation at all, and it was all the more reason that I should find Phineas quickly. I'd only met Slugger once before, when he was leering over the body of a dead matelot — and it wasn't to see if he could bring him help.

'Hook it!' he told me with a gesture that made his point quickly.

I promptly hooked it.

*

I have a nodding acquaintance with Mrs Tutman, whose lodging house is well known to me. She has all sorts there, sailors from foreign parts, dockers, professional beggars, even gentlemen down on their luck. They all sit round an evening table to enjoy what passes for food, but there is little communion amongst them; they all come from situations so different and so grim that they have nothing to share and nothing to which they can look forward, save being able to save the next fourpence for a night's sleep. What the deuce was Phineas doing here?

Mrs Tutman is not like the Widow Snook. She is thin and determined and suspicious, the first on account of her lack of cooking talents, and the second and third because of where she lives.

'Me chimneys are as clean as new,' she snapped.

They weren't. I'd heard from a fellow sweep that there'd been three chimney fires in the last two months there. 'Mr Phineas Snook, if you please,' I said. I had to find him quickly.

'Round the back, up the garden stairs.' She closed the door before I could even thank her.

I picked my way through the rubbish piled up in the entry to the small yard where only one struggling daisy and some dandelions in the cracks between the stones suggested its pretensions to the name of garden. Nevertheless, compared with what I'd once glimpsed of the rooms inside the front of the house, this looked luxurious. A flight of wooden steps — one missing — led up to what must be Phineas' room. There was a small platform between the steps and the shabby door, and sitting impassively on guard was Phineas' stalwart companion. I'd recognise that cat anywhere.

It was Cockalorum.

I'm not one for cats, but Cockalorum is different. He lives up to his name, being aware of his own importance. He's a tabby to look at, but not the soft and cuddly kind. Cockalorum is a lean and learned cat, who takes himself very seriously. He's acquired enough knowledge in his short life to survive all that London's dark side can throw at him. He knows who's good and who's bad, whom he likes and whom he dislikes. Phineas is at the top of Cockalorum's list of likes. Indeed, he seems to be the only person on it.

Cockalorum was watching me suspiciously as I climbed up the steps towards him. When I went to try the door handle though, he stretched a warning paw that sent a message that he was provided with long claws for good reason. Even Slugger must think twice about upsetting Cockalorum.

'Cockalorum,' I addressed him politely to avoid any fast-moving claws, 'mind if I knock on the door?'

I did so, but there was no reply. I sighed and turned to go. 'Tell him Tom Wasp wants to speak to him, Cockalorum. It's urgent.'

*

Where would I find Phineas? Street folk have a hard life, depending on weather and many other things. The streets are working territory to thousands of people. Long before dawn we sweeps are out calling the streets, armies of smallholders are paying their halfpenny tolls to cross the bridges to reach London's markets, coffee stalls are busy and markets are humming; then housemaids drag themselves from their beds to light the fires, and workers of all sorts are flocking to their places of toil. They have no time to stand watching street entertainers, so *they* arrive later, when visitors, shoppers and men of business are willing to stand a moment to admire and pay for their genius.

Gone are the days when to be a clown or fool or jester was a noble profession. Phineas told me once he began his working life as a clown, but by our times such a profession has lost the respect of monarchy and people alike. Now he's a street entertainer, and sings and plays the pipe like the fools of old, just as Richard Tarlton was the king of clowns at the court of Queen Elizabeth, according to Clara. I've no doubt that Phineas would do well at cheering Her Majesty Queen Victoria up after the loss of her husband Prince Albert, such is his power to sing and dance and play his music that one can both laugh and weep with him. Phineas told me once: 'I can play the lute, the tabor, the pipe, I can sing merrily, I can sing of love, I can juggle, I can dance and I can jest — but I don't like jesting. Jokes are like daggers but they strike with the tongue.'

I decided to try one of Phineas' favourite spots for his performance, and that's by the Tower of London. On a good day the Tower gets many visitors and while they wait at the entrance for the next tour to take them to see the armouries and the crown jewels, Phineas often entertains them. His reddish-brown pantaloons, hose and fool's cap with its jaunty feather fit well with the Tower, for the Tower has been host to many kings and queens. It's true that not many of them would have been in a mood to enjoy fools, as they were imprisoned there and in fear of their lives.

On a sunny day outside that glorious building, it's easy to forget that. I wonder sometimes whether the lot of those kings and queens was really any different from ours. Death is with us all, so the only difference is in the merrymaking; the kings and queens had their feasts and dances, and we ordinary folk have our coffee houses, our music halls and those moments of silence when we watch the old river Thames flow by or look at the flowers in Victoria Park.

The last tour of the Tower was at four o'clock; I had passed no clock but it must be about that time already. I hurried along Postern Row, which borders the great ditch that surrounds the Tower, then looked down Tower Hill. There I could see the queue leading from the ticket office back across the bridge to the green sward of the Hill which is where Phineas often performs. To my relief I heard him singing and saw him dancing. The queue seemed to be taking little notice though, pressing ahead to pay for their tickets.

The Reformists amongst us frown on music and dancing, but what else can we do to let the good Lord above us know we appreciate Him? I watched Phineas for a while as he danced, knowing he cared not a whit if no one applauded him or even if they jeered at him. He's generous of heart and spirit. I saw him once pick a wild rose in Wellclose Square and give it to a beggar girl. He had no money to give but there were tears in her eyes as she thanked him. He's an ordinary sort of man when he walks alongside you in his everyday clothes, but while he sings, dances or plays his whistle or pipe, then he's over the hills and far away.

Someone told me his songs were often those of Mr William Shakespeare, who used to write his plays around this part of London. They certainly aren't to current taste. No *The Captain and his Whiskers* for Phineas. As I walked down Great Tower Hill, I could hear him singing *Sigh no More, Ladies*, and wondered if that meant he was still worrying about Hetty. He often dances out his love for her. He's in his own world then, a world he would like — I fear in vain — to share with Hetty.

He caught sight of me watching him and stopped his song immediately. 'Hey nonny, Tom Wasp,' he cried out.

I knew by that he was still in his world of song and merely taking time off to talk to me, and quickened my step.

'What news of Hetty?' he asked anxiously, as I joined him.

'She is well,' I told him. That was true enough and much relieved, he danced a few steps. He asked me to wait while he changed into his everyday clothes at the nearby Lion tavern, with which he has an arrangement.

Clowns usually paint their smiles and whiten their faces, but they may not smile underneath, poor souls, as they try to earn pennies to eat. Fools are different and Phineas' face is there for all to see; it's the most changeable face I've ever seen, whether he's laughing at the glories of this world or weeping for the loss of a butterfly. When he returned from the tavern he was still smiling with pleasure at the news I had given him, and off we set, at his suggestion, to his lodgings. I hesitated about telling him the terrible murder of Mr Harcourt as he walked merrily at my side, swinging his bag from which the fool's cap's feather peeped out.

To me, Phineas is in some respects a modern-day Richard Tarlton, whose picture hangs in Dolly's famous coffee room opposite that of

Dolly herself. In the drawing, Tarlton too has a pipe and tabor but he was known for his jests as well as for his bawdy jigs and songs. Tarlton wanted to make the world laugh. I'm not sure what Phineas wants, but I hoped he'd find it one day.

'I've bad news to tell you, Phineas,' I finally said as we reached his lodgings.

He looked alarmed. 'Mr Harcourt is going to wed Hetty?'

'He is not.'

'That's good news,' he said with relief, 'not bad. Tell her ...'

'Tell her what, Phineas?' I asked.

He smiled. 'That I will make a willow cabin at her gate.'

'I don't follow you,' I said.

He'd retreated into his own world again. 'That's all I could offer her, apart from a blackbird to sing at dawn and a nightingale by night.'

'She's had a nasty shock, Phineas. She needs help.'

Instantly he was practical. 'What help? What shock?' he asked as we climbed the steps and entered his room.

Cockalorum purred at me benignly as we entered, perhaps because I now had his beloved master's sanction to come inside. He even allowed me to take the rocking chair on which he had been sitting.

I took a deep breath and began. 'Mr Harcourt is dead, Phineas — and his widow grieves.'

Apart from his trade, Phineas is no fool. He stared at me. 'Hetty's safe then. So Mr Harcourt was married — I knew he was a rogue. Yet for every man's death, we should weep, Tom.'

'There's worse,' I said. 'He was murdered, Phineas, and the peelers will want to talk to you, because you're a friend of Hetty's.' That was all I could say, as I had no idea why they should have fastened on Phineas — unless the connection with Slugger Joe was known to them.

26

Phineas looked puzzled. 'That's terrible news, but Hetty has many friends.'

'Even so, the peelers may ask you where you were last night.'

He answered readily enough. 'I was asleep.'

'Anyone vouch for that?'

He chuckled. 'Cockalorum.'

'Between what times were you here?' I persevered, determined to make him realise how serious this was.

He considered this carefully. 'I have no watch, but I heard midnight strike and remained until dawn.'

And that was as far as I could get. I was worried though, because it seemed to me that a whole sack of soot might come tumbling down when the City of London police got going — especially when they found out that Slugger Joe was in the picture. Phineas wouldn't be worried, of course. He would be blithely sure that because he knew he was innocent, the police would believe that too. Cockalorum must have been of the same opinion because when I left he gave me a smug and supercilious look as if to say I need not come bothering them again. I hoped I wouldn't, but Phineas might not stand a chance if Inspector Harvey had a bee in his bonnet that he was involved in Mr Harcourt's murder.

When I reached Hairbrine Court again Ned was waiting for me with the kettle already on the coals and the sausages ready to cook, but I was still concerned. If Phineas wasn't going to take care of his interests, then I knew I must — even if it meant treading on the toes of the City of London Police.

'What's wrong, guvnor?' Ned asked, so I explained that it was possible that the City police might think Phineas wanted to kill Mr Harcourt.

He shook his head. 'No, it was one of those crack-brained Ordinaries.'

'You may be right about that, Ned, or maybe it was one of them hired Flint's mob to do the job.'

Clara had said that the Ordinaries were the last to leave, and Mr Harcourt was being supported by three of them behind the other four. But that was at the Queen's Head Passage entrance — how and why was the body in the log store outhouse? *That* raised some very nasty thoughts that would horrify Clara and cast an even worse shadow over Dolly's: had one of her staff killed him? Then I realised that it could equally well be Flint's men waiting in the dark of the yard entry to pounce on Mr Harcourt as he emerged. There was no doubt in my mind that I would have to return to Dolly's tomorrow and not just to clean those chimneys.

Ned looked worldly-wise — as indeed he is, in most respects. 'Flint's mob, for sure, guvnor.' But I heard him mutter, 'I reckon that Boy in the alley had something to do with it.'

*

We went to fetch Doshie and the cart the next morning, bright and early. Doshie is our faithful old horse whose stable is just round the corner in Blue Anchor Yard. We have an arrangement with the tavern keeper there and Doshie seems quite happy with it.

As it was so early, Clara wasn't about when we reached Dolly's, but a yawning maid let us in. By now Dolly's chimneys and I were old friends. Like Clara herself, there are no bends and slants to them. They're straight up to the clear sky of our Lord above and so we were quickly done with our machine. Ned was quiet about his work until we cleared our cloths and soot bags into the cart and returned to the kitchen.

There, ready to light the fires for the day were the kitchen and chambermaids who were their usual welcoming selves — despite the presence of Jericho Mason, Dolly's chief cook. Today even Jericho's dour presence couldn't stop the chatter about the murder and opinions on who might have been Mr Harcourt's killer. Ned was basking in the attention he was receiving (and the fresh muffins that came with it) and relating for the umpteenth time every detail of the gory scene we'd come across yesterday. Clara's staff were listening avidly as they had felt cheated at being refused entry to the murder scene until after all the peelers had left and the body been removed.

Jericho was the only person at Dolly's with whom I have failed to see eye to eye, and not just because he's over six foot tall. He makes wonderful pies and broils the best chops and steaks in London. He's a tall, strongly-built man to say the least, with the brawniest arms I've ever seen. Slugger Joe would employ him immediately. He puts his heart and soul into his work, but no one dares cross him when he's off duty.

'Ain't you finished yet, Wasp?' he grumbled as I returned. 'And what about this gridiron, eh? Expect me to cook on that, do you?'

'That's burnt bits of steak, Mr Mason,' I told him amiably, 'not soot. But I'll clean it for you.' I have a way with cleaning things, not just chimneys. I can often wipe a situation clean with just a few words too. For a moment I thought he'd carry on the argument, but seeing as how no soot can produce a lump half an inch thick on cooking utensils he graciously accepted my offer. He watched me with folded arms while I scrubbed and so I could tell he was weighing up what to complain about next.

I plucked up my courage. 'Mrs Pomfret mentioned you were here last night when the Ordinaries left. Hear any set-to in the yard, did you?'

His arms slowly unfolded and the fists were clenched. I took a step or two back.

29

Surprisingly — and to my relief — the answering growl was a simple 'No.' Then after further consideration, he added, 'You're from the docks, aren't you, Wasp?'

I agreed I was, as St Katharine's and London docks are not far away from where we live.

'Heard of a bloke called Phineas Snook?'

Not again! 'He's a pal of mine.'

'Tell him to watch out.'

'Why's that?' I asked as lightly as I could. Was this a warning or advice? With Jericho I could never tell from his tone because it's always threatening.

'What?' He stared at me oddly. Then: 'Tell him to keep away from here.'

There was no doubt about his intention on this occasion. It was a definite threat and I shivered at the thought that there might be mysteries inside Dolly's of which even Clara was unaware.

The kitchen was beginning to be busy. Tradesmen were hollering at the rear yard door, delivering meat and vegetables; the waiting staff were beginning to arrive through the side door that also opened into the yard. They would be as anxious as usual to get the most tips out of the breakfast business and today to hear the latest news on the murder. The two chambermaids who lodged at Dolly's were awaiting hot water to take up to the hotel rooms and agog to pass on any titbits of information to hotel clients.

This, I thought, would be a good time to speak to William Wright — if I could find him. Someone had killed Mr Harcourt, and it could have been one of the Tarlton Ordinaries. I couldn't forget what Clara had said: that William had *asked* to serve them yesterday evening. Was that just to save Hetty from doing so, or for his own reasons? And what else might he have heard than the little she had told me? The sooner I talked to him the better, given that waiters need their tips and workers would be coming in for breakfast very shortly.

William's a bright and polite young man of about twenty-five, the son of a smallholder out Blackheath way and eager to make good in the City. He's slim, rather like a chimney brush: a long pole with a head of bushy dark hair. He moves like one, too — I've seen him swaying along with eight or more plates of chops balanced on one arm. He's here and gone in a flash when he's working and even now was fidgeting to get back to his work.

'I've told all this to the police yesterday, Mr Wasp,' he said plaintively. 'I told them I was here until well past midnight and didn't hear anything after the gentlemen had finished their caterwauling outside. Can I ask what your interest is?'

It wouldn't do to mention Phineas, on account of William also being an admirer of Hetty, so I tried to be careful.

'It's this way, Mr Wright,' I said. 'Me having found the body the police are naturally eager to prove I murdered this man myself.'

'Did you?' he asked, more startled than anxious on my behalf. 'He was an unpleasant man anyway. No one would have blamed you.'

'Unpleasant to those he met in his line of work, or by his way of treating ladies?'

'By gum, both!' He flushed red. 'I'd a mind to speak out. He was that rude about ladies when Mrs Fortescue tried to join them. And he didn't treat Hetty well, he must have been three times her age, and treated her like she was off the streets. He was an old goat and now Mrs Pomfret says he wasn't a widower, he was married.'

'How was he when you served the Ordinaries yesterday evening?'

He shrugged. 'Old boozers playing games, like they always do.'

'Quarrelling?'

He became guarded now. 'They were excited over something to do with that Tarlton. There was some joke about lechery and Tarlton liking it. They always talk about how well their books are doing, old books and that sort of thing. That wolf Harcourt was boasting about something. No wonder he got himself murdered. He shut up when he saw me.'

'Boasting about Miss Hetty?'

'No. Some book or other. I served them their port and Stilton then left them to it. Shouting their heads off, they were. They'd had so much tipple they were falling down the stairs when they left.'

'Mrs Pomfret says they all left more or less together by the front entrance about midnight and Mrs Fortescue rushed out to join them. What happened to them then?'

'Wouldn't know,' he said, but I felt his attention wasn't on me.

We'd been sitting at one of the tables in the restaurant, and Hetty was coming through the door. She wasn't rushing to serve a table but coming towards us, smiling. *She walks in beauty like the night* — I read that once, in a poem. Hetty brings the sun with her, though, not the night.

Seeing William with me she was putting on airs, for she knew she made a pretty picture with her fair hair, blue eyes and the lace cap set off by her black lady waiter's full-skirted dress. Her heart-shaped face looked proudly at us, as though daring you *not* to admire her. At heart she was a kind girl, a good daughter to Clara, but she hadn't yet learned all the ways of the world.

William's expression as he gazed at her was one of adoration, and even Ned, not quite yet at the age when beautiful young ladies can catch at his throat, had his eyes glued to her.

'Dear Mr Wright,' she said sweetly. 'Mother asked if you could assist her in the office.'

A look of anguish crossed his face not because he wanted to avoid work, but because he would have to leave his goddess. Indecision held him motionless but at last he left us leaving Hetty to ask me anxiously:

'Mr Wasp, have you spoken to Mr Snook?'

'I have, and have told him about Mr Harcourt's terrible death.'

She looked distressed. 'Is he upset with me because I dallied with Mr Harcourt?'

'Not with you, Hetty, only with Mr Harcourt, and he is not alone in that.'

She looked downcast. 'I don't see why,' she said mutinously. 'I'm eighteen years old and quite grown up.'

'We make mistakes whatever age we are.'

'I didn't know Mr Harcourt was married,' she said in a burst of confidence. 'He said he was a widower and that he would marry me and I believed him. Otherwise ...'

She broke off and there was a sudden smile. 'I didn't really want to marry him. But oh, Mr Wasp, he was a *gentleman*.'

'No, Miss Hetty, he treated you as no gentleman would.'

A small giggle. 'He wanted to take me to Cremorne Gardens.'

'Then it's as well you did not go.' Cremorne Gardens is notorious for its shady paths and hidden corners, from which many a girl has emerged no longer a maid. 'Mr Wright or Mr Snook would take you there and not beguile you into dangerous paths.'

'Phineas.' She went very quiet. 'Did he speak of me kindly?'

'He did. He said he would give you a blackbird to sing at dawn and a nightingale by night.'

A tear ran down her cheek. 'He would not say that if he knew ...'

But she would say no more.

I left Dolly's greatly troubled. It seemed that the mysteries inside Dolly's were not confined to staff and customers. They were close to Clara herself.

CHAPTER THREE

Tuppence for a Book

St Paul's Churchyard is busy all day long and every day, with the shops, coffee houses, schools and houses surrounding the iron railings of the churchyard itself. Only on a Sunday does the scene change, as the pious come to worship Our Lord in His great cathedral and Paul's Chain is put across the main carriageway to still the noise of the carriages. This was a Saturday though, and so as usual every stallholder was shouting of the glory of his wares, children were yelling either in excitement or tears and every horse, carriage and growler in London seemed to be clattering over the granite stones. Inside the cathedral, however, our Lord was beckoning those who wanted to find peace.

Once, this whole area had a religious bent, and the streets about it showed their reverence by taking names like Amen Corner and Paternoster Row, and all the booksellers and publishers were dedicated to religious books. Nowadays, the chief sign of religion outside the cathedral itself is several sellers of Biblical tracts, ordering passers-by to heed their God amid the temptations of silks, flowers and cigars around them and threatening hellfire to those who fail to listen. As we passed the gate of the Churchyard gardens, one looked ready to thrust a sheet at any newcomer, and a very stern, tall and terrifying man he looked.

'Where will you spend eternity?' he thundered at me. 'Tread not the sinner's way.' He stepped back, thrusting the tract at me from arm's length — he didn't like my smell any more than anyone else, however much he wanted to bring me to our Lord. My own view is that there is enough to scare us in this world without such fearsome people blighting our days unnecessarily. One look at the glory of the cathedral itself does more than a tract to remind us of Our Lord's wishes.

'Thank you kindly,' I replied, believing it best to be polite when I can, but he had already turned his back in search of his next victim. Furthermore, I might need a slice of God's word with me where I was going.

Ned and I trundled our handcart, which carries the cleaning machine, along Paternoster Row to Hart House, where Mr Harcourt lived and worked and where we were expected for chimney sweeping. Clara told me the house was named for a famous actor at Drury Lane, a great-nephew of Mr Shakespeare's.

Many's the time I have peered in the windows of Harcourt's Antiquarian Bookstore, admiring the strange volumes that appeared there. As with human beings, some books are desired for their outer covers, some for their hearts, the matter that lies within. The old book market casts its web far and wide to catch the one person who might love a battered dusty tome that had lain forgotten for years. Mr Harcourt must have loved his bookstore greatly to live above it when he couldn't be with Mrs Harcourt in the countryside.

Today I noticed that the blinds were not down, as was the custom on a death. Nor was there a wreath on the door. I paused when we reached the area steps at the rear of Hart House, where the kitchens and storerooms lay. This had been the home of a man who had died a horrible death and it seemed right to take off my topper for a moment. Seeing me do so, Ned dutifully pulled off his own cap, sending a shower of soot floating around us. Once inside and our cloths laid, we did our duty by the chimneys after which Ned was able to put on his usual waiflike look of 'I haven't eaten for two days', which always goes down well with the lady servants. He has a keen eye for those who might take pity on him under the delusion that his cruel master was still pushing him up chimneys.

It was thanks to Clara Pomfret that I was here, as the baker who also delivers to Hart House had, at Clara's request, passed on the information that it was time for me to call there again. It is sad that even in times of tragedy the routine of life must roll on; fires must be lit, chimneys swept and delivery men kept informed of local news. This was a good opportunity to find out more about Mr Harcourt and with good fortune to see Mrs Harcourt, who must be staying here. Where better to begin than in the kitchen?

Ned busied himself with a muffin, and I studied the servants with whom I shared the kitchen table. I can tell a lot about the heads of a household from its servants. At one end of the table sat Mr Parker, the butler — a grand name for his role in this size of house — at the other the housekeeper Mrs Birch, and there were two maids and a footman. I'd also glimpsed a young lad working outside in the yard. I can't speak for him, but these five were as haughty and stiff as if they'd never had a night out at the music hall. There was nevertheless much eager chat about the murder of the late master, but not much hint of his being mourned. They seemed more interested in a broken sash window pane that had just been noticed. I spent some time retelling the story of finding Mr Harcourt's body, but I had to work hard for any reaction. Ned, being mischievous, made the story more lurid:

'*Bucketfuls* of blood there was,' he informed our audience with relish, setting to on his second muffin. No one pointed out that Mr Harcourt had been strangled, not stabbed.

Following his example, I was just at the point of telling them how I was nearly put in chains and marched off to Newgate prison when a great rumpus of shouting and shrieking broke out above us.

'Godamercy, what's that?' screamed Mrs Birch, as another screech came from upstairs and I could hear heated women's voices.

'I've been robbed,' someone was shouting. 'Police. I want the police!'

'That's Mrs Harcourt,' Mrs Birch cried, exchanging a look with Mr Parker, who broke out of his solemnity to yell at the boy outside to fetch a copper. With one accord he and Mrs Birch rushed to the stairs that led to the upper floor, with me following them as fast as I could and the two housemaids close behind me.

When we reached the door into the bookstore the hubbub was still in full cry, but as the doorway was blocked by Mrs Birch and Mr Parker, I had to squeeze my way round them to see what was happening. Two ladies, both of mature years, were prowling around each other like pugilists sizing each other up for the big fight, and shouting at each other so loudly I couldn't make out a word. One, a full-figured lady of medium height, I recognised as Mrs Maria Fortescue, Mr Harcourt's assistant in the bookstore and apparently his erstwhile lady friend; the other, a tall, thin, severe-looking lady, must be Mrs Harcourt — although it wasn't a widow's grief written all over her face, it was rage.

'You old bitch,' she was yelling at Mrs Fortescue. 'You're nothing better than a moll. Get back to walking the streets where you belong. What are you doing here, anyway?'

Mrs Fortescue stood with arms akimbo, clearly determined to give as good as she got. 'Think I've nothing better to do than throw books over the floor, you old cow? I came to pay my condolences, but I see they are not required.'

Peering down, I saw that most of the floor was strewn with books thrown down anyhow without regard for their contents; some looked as though they'd been wrenched open, journals lay around higgledy-piggledy, and volumes of what looked like manuscript had been tossed down so carelessly that their pages were lying loose. This, I realised, must be connected with that broken window pane.

'Condolences? Madam, custom requires them to be paid *after* the funeral, not before. Tell me, where is it?' Mrs Harcourt shrieked.

'If there was anything, the thief took it,' Mrs Fortescue shouted in return, glaring at us all.

Mrs Harcourt ignored this. 'Where have you hidden it?' she screeched, pushing her adversary out of the way to gain access to the shelving Mrs Fortescue was blocking. 'It's mine.' She cast a quick look at its contents then began to stomp around the shop, delving into the unhappy-looking piles on the floor, perhaps in the hope that whatever it was she sought would suddenly appear at the top. This was strange as she didn't look like the kind of lady who would cry over losing one book out of so many. Nor did she look like a lady who had just lost her husband.

'What's been stolen, Mrs Harcourt?' asked Mr Parker, clearing his throat in a business-like manner as befitted his position as butler.

Mrs Harcourt turned on him. 'Nothing to do with you, Parker. Why didn't you discover this outrage earlier?'

Mr Parker drew himself up to his full height. 'The bookstore is not our responsibility, Mrs Harcourt. Mr Harcourt was most particular about that.'

Mrs Fortescue, who had been doing her own share of prowling, took advantage of this lull in the storm. 'The manuscript you require, Mrs Harcourt, is not here and never was,' she snapped. 'All that thief took was some poetry in what appeared to be Christopher Smart's handwriting, enclosed in a folder entitled *Jubilate Agno.* I remember seeing it displayed on the counter early on the Wednesday afternoon before I left the bookstore.'

'Before he gave you the boot, you mean,' Mrs Harcourt jeered.

Mrs Fortescue took no notice. 'Mr Harcourt cannot have sold the manuscript to which you refer later that afternoon, or the sale would be recorded. For the Smart folder the thief has left a mere tuppence. *Your* manuscript is not here.'

'Nonsense,' snorted Mrs Harcourt.

Mrs Fortescue shrugged. 'Look at this, if you don't believe me. Here's the tuppence.' She pointed, and being near the counter I could see three halfpennies and two farthings neatly piled up.

Mrs Harcourt was not impressed. 'There's more missing than a mere poetry folder. Mr Harcourt,' — she remembered to cross herself — 'may he rest in peace, told me some days previously that the manuscript would be arriving that afternoon. And *that* is why he asked me to come here yesterday morning. Only to find out he had been *murdered.*' A handkerchief was applied to her eyes.

'As I informed you, I wasn't here for the whole of Wednesday afternoon,' Mrs Fortescue said icily, 'when — *if* — it arrived.'

'Bitch. You've stolen it. Do you think I don't know what went on? You shared his bed for long enough, and when he didn't fancy a scraggy old woman like you and turned his attentions to Miss Pomfret, you took your revenge and stabbed him to death.'

This mention of Hetty was a vicious switch of attack. Mr Parker's eyes were popping out of his head — this being a situation to which butlers aren't accustomed. Mrs Birch's mouth fell open wide in shock, and the housemaids were giggling nervously. As for me, I was thinking that I would find where the cracksman — assuming there was one — had made his entrance through that broken sash. None of the servants had spoken of hearing any disturbance during the night, which suggested the cracksman was a professional.

While everyone's attention was on the two pugilists, I managed to slip into the rear room of the bookstore which had also served as Mr Harcourt's office, judging by the furnishings. There I could see the missing window pane, obviously neatly cut with a glass-cutter's stone, and the window still ajar. It didn't take a Scotland Yard detective to see that this room too had been ransacked. Piles of books and journals adorned the floor here, just as in the room I had left.

What interested me most, however, was that tuppence on the counter in the front store. What kind of burglar breaks in during the night to buy a book that he must want very urgently (and cheaply) and then leaves money for it?

*

Mrs Harcourt insisted Mrs Fortescue remained until the City of London Police arrived, but if she was hoping that they would arrest Mrs Fortescue for the murder of Mr Harcourt, she was disappointed. Burglary being a common offence in this noble city of ours, just one bobby had been allotted to this crime and he was not interested in murder. He was an aged constable by modern standards, and I recognised him as Billy Russell, who had risen from being one of the old watchmen charlies to the status of a City constable. Billy smiled benignly on the world, and recognising each other we exchanged a few merry words much to Mrs Harcourt's fury.

'Do your duty, my man,' she commanded. 'Arrest this person.'

'Which person would that be?' Billy asked, studying each of us one by one very slowly and very carefully. I could tell he didn't like being called 'my man'.

'This one.' Mrs Harcourt poked Mrs Fortescue, who had taken heart at seeing Billy's reluctance.

'Arrest this lady for what?' He was puzzled — or appeared to be so.

'Look around you,' she replied impatiently. 'A robbery during the night and *murder*. This woman stole my property and murdered my husband.'

'If it was done during the night, how do you know it was this young lady?' Billy looked benignly on Mrs Fortescue, who must be forty at least. 'And where's this murder been done? I ain't seen no body.'

'Then arrest her for theft,' Mrs Harcourt cried. 'Perhaps she stole it this morning, not during the night. The woman was working here.'

Billy thought this through carefully. 'If she were working here, ma'am, she wouldn't have needed to break in, would she?'

'She's thrown all these books around to confuse us. She is the only person who knew the manuscript was here.'

Billy shook his head regretfully. 'If it isn't here, I can't arrest no one. There's no evidence it *was* here, see? I'll have to make a report.' He slowly withdrew a notebook from his tunic pocket.

'Of course the manuscript isn't here. She stole it!' Mrs Harcourt's voice rose to a shriek. 'But she's a *murderess*.'

This only resulted in Billy's need to make a second report. Then he carefully replaced his notebook in his pocket, and walked out of the door.

Mrs Fortescue was sobbing with relief, so I escorted her across the road and under the archway to Dolly's, where I knew Clara with her kind heart would look after her. We took the front entrance to avoid reminding her of the yard where Mr Harcourt had died. Mrs Fortescue was not capable of telling Clara herself what had just happened at the bookstore and so that would be left to me.

By this time it was nearly eleven o'clock in the morning, so I had sent Ned home with the cart with chimney sweeping over for the day. Luncheon customers were beginning to gather at Dolly's and many of the booths were already full. I could see Hetty whisking around, skirts swishing, as she and the other waiters hurried to and from the kitchens.

There is nothing as good as the smells from kitchens. They seem to reflect the cooks and those who employ them. Dolly's kitchen smell was warm and inviting, the rich harvest of Clara's influence. Even Jericho's dour presence didn't affect that, nor even the thought of the murder that had taken place here so recently. A murder that must be connected to Dolly's. No vagrant of the night would have dragged his victim into the yard, and no robber chancing upon Mr Harcourt would have left that watch and albert behind him.

'A burglary, Mrs Pomfret,' I began (formally, as Mrs Fortescue was present), once we were all settled in Clara's greeting room. 'Mrs Harcourt thinks a manuscript has been stolen and she made unfortunate accusations against Mrs Fortescue.'

Clara looked grave. 'I don't like this, Mr Wasp. A robbery at his bookstore when Mr Harcourt was murdered so recently — and when we had so many booksellers and publishers here that night. It can't be a coincidence.'

I saw a light shining on the situation. 'Phineas Snook can't be connected with *that*, Mrs Pomfret. He has nothing to do with books.'

'That terrible woman accused me of murdering Mr Harcourt,' Mrs Fortescue moaned. 'But I could not have done so. I merely asked him to escort me to my home on the corner of the Churchyard that Wednesday night. He agreed, so the other gentlemen left, but then after walking a short way along Queen's Head Passage Mr Harcourt changed his mind and said he was returning straight home, which of course is in the opposite direction. That left me alone, and I ran through the Passage to Newgate Street where seeing my distress a gentleman and his wife kindly escorted me home. My maid will confirm that. Mr Harcourt turned towards the Row, but,' she sobbed, 'met his tragic fate instead.'

I saw an opportunity to find out more about why Mr Harcourt might have been crowing that evening as William Wright had told us. 'Did Mr Harcourt mention anything unusual about his work that you might not have known about?'

'He was always boasting about some great find,' she replied snappily. 'It's possible he expected one to arrive, but if so it did not do so before I left.'

Clara looked at her sympathetically. 'You come with me, Maria, and I'll settle you down with a nice cup of tea in my parlour.'

After she had done so she returned to me sitting in state alone. 'This could mean trouble, Tom. It looks as if that murder must have been connected with the Ordinaries' meeting. Phineas Snook can't have had anything to do with it because he wasn't here.'

I braced myself to be tactful. 'But *anyone* who was here could have killed him.'

Clara looked at me steadily and not very warmly. 'You're thinking of William, aren't you, because he cares so much for Hetty? But he wouldn't, Tom, and nor would any of the rest of my staff. And no woman, certainly not Maria, could have strangled him.'

I had to point out the other possibility. 'As we said earlier, Clara, there's Flint's mob.'

'That brings us back to the Ordinaries,' Clara retorted. 'They could have hired Flint and they're coming for luncheon today. That's not usual, Tom, and I believe they're gathering to talk over what's happened. They *know* which of them killed Mr Harcourt. They probably know about the burglary at Mr Harcourt's shop and this missing manuscript.' She broke off and looked at me in a most meaningful manner. 'Do you think you …'

I caught her drift. 'They won't welcome a chimney sweep, much as I'd like to be there.' I would indeed. If Clara was right, and one of the Ordinaries was Mr Harcourt's murderer, then that would lift the shadow over Dolly's. Not that that had done any harm to trade; customers were flocking in, drawn by the ghoulishness of the crime that had taken place in the yard. But that didn't help Clara, presiding over an establishment where everyone looked at his neighbour wondering whether he was working or dining with a murderer. Suspicion eats away at the heart of a place like Dolly's.

'I wouldn't be welcome either,' Clara replied. 'But women can be invisible and so can you.'

'How's that?'

'That serving room next to the coffee room where the Ordinaries meet,' she continued. 'A dumbwaiter brings food up from the kitchen, and there's a hatch to the coffee room for quick service. The waiters collect it from the sideboard inside the room. You could sit in the serving room, well out of sight. I'll do the serving both from the dumbwaiter and the sideboard.' She managed a laugh. 'They'll be disappointed that I'm not Hetty, but that can't be helped.'

'Clara, you're a golden nugget to a mudlark,' I said thankfully, as I followed her up to this serving room. I knew enough about the mudlarks on the banks of the Thames to know that treasure like that was rare indeed — and so was Clara.

The smells arising from the kitchens made me hungry while I was waiting for the gathering to begin. At last Clara bustled in, to warn me that the Tarlton Ordinaries were arriving and I should be sure to keep out of sight. Luckily the aromas of Jericho's steaks and mutton chops would override any slight odours from my clothes, and anyway the Ordinaries would be more interested in their tankards of ale.

Minutes crawled by but at last I heard one or two of them coming up the stairs, then the rest like marching soldiers. Seven of them, Clara had told me, now that Mr Harcourt was no more. I mentioned earlier that I'd once seen Mr Harcourt at Dolly's; on that occasion Hetty had pointed out to me with great awe this tall gentleman with piercing eyes and a haughty manner. I had also heard that night the booming voice of one of the other Ordinaries and been told it was that of Mr George Timpson. Now I heard it again; he was introducing the luncheon. I had been expecting an urgent discussion of Mr Harcourt's murder, but instead he declared loudly:

'Gentlemen, let tabor and pipe commence.'

There followed the sound of the tabor and the shrill noise of a pipe. The tune was familiar — perhaps I had heard Phineas play or sing it. I leaned forward as far as I dared and glimpsed Mr Timpson at the head of the table and one of the other gentlemen on the far side of the table, who was on the plump side with rosy cheeks. I could also see the backs of the two gentlemen on the near side of the table. There must have been two other gentlemen, whom I could not see without disclosing my presence, and the seventh member seemed to be progressing around the room with a tabor and pipe.

The unusual aspect for a gentlemen's gathering was that the members — I presumed all of them — were wearing green and red floppy fool's caps, like the jesters of old. The seventh member was wearing a large old-fashioned cap just as Richard Tarlton did in the drawing of him hanging in the coffee room. Gentlemen in clubs often have rituals, but this one seemed strange indeed, especially for a luncheon meeting. They must take their commitment to Richard Tarlton very seriously. The music from the tabor and pipe was stirring and I wished I could have been inside the room to see more clearly all these grave and important gentlemen wearing their floppy ears. Gentlemen are all boys at heart.

The music came to an end, but it seemed the ritual was not yet over. Surely Mr Harcourt's death deserved more urgent attention?

'A toast,' declared Mr Timpson, who was a large and corpulent gentleman. 'A toast to Her Majesty Queen Elizabeth.' I saw him standing and the other gentlemen were following suit as he held his tankard aloft. 'And a toast to our beloved clown, Richard Tarlton.' Then: 'You may sing, gentlemen, you may sing.'

I had thought he made a mistake over the queen's name and that our Queen Victoria might not be pleased, if she had known, but then I realised that Queen Elizabeth was as much as queen to Mr Tarlton as Queen Victoria is to us. The song they chose was no wistful melody as Phineas sings, but the round Clara had mentioned, with all seven voices coming in in turn with:

He that will an alehouse keep
Must have three things in store

ending up with a rousing: *Nonny hey nonny, hey nonny no.* This must be a tribute to Mr Tarlton and to his Castle tavern, that was on this site until the Great Fire so many years ago. It was joyous singing, and not as lewd as the tavern songs heard at Paddy's Goose on the Highway, but even so I was mystified by its light-hearted tone, considering the circumstances. Perhaps such levity was a mask. With each of them being suspects for Mr Harcourt's murder, there would be unease at any open discussion.

Clara was distributing the first of the dishes now, a fine selection of whelks and mussels, and it was only when these were disposed of that Mr Timpson addressed the meeting again — seemingly reluctantly.

'We are here,' he told his fellow diners, 'to mourn the loss of Mr Arnold Harcourt.' A pause, with a tentative 'hear, hear' from one of the two gentlemen with their backs to me.

'We were all here that fateful evening,' he continued, 'and we have doubtless all spoken to the City of London Police. I take it that we can assume that none of us saw who killed Harcourt?'

No one replied and Mr Timpson was forced to continue himself.

'As you know, four of you were ahead of Mr Harcourt, and walked through the archway to the Row, whereas Mr Manley, Mr Splendour and myself remained briefly, supporting Mr Harcourt. However, you may all wish to clarify your movements.'

It appeared, from what I could hear, that the group of four had gone their separate ways after reaching the Row, and despite the best efforts of the other remaining three, seemed therefore to be excluded from immediate suspicion. Mr Manley and Mr Splendour seemed to be the two gentlemen with their backs to me on the near side of the table.

'We were only with him because he was tipsy,' one of them said anxiously. 'We were concerned that he might take a fall, having dined well. Then it turned out that he was well enough to escort that woman to her home. We three left him then.' A pause. 'Didn't we?'

'*I* certainly did,' Mr Timpson boomed. 'I left you two gentlemen with Mr Harcourt and that woman and decided to take a short walk to the Churchyard to admire the cathedral by night.'

'I do not recall that,' the gentleman with his back nearest to me replied instantly. 'I myself was the first of us three to leave. You will remember, Mr Manley —' He turned to the neighbour between himself and Mr Timpson '— I had unfortunately left my umbrella behind and went back into Dolly's, leaving you two with poor Harcourt. When I returned there was no sign of any of you.'

'You were most definitely there when I left,' Mr Timpson boomed in response. 'Wasn't he, Mr Manley?'

Mr Manley was most anxious to assure the company that he really could not recall this. All he remembered was that he had departed the very instant that Mrs Fortescue and Mr Harcourt had begun the walk to her home in the opposite direction.

'I,' he concluded, 'always take a breath of fresh air by the Thames when out during the hours of darkness. It is most inspiring.'

The Thames air is not the kind of breath I like for refreshing my brain, but the murmur of the six other gentlemen suggested they were in complete agreement. A heated discussion now broke out between the three men as to who had departed first after Mr Harcourt had agreed to escort Mrs Fortescue to her home. All they agreed on was that none of them was anywhere near Queen's Head Passage after Mr Harcourt had abandoned Mrs Fortescue.

If one of those three gentlemen had been Mr Harcourt's murderer, I reasoned, they would have been expecting him to return through Queen's Head Passage after leaving Mrs Fortescue's house and might have waited there; his decision to leave her at such an early point would have made this a much shorter interlude. It occurred to me, however, that there was only Mrs Fortescue's word for it that she was indeed abandoned. And where, in all this, might Flint have played a part? He, or Slugger, could also have been lurking in the shadows for an opportunity to pounce on their victim.

The argument was continuing. Everyone was shouting at once, which was most inconsiderate of them as I could not distinguish who was saying what.

When they at last fell silent Mr Timpson looked most grim. 'To our muttons, gentlemen. We now know that there was a burglary at Harcourt's store last night and a manuscript is apparently missing. Once it is found, who is going to approach Mrs Harcourt on behalf of us all? Or — dare I say it? — does one of us know all too well what the position is?'

I expected another outcry, but none came. Instead there was what seemed an appalled silence.

At this unfortunate moment, Mrs Fortescue must have tired of her lonely position in Clara's parlour, for I had heard the door open and her voice proclaimed loudly, 'Gentlemen, if you are referring to the manuscript which the late Mr Harcourt was so delighted to receive, there is still no sign of it.'

There was a startled pause, perhaps because a lady had once again dared to interrupt their grave and ordered proceedings, but perhaps because they were assessing the situation with all speed, as chairs were scraped back to rise to their feet in tardy politeness.

Mr Splendour, who by elimination I discerned was the second gentleman on Mr Timpson's right, broke the shocked silence. 'My dear Mrs Fortescue, we can hardly take your word for that. Mr Harcourt might not have taken you into his confidence over where he had put the manuscript on receipt.' Another pause. 'I have heard that one item was taken during the burglary. What was that?'

Mrs Fortescue was clearly about to make the most of this moment, judging by the sudden tension in the room. 'Only poetry thought by Mr Harcourt to be by Christopher Smart. Nothing else. Either Mrs Harcourt is correct that the manuscript in which you are interested was stolen or its existence was a tale concocted by Mr Harcourt to fool you all.'

At that there was an outcry of 'Nonsense.' Amongst the babble that followed, however, I thought I heard the name Phineas Snook. If so, no one commented, but it filled me with fear. Whatever this mystery was — if there was one at all — I could not see how Phineas could be involved. And yet the City of London police knew his name and so did Constable Peters. How could a street entertainer, even one in love with Hetty Pomfret — be connected with these gentlemen? I listened uneasily, but there was no further mention of him.

When the rumpus died down, someone I could not see asked for further information about the burglary. 'Madam, are you *sure* the folder of poetry that was taken was by Smart?'

'I am,' Mrs Fortescue replied firmly. 'It was acquired by Mr Harcourt only recently from a prominent Spitalfields dealer. The robber paid tuppence for it.'

There seemed an air of relief in the room, as like Cockalorum they smoothed their ruffled fur, and sank back into their seats although she had not invited them to regain them.

'Christopher Smart,' Mr Timpson declared in an offhand manner. 'A friend of Dr Johnson of course.' Then he added, 'Is it not possible that the same person who acquired that for tuppence also stole this other manuscript?'

'Perhaps,' Mrs Fortescue snapped.

Mr Timpson was not deterred. 'Or as you were such a valuable assistant to Mr Harcourt, you would know if he had kept the manuscript in some secret place. You knew his most *private* business.'

I heard Mrs Fortescue hiss with fury. 'You, sir, are not a gentleman.'

'And you, madam, are no lady to keep the truth from us,' Mr Manley, the anxious gentleman, declared passionately. 'We have a stake in this matter. We are the Tarlton Ordinaries.'

Who all, I thought to myself, seem remarkably unconcerned that one of their number had been brutally murdered and that at least three of them must be under investigation by the City of London Police.

'Ordinaries?' Mrs Fortescue jeered. '*Very* ordinary. You, gentlemen, are the clowns, not Richard Tarlton. If there's anything missing you exalted booksellers and publishers would surely know what it was, whereas a mere assistant would be kept in ignorance. Perhaps Mr Harcourt was murdered because of this imaginary manuscript — and by one of you.'

With that challenge, she departed, judging by the sound of the door slamming, and there was silence. I could see Mr Timpson looking round the table and the other gentlemen in my restricted view leaning forward to look at their neighbours, just as paintings show the Disciples at the Last Supper. Whom to trust? Whom to doubt? Was this too a case of betrayal by friends? Was Richard Tarlton in the portrait on the far wall peering down sadly at his Ordinaries? Did *he* feel betrayed?

CHAPTER FOUR

Meeting the Ordinaries

I spent an uneasy night dreaming of being pursued up a chimney by an army of angry gentlemen wearing fool's caps, jerkins and hose. When Ned bounded into the room to wake me up, though, it was Phineas who came immediately to mind. Why was his name cropping up so often?

Being Sunday, there were no chimneys today and Ned had announced his intention of enjoying the pleasures of Victoria Park. I had suggested the pleasures of the public baths, but they did not appeal. I decided to face my fears and find Phineas again.

Even though it was Sunday, he would probably be at work, so I once again set off to Great Tower Hill to see if he was a-dancing there. The only way to settle my mind was to question him more closely on his movements. I had been told he hadn't been seen at Dolly's that day, but had he been in the Row? He would tell me, as he doesn't know the difference between truth and a lie — this because he doesn't know what a falsehood is.

As I reached the Hill I could see him in the distance, dancing with his pipe to his lips. Seeing him so cheerful in the morning air made it hard to believe that anything might be amiss with him.

He stopped as I approached. 'Good morning, Tom. Two peelers came to see me yesterday at my lodgings, just as you said.'

'What did they ask you?' At least Phineas was still here, not taken off to Newgate prison. Fortunately this was Metropolitan Police territory, which meant the City of London would have to consult before they acted.

'Whether I had killed Mr Harcourt, but I told them I hadn't.'

This was alarming. 'Why did they think that? Did they have evidence or just because you didn't like his behaviour to Hetty?'

'Yes.' Phineas began to look worried. 'Hetty was upset because she told the police that I disliked Mr Harcourt.'

This sounded ominous, but there must be more to it than that for them to question Phineas. 'Do you know why the Tarlton Ordinaries would be talking of you? Have you met them?'

He looked at me, puzzled. 'I don't think so.'

He began to hum and I knew I would get no answer if I asked him whether he had been in Paternoster Row on Wednesday evening. He told me he had been at home at midnight and Phineas always tells the truth, so I believed him. And yet something wasn't right.

The sweet sound of his voice filled the air with *There was a Lover and his Lass*, but I was still worried. How, for instance, did Phineas know Hetty was upset if he hadn't seen her since Mr Harcourt's death? It suggested that he paid more visits to Dolly's Chop House than I had thought — and perhaps more than Clara had thought, too. I wondered what the police had made of Phineas as I walked back to Hairbrine Court. So far I had been giving thought to who killed Mr Harcourt, but it occurred to me that no one had talked much about Mr Harcourt himself. He wasn't a man who was greatly liked, what with his treating Mrs Fortescue so cruelly and trying to seduce young Hetty. Nor did he treat his wife well. But as with apples, most unlikeable people are only half bad. He must have had his good moments or he couldn't have charmed Hetty into liking him. Was the Mrs Harcourt I had encountered once her husband's tender sweetheart? Did he find pleasure only in his books? Did he truly love Mrs Fortescue, once? Did he have love for Hetty or merely lust after her body? Did he see himself as the King of Paternoster Row? Was that why he had boasted about a manuscript he might never have possessed? Was he killed for revenge or in defence of Hetty or for a manuscript he might or might not have possessed?

I had been looking forward to reaching Hairbrine Court and having a glass of ale with Ned, or perhaps a cup of tea if our money box could afford a new packet, so that we could talk things over instead of my worrying alone. Ned doesn't say much as he isn't good at conversation, but what he does say always sets me thinking hard.

That had to be postponed. There waiting for me was not only Ned, but Constable Peters, looking as usual like a schoolboy off to Sunday school, only happier. Ned had given him a glass of my ale and very peaceful and comfy they looked.

'You'll be getting me a bad reputation calling here, constable,' I joked. I knew this must be important though, this being a Sunday when he must like being at home with Mrs Jessica and Master Bertie.

'The Detective Department's had a request from the City of London Police, Mr Wasp. They want permission to come on to our territory over this Harcourt case.'

That set the alarm bells ringing.

'They might want to interview you again — and others,' the constable added, not looking me in the eye.

I knew what he meant: Phineas. And that couldn't be just because he'd warned Clara about Mr Harcourt's attentions to Hetty. 'Were you the peeler who spoke to Phineas?' I asked him outright.

He blushed even rosier. 'Yes. I wasn't ordered to do that, but after you told me about the case, I really wanted to talk to him about Slugger Joe. We can't arrest Slugger without evidence, so every time he slips through our fingers like a blessed eel. Phineas told me Slugger won't force his way into his lodgings because someone called Cockalorum scared him off.'

I grinned. 'Cockalorum's a cat.'

He didn't believe me. 'A cat wouldn't scare Slugger.'

'Cockalorum would. When in fighting mood, he'd scare anybody.'

The constable laughed. 'Even Flint?'

'Not knowing who he is, I can't say. Now, as to Mr Harcourt, Phineas says you asked him if he killed him.'

'That wasn't me. That was Inspector Wiley of H Division. He came with me.'

I groaned. Inspector Wiley — although I always think of him as Sergeant Wiley, he being of that rank when I first encountered him in the River Police — is good at heart, but he and I don't see eye to eye, him being the sort of copper to whom a man is guilty until proven innocent rather than the other way about.

'I talked to Sergeant Williamson about it,' Constable Peters added awkwardly. Sergeant Williamson is the brilliant detective at Scotland Yard who has had a role in many famous murder cases, including the tragic Road murder, where he assisted Inspector Whicher. 'He agreed we should let the City of London come on to our territory. He's told me to keep an eye on them though, and they can't arrest anyone here without our being present. And we've been given the same rights on their territory over this case if Slugger and Flint are likely to be involved.'

That sounded sensible to me, but I was wondering how a mere chimney sweep like myself came into this.

Constable Peters gave me the answer to that. 'Sergeant Williamson wants me to do some nosing around on this Harcourt case now that we have this joint arrangement but I don't want to look too formal about it. So I'd like you to be present tomorrow when I do so, Mr Wasp, seeing that you know Phineas and Dolly's.'

This was very flattering, but I tread cautiously over rough stones. 'You're not planning on suspecting Mrs Pomfret, are you?'

'No. It's the gentlemen who were at Dolly's that night with him, the Tarlton Ordinaries. I'm concerned, Mr Wasp. The City of London's divisional Inspector Harvey doesn't see them doing the job themselves. He's either looking elsewhere or at their hiring Flint.'

'Either might lead him back to Phineas,' I said, 'as Slugger is friendly with his mother. What's his line on Flint though?'

'Mr Harcourt had regular dealings with Lairy John.'

I gasped. That was a bucketful of soot in my face all right. Lairy John, as well as being one of Flint's two deputies, was no mere dolly-shop fence; he was working out of Spitalfields, which meant he had the best of both worlds: the takings of the thieves' dens of east London, but not beyond the pale for those of west London, too.

Spitalfields and Lairy John ... What had Mrs Fortescue said? That the poetry folder bought for tuppence and thought to be by this Christopher Smart had come from a prominent Spitalfields dealer. That must surely be Lairy.

'So this missing manuscript Mrs Harcourt's so worried about ...' Constable Peters began.

'Might have passed through Flint's hands — and Slugger's bloody ones too,' I finished for him.

'The trouble is,' the constable said awkwardly, 'the City blokes aren't thinking it through.'

I saw his gist. 'Which one of those Ordinaries hired them, you mean.'

He nodded. 'Which is why I'd welcome your presence, as a concerned friend of Mrs Pomfret as well as the person who found the body.' He winked at me.

Thanks to my unofficial attendance at the Ordinaries' meeting yesterday I was able to tell him whom, in my view, he should speak to first: Mr Algernon Splendour, Mr Thomas Manley and Mr George Timpson, the three who were escorting Mr Harcourt as they left Dolly's. They would have been thinking he was with Mrs Fortescue after they left him, but in fact he was very shortly on his own and still near Dolly's. Right where any of the Ordinaries could have attacked him — or Flint's men. Or, I had to admit, anyone in Clara's staff who had reason to want Mr Harcourt dead. Like William Wright.

*

The premises of Messrs Timpson and Timpson in Paternoster Row were very grand and formal, for a publisher who aimed at the popular market rather than the educational market like Messrs Longmans. Rotary steam printing presses and modern typesetting have made books so much cheaper now that everybody wants to read (except Ned, who thanks to the local ragged school can read but seldom does). Clara giggled when she told me Mr Manley maintained that the word *literature* did not apply to Mr Timpson's list of penny dreadfuls, cheap novels and reprints, and Mr Splendour did not recognise any work written after the death of Good Queen Bess as having literary merit. As I have never been sure of what publishers do, except take manuscripts from an author, give them to a printer and arrange for someone else to sell them, I was most interested to visit Timpson and Timpson on several counts.

The lofty red brick building in which their offices were located was close to Hart House where Harcourt's Antiquarian Bookstore was housed and Timpson and Timpson seemed to look down in scorn upon the pedestrians and traffic beneath. When Constable Peters and I entered on Monday morning, it seemed to be full of earnest young gentlemen in smart waistcoats looking most important as they hurried up and down stairs clutching books, papers and ledgers and seemingly rapt in admiration for the valuable work which they were helping to immortalise in print.

Everyone in the reception area seemed far too busy to speak to us, not realising that Constable Peters was from the police. At last one young man took note of us and managed to find a moment to enquire our business. He looked shocked at the very idea that Mr Timpson himself might have spare time to waste on us, police or not, but fortunately I could hear the familiar booming voice. He and a lady visitor were descending the stairs, with the skirts of her dress swishing as she expressed her gratitude for his condescension in publishing her humble work.

'It is mankind who will thank you, my dear madam,' Mr Timpson assured her as they passed by us.

From the gravity of his voice, one might think that Miss Jane Austen herself had returned to life, although this tiny lady in an old-fashioned walking dress was more likely to be the proud authoress of one of the still popular three volume novels.

On his return from ushering her into the Row, Mr Timpson, looking most imposing in his morning coat, deigned to take note of us. 'Who is this?' he enquired of his clerk.

Constable Peters, normally the most peaceable of men, took objection to this and made no bones about who we were. 'Mr Thomas Wasp and

Constable Peters from the Detective Department of the Metropolitan Police. Here about the death of Mr Arnold Harcourt.'

Mr Timpson quickly reassessed us and wisely did not enquire why a sweep should be involved; instead he ushered us to the first floor. I was awarded a chair at the rear of the office, which suited me well because I could observe without getting in Constable Peters' way.

'I trust this tragedy of Mr Harcourt's death will convince you that something must be done,' Mr Timpson informed the constable solemnly, 'about the ruffians who invade our streets.'

If the severity of his tone was meant to impress us, it failed. 'He wasn't murdered by some ruffian, sir. We believe his death could have been planned,' Constable Peters told him. 'He doesn't seem to have been a popular gentleman.'

Mr Timpson stiffened. 'Nonsense. Arnold Harcourt was the most popular man in the Row.'

'With the ladies?' the constable enquired, with his face looking as innocent as ever. 'I'm told that evening a distressed lady interrupted your proceedings at Dolly's Chop House and that Mr Harcourt also made advances to Miss Pomfret.'

Mr Timpson was taken aback. 'Ah well, we gentlemen, eh?' A hearty laugh, in which we did not join. 'That may be so,' he added hastily. 'I spoke of course about his professional reputation.'

'I'm told you escorted Mr Harcourt part of the way to his home.'

'I did, until that very distressed lady, Mrs Fortescue, intervened. Mr Splendour, Mr Manley and myself then departed.'

'Together?'

'Separately,' Mr Timpson informed us. 'I myself was the first to leave and took a brisk walk round the Churchyard. I can't speak for Manley and Splendour.'

I wondered what their stories would be today, remembering the interesting argument at Dolly's.

'You had no disagreements that evening at the supper you all attended?' the constable asked.

'Where the deuce did you get that idea?' Mr Timpson laughed heartily again. 'We meet to honour one of the greatest fellows in the drama history of our country, Richard Tarlton. Nothing to argue over. He was greatly respected in his time and for long thereafter, pals with Sir Francis Walsingham, Sir Philip Sidney and even Queen Elizabeth herself. He wrote treatises, poems, and only had to put his head round the curtain on stage to have the audience cheering and laughing.'

I decided to make my presence felt. 'Do you publish his writings, sir?'

He didn't like that question. 'We live in a different age. I publish for the millions.'

'Yet you attend the Tarlton Ordinary Club?' the constable observed.

'I publish as a business,' he snapped. 'My private interests differ. They keep an excellent table at Dolly's. We've had dukes, earls, playwrights, actors as members in the past — all dedicated to keeping Tarlton's memory alive. It's a joint responsibility. And therefore,' he said, 'as there was a burglary at Harcourt's place on Thursday night, I'm entitled to know what's happened to the missing manuscript.'

'I've heard talk of that, sir,' I told him, 'but what it is and who has it don't seem to be known.'

'That is unfortunate, my man.' Mr Timpson glared at me. 'Mr Harcourt often boasted about some great find of his. If we passed him in the Row or took coffee with him he always had some such tale and usually nothing came of it. Given that he was murdered however, we must allow for the possibility that on this occasion he was right. And that, constable, surely affects your case.'

The constable seemed to be encouraging me to continue, so I spoke again. 'What was the subject of this missing manuscript that concerns you?'

'Harcourt gave us no details,' Mr Timpson replied stiffly.'

'Something obtained from Lairy John, perhaps?' the constable enquired.

That shook him. 'Absolutely not.'

He didn't enquire as to who Lairy John was, I noted.

*

Next we made our way to call on Mr Thomas Manley, whose premises were hardly to be compared with Mr Timpson's, although they too were close by in the Row. We were directed upstairs by a young man in his shirt sleeves on the ground floor who appeared to have nothing to do with Thomas Manley Limited. On the third floor there were three doors of which one was open and occupied by another young man sitting on a high stool with a ledger propped before him. A bookcase stood nearby with a few dusty slim leather-bound volumes on its shelves, which spoke of long ago days in the publishing world and several with names unfamiliar to me, such as Geraldus Flowerflook's *Rainbow: the End, the Beginning*.

The young man looked surprised at having two visitors but he laid down his quill and informed us that he would see whether Mr Manley was free. From the look of this office, it seemed to me that Mr Manley would be free quite a lot of his time, but the youth bounded forward with such eagerness you'd think he was announcing Mr Charles Dickens and Mr Wilkie Collins.

The inner office revealed Mr Manley himself, who rose from his desk with a creditable imitation of a busy publisher. Previously I'd only glimpsed his back and part of his profile, and now I saw an earnest face and dreamy eyes. Determined, though.

He spoke rapidly as though this was a well-rehearsed speech for greeting visitors — if there were any. 'Ah yes, gentlemen,' he began, 'I take it you have brought me some of your work. We are a small but ambitious company dedicated to our duty to literature. We print only the best, by which I mean books that have contributed or will contribute much of value to mankind.'

Grand words, but I couldn't help noticing that the cuffs of his shirt were frayed.

'Like Mr Kingsley's *Water Babies*,' I commented knowledgeably. 'That shows what a hard life a climbing boy has.'

'Indeed.' Mr Manley looked uncertain about this departure from his script.

'We're here,' Constable Peters rescued the floundering publisher, 'to ask about Mr Harcourt's death.'

Mr Manley looked alarmed. 'I've explained to the police already.' His voice rose. 'I know nothing of that. He and Mrs Fortescue were about to walk along the Passage to Newgate Street when I left. I cannot answer for my two colleagues' movements,' he added firmly. 'I did not see either Mr Timpson or Mr Splendour after I departed. I left them there as I felt the need of inspiration before I retired. I walked over to Doctors' Commons and down the Thames riverside before returning here. I have rooms on the floor above this.'

He seemed very nervous now, and his eyes were like a sparrow's, dodging everywhere rather than looking at us.

'This manuscript that seems to be missing from Mr Harcourt's shop — what was it?' the constable began.

Mr Manley looked trapped and tried a light laugh. 'It depends to which one he referred. Harcourt had so many and he really knew very little about true literature. He was an antiquarian bookseller, as is Mr

Splendour. I have little in common with them. The words of the past may have great interest, but the words of the future are precious jewels for us to nurture and treasure. Literature is a continuous story. Each great writer plays his part.'

'From William Shakespeare to Mr Dickens,' I contributed, as Constable Peters was looking mystified.

Not for long. 'What about that poetry book the thief bought for tuppence? Would that be valuable?' he asked.

Mr Manley seemed to me relieved. 'I doubt that very much. Smart is not a popular poet at present. His slender output, unfortunate mental problems and dissolute way of life do not appeal. Hardly the moral standard we seek for this company.' He looked forlornly round his empire of cheap rickety furniture and the meagre row of books.

'What about works by Mr Tarlton?' I asked him, hitting my target.

'A *great* man, a great fool,' he stuttered. 'But manuscripts — no, certainly not. There are none. So little of his writing has survived, and even if more came to light it would be of little interest. Do consult Mr Splendour or Mr Timpson or the other Ordinaries.' He brightened at this solution. 'Far more expert than I am but they would agree — Tarlton — little interest now …' He stopped in mid flow. 'Except to the Ordinaries of course,' he added unhappily. 'Admirers, but nothing of value — no.'

'Mr Harcourt couldn't have been killed because of this manuscript, then?' Constable Peters asked firmly.

'Certainly not,' Thomas Manley said miserably. 'Most unlikely.'

*

The last Tarlton Ordinary we had to visit this Monday morning was Mr Algernon Splendour, a gentleman I looked forward to meeting if only because of his name. He, like Mr Harcourt, was an antiquarian bookseller and since his premises were opposite one another they must indeed have been rivals. Their window displays were quite different, however. Mr Harcourt had set out to attract as many people's attention as possible and thus had many more books displayed than Mr Splendour, whose range was far less wide and looked eager to boast of their exclusivity.

He was a tall, elegantly dressed gentleman in his forties, who seemed to have a perpetual smile as though wishing every customer to know he was their friend. His eyes, however, were those of a good-natured hawk eyeing his victims. Nevertheless, he was a true gentleman and ignored the quaint appearance of a chimney sweep at the side of a policeman. Indeed, he closed the shop and escorted us upstairs to his own library and office, ushering me to an armchair by the window. From this I could see Harcourt's Antiquarian Bookstore across the way, which made me think all the more about the desolation I had seen within it.

Constable Peters took a different line with Mr Splendour than he had with Mr Manley or Mr Timpson. 'Our way of thinking is that this garrotting could have been the work of one of those gangs working round here,' he confided to him. 'That's what Mr Wasp here thinks.'

Did I? Mr Wasp was flattered by this, but kept a modest face and said nothing.

'The murder must have taken place after Mr Harcourt left Mrs Fortescue on her own,' he continued, 'and walked back past Dolly's towards his home. Just unlucky, he was. Do you live here in Paternoster Row, Mr Splendour?'

'I do. Of course,' Mr Splendour's smile grew somewhat fixed. 'Poor fellow to be so unlucky. It could have been me. I had returned to Dolly's to retrieve my umbrella, I spent some ten or fifteen minutes in there and when I came out there was no sign of Harcourt. He must already have been attacked. Perhaps Timpson or Manley can tell you more. I left them with Harcourt as soon as I recalled that I had foolishly left the umbrella inside. It had been a most enjoyable evening,' he added without conviction.

'Because Mr Harcourt told you about the special manuscript he had?'

The smile became a grimace. 'Pure hogwash, gentlemen. *Special?* We laughed about that. As so often Harcourt had claimed to have found a great treasure for which the world had long been waiting and that evening it was no different. He expected so much and received so little.'

'And yet there was a burglary the following night at Mr Harcourt's shop, perhaps the result of his murder?' the constable asked with interest.

The grimace remained in place. 'The robbery could have been entirely unconnected.'

'Unless this great treasure was stolen,' the constable pointed out.

The smile vanished as Mr Splendour considered this. 'Perhaps I should tell you precisely what Harcourt's expected find was on Wednesday evening — and there were so many such finds.'

'Perhaps you should,' Constable Peters agreed. So did I.

'Harcourt asked us to keep it secret, but I see no harm in telling you now that Mr Harcourt is no longer here to swear me to silence and the manuscript has disappeared. How much do you know much about Richard Tarlton?'

'Nothing, sir,' said Constable Peters. His answer was good policy.

'The tragedy of our literary world is that for every well-known author of the day,' Mr Splendour said, 'there is a myriad of people who are only a fraction inferior but they are quickly forgotten. It was so in Elizabethan times. One must also consider the numbers of possibly brilliant poets of the past — or indeed the present — who could only sing their work in their minds because they were never taught to write and read. There were also dramatists whose plays were performed to public acclaim but were never printed.'

I thought of street entertainers like Phineas, whose gifts could not reach those that did not know of him.

'Consider William Shakespeare,' Mr Splendour continued grandly. 'And then consider the Tarltons, the Richard Greenes, the Thomas Kyds — they are seldom remembered now by the general public. Little of the work of such dramatists now exists and even if it did, their scripts would be not be worth a great deal even to us antiquarian dealers. Mr Harcourt that evening was boasting of receiving some hitherto unknown small fragment of Tarlton's work. It was only of moderate interest to us — and certainly did not fill us with emotion, nor would it have filled our pockets with gold,' he added hastily.

'So Mr Harcourt's murder could not have been connected with this missing manuscript,' the constable observed.

'Certainly not.' Mr Splendour said vigorously. 'Dreadful murders such as this are not committed in the name of literature. No, you will find that a gang is indeed responsible and if not, then I should explain that Mr Harcourt's private life was not above reproach. He was greatly attracted to ladies — a motive for murder hardly unknown over the ages.'

'I'll bear that in mind,' the constable told him. 'Now, this unnamed fragment,' he continued doggedly, 'even if it wasn't worth much, would he have bought it through the fence he used?'

The smile disappeared instantly. 'Fence? My dear sir, we are reputable booksellers. We never deal through Lairy John.'

He didn't need to see the expression on our faces as he realised his mistake immediately and the smile hurried back. 'My dear sirs, it seems I have donned the thumbscrews of my own free will. Very well.

Mr Harcourt's acquisitions were, I fear, *sometimes* subject to the need for scrutiny. This was no exception, but I assure you, gentlemen, that I am not of Mr Harcourt's ilk in that respect — *whatever* trifle he had considered might be of interest to the Tarlton Ordinaries.'

*

Constable Peters felt justified in taking a hackney carriage to his home and kindly offered to take me with him. The cab driver was not pleased but I offered to alight in Royal Mint Lane rather than his risking his horse and vehicle on the stones and other dangers of Blue Anchor Yard.

'My thanks to you, Mr Wasp,' the constable said to me as I was bowled along in state. 'I'd wanted, as you might put it, to get to know the chimney flues we are dealing with. Justice has to be done, whatever the price.'

For a moment I thought he meant I was about to be arrested, but then I realised what he was hinting. Phineas Snook was under suspicion.

The cabbie was duly grateful to set me down in Royal Mint Lane. Strange things happen east of the Tower even when, as now, we were blessed with the sunshine of day. I know this area though. I know its ways. I know its poor and I know the evil that men can do around here. I walk through it and no one stops me as a rule, save when I meet the Slugger Joes of this world.

As I did today. He was lounging in the entry to Hairbrine Court. Under his filthy cap, his long hair, as black as his heart, was tumbling round his face as he towered over me. I thought I was going to have my neck wrung like a chicken who'd walked into Smithfield market by mistake. Instead, he put a heavy hand on my shoulder. It pressed down on me so hard that I was bent over, lopsided.

'There's things happening, Wasp,' he growled, 'that are none of your business.'

'Who decides that, Slugger?' I asked bravely.

'Flint. He wants you to appreciate that. And — ' He jabbed me in the chest. ' — I know where you live, Wasp.' A pause. 'You and that Ned of yours.'

I went cold. Ned is my weak spot and Slugger knew it. Ned's a sharp lad who can look out for himself, but he's no match for Slugger Joe and still less for Flint, whose face and name I did not know. He was everywhere and we feared him.

'Phineas Snook,' whispered Slugger in my ear so close I felt his hot breath licking at my face. 'Forget him.'

CHAPTER FIVE

The Lover and his Lass

After my legs had finished shaking from the encounter with Slugger Joe, I tried to make sense of it all. First, there was Flint, who could very well be at the top of this tangle of twisting flues. Slugger was his deputy and therefore it was almost certainly Flint who had given orders to warn me off Phineas. That raised the question of why Flint should be interested in Phineas — which could be the reason that Slugger had blessed the Widow Snook's home with his presence.

Dealing with Flint, even just in my mind, was like stabbing blindly at a fish in the murky waters of the Thames. The fish would have nipped off like a shot. And yet Flint had to keep swimming around if he was to know what his mob was up to. That thought made me shiver. Flint's jaws could snap shut on Ned and me at any moment and we'd never see them coming.

An even darker possibility galloped through my mind, preposterous though it was. If Slugger's visit had nothing to do with Flint, could Phineas himself have asked Slugger Joe to remove Mr Harcourt from this world, in order that Hetty should be troubled no longer?

I tried hard, but the devil doesn't take no for an answer, so I had to question myself most rigorously: did I think Phineas Snook could have become desperate enough to kill, if Hetty was falling for the charms of Arnold Harcourt? To my relief, no. Could it have even occurred to him? No. Phineas doesn't think that way.

I heard the devil sniggering, though, and he jeered at me. Why should Slugger Joe be ordering me not to talk to Phineas if he had nothing to do with Mr Harcourt's death?

I stood up to him fair and square. Perhaps Slugger had wormed his way into the Widow's house merely because he wanted the Widow all for himself and didn't want Phineas living there, too. Or Cockalorum. I thought I'd seen the truth of it, but even then the devil sneaked back. Phineas must have seen Hetty very recently, as he was aware of her upset at Mr Harcourt's death. Hetty had confessed to me that there was something that Phineas did not know — 'he would not say that if he knew,' were her words. If he knew *what*, I wondered, and how was Hetty involved? I had no answers, only fears and a dogged faith in Phineas' — and Hetty's — innocence.

I dragged myself up the steps to Ned's and my safe haven, our home. I pushed the door open — but it was to emptiness. Ned wasn't there.

Fear pierced me like a toasting fork. Slugger Joe had threatened me — and now Ned had disappeared. In vain I told myself he must be out buying (or pinching) supper, or earning himself enough to pay for it (in his way, which doesn't always accord with the way the law sees things). Terror strikes like lightning, choosing its targets, setting fire to hope, destroying, killing, and scaring; then it leaves, well satisfied with the results. That Ned's disappearance had to do with Slugger Joe I had no doubt, but where would he take him? To Widow Snook's? No. Mrs Snook, for all her faults, would not tolerate the abduction of a child, even one of Ned's age.

Would Phineas know where Slugger lived when he wasn't with Mrs Snook? Trying to convince myself that this was the answer, I stumbled and hobbled my way to the Ratcliffe Highway and over to John's Hill, heart beating within me as I hurried through the entry to the rear of the lodging house. There was no sign of Cockalorum. Had Slugger already been here? I began to see his sinister hand everywhere as I pulled myself up the steps, half falling against the door, which was ajar.

I steadied myself — and stopped short as joy stabbed me instead of fear. Cockalorum was curled up at Ned's feet as he swung his legs to and fro from the rocking chair and Phineas looked on benignly from his old armchair.

'Hello, guvnor' and 'Hey nonny, Tom,' came from Ned and Phineas in unison as tears filled my eyes. Phineas was as pleased as Mr Punch to see me, although Cockalorum gave me a token hiss as Phineas yielded his armchair to me and went to sit cross-legged on the bed.

'What you doing here, Ned?' I asked, choking with relief.

Ned looked surprised. 'I met Phineas on the way home and he asked me to tea. He had something to tell me, guvnor. He'd heard that I'm going to be Jack-in-the Green in the May Day procession.'

'That's good news indeed, Ned.' I'd known for a while but had been keeping it a secret to tell him on a special occasion. Now it was out I was delighted to see his happiness. Jack-in-the-Green has a proud place in our annual sweeps' day on the first of May, less than two weeks away now.

'They've asked me to dance in it, too,' Phineas told me. 'And I went to Dolly's yesterday to ask Hetty to be Queen of the May for our procession. She said she'd already been asked to be in the City Sweeps' procession, but she preferred ours. William won't like that.'

We sweeps organise our own processions for our own areas and most enjoyable they are.

I had been worried for nothing. Ned's absence had a simple explanation and Slugger was nothing to do with it. 'My thanks to you, Phineas,' I said, wholeheartedly.

'What for?' he asked.

'I thought Slugger Joe had nabbed Ned. He had a word with me tonight.'

'Joe? Oh.' Phineas' face clouded. 'Did he hurt you?'

'Only threats,' I said for his sake, although threats can pierce like slivers of glass.

'Is he the reason you left your ma's house?'

Phineas chuckled. 'He doesn't like Cockalorum.'

The cat stirred, stretched and yawned — but then I saw those claws tighten.

'Slugger warned me to keep away from you, Phineas. Why's that?'

'I'm sorry, Tom. I don't know. But it's bad news.'

That made me even more uneasy. Something was askew here. Phineas wasn't looking me in the eye.

'Does Slugger know something about Mr Harcourt's murder?' I persevered.

'He thinks you do, Tom,' he muttered.

That set me rocking, as well as Ned. 'Why's that?'

'You won't like this, Tom. He says you must have killed him because you pretended to find the body.'

'He didn't kill him. I'd have seen him do it,' Ned yelled indignantly.

I had to stop this, knowing how hopeless Phineas was at recognising lies. 'That's a damp squib, Phineas. Why would I want to kill him?'

'You wouldn't,' Phineas said stoutly, 'and I told Joe he was wrong. Why would anyone want to *kill* Mr Harcourt?'

'Plenty could *want* to, Phineas, especially people who love Hetty, but they wouldn't *do* it.'

Phineas cocked an eye at me. 'Jericho Mason might.'

That took me by surprise, as I never thought of Jericho as one of Hetty's admirers. 'You mean William Wright, don't you?'

'*And* Jericho.'

Phineas might be better acquainted with Dolly's Chop House than I had realised, so I asked him outright. 'When were you last at Dolly's?' If Hetty wasn't giving me the full story, Phineas would.

But he didn't like that question. 'The peelers asked me that,' he said shortly.

'And now I am, Phineas.'

He didn't reply, though. He just stretched out to pick up Cockalorum and began to stroke him. I would get no further.

Ned was annoyed with me on the way back to Hairbrine Court. 'Why did you upset Phineas, guvnor?' he asked crossly.

'It's for his own sake, Ned,' I tried to explain. 'We don't want him mixed up with this, and he doesn't always understand what's going on.'

He eyed me keenly. 'Think he stove that bloke in?'

'No, Ned, I don't, but something's stuck up that chimney.'

*

If Phineas wasn't going to tell me about his visits to Dolly's I would have to question Hetty herself and with Slugger on the prowl the sooner the better. Ned and I had chimneys to sweep first, but I was able to reach Dolly's by about ten of the clock on Tuesday morning, well before the luncheon trade began. Ned had gone off on his own with the cart after promising me that he'd go nowhere near Slugger Joe's working area.

When I arrived, Jericho Mason was in the rear yard emptying a bucket. He scowled when he saw me, but let me pass by him without comment. I felt his eyes drilling into my back nevertheless. This was no time to ask him about his romantic fancies.

Clara was coming down the stairs as I went inside and must have been very glad to see me because she immediately took me straight to the greeting room without even asking why I was there. 'What with Hetty being upset, the police here again and William all over the place it's a shambles here,' she lamented. 'He served a treacle pudding with gravy instead of a mutton chop to Mr Splendour yesterday, one of his best customers.'

'What's amiss with him?' I asked.

'You know that, Tom. It's because he's set his cap at Hetty. Maybe his heart as well.'

'I'm told Jericho Mason's heart is set on her too.'

'She wouldn't look twice at Jericho,' Clara snorted.

'That don't mean *he* isn't looking at *her*.'

She sighed. 'Neither of them would gain anything from killing Mr Harcourt.'

'A man with a passion forgets that. And a lady too, in this case.'

'Poor Maria. I met that housekeeper of Mr Harcourt's again yesterday, Mrs Birch,' Clara told me. 'She said she'd always thought there'd be murder done in that house.'

'To do with the bookstore or the house?'

'Both, Mrs Birch said. She says he paid her extra not to tell Mrs Harcourt about Mrs Fortescue because she never came up here in a month of Sundays. But she did visit a week or two ago and must have realised what was going on and ordered Mr Harcourt to get rid of Maria. Even then she stayed on working in the bookstore. When he told her to leave last Wednesday, they were shouting at each other so loud Mrs Birch thought she'd have to tell Mr Parker to intervene.'

'But Mrs Fortescue came back to the bookstore the day after the burglary.'

'Yes. She says she didn't know Mr Harcourt was married, and only found out when she came to pay her condolences — and that's not usual, not before the funeral.'

'Perhaps she went to look for that missing manuscript.' I couldn't take this further because at that moment Hetty came in. It was a downcast Hetty, though, without her usual air of bringing the sunlight with her. Far from it. I could see she'd been weeping.

'I want to talk to Mr Wasp alone, mama,' she pleaded. Clara pulled a face at me as if to say 'you go gently on her' and then reluctantly closed the door behind her.

Hetty sniffed, sat down, stopped crying and clasped her hands in her lap looking like Ned does when he's something to confess.

'You do like Mr Phineas Snook, don't you, Mr Wasp?'

'Very much, Hetty. He's a good man.'

'So is William.' A pause. 'You don't believe Phineas could have killed Mr Harcourt, do you? All because of me?'

'No, Hetty.'

'I'm glad because he was very upset when I told him Mr Harcourt was taking me to Cremorne Gardens. I didn't mean to go. I only said it to make Phineas jealous. That wasn't kind of me, was it?'

She looked at me so appealingly that I had to put her mind at rest. 'No, but we all say things we shouldn't sometimes when we're in love.'

I couldn't fully remember how that felt, but it seemed to be right.

'Am I in love?' She frowned. 'I'm not sure I am. I like Phineas very much, but I like William too, so how do you know when you're in love?'

I thought very hard about what to say. 'You're dancing inside your heart when you're together.'

76

She considered this. 'Does one have to dance all the time?'

I had to tread gingerly. 'No, because other things get in the way. But mostly you dance. Like when you see him coming towards you, or when there's a joy you share with him, or when he leaves you — only that's a different sort of dance.' I was getting so tangled with this that I wasn't sure I was helping, but she was paying great attention.

'I don't think I dance in my heart with William, although he does say such nice things. So did Mr Harcourt, although I didn't like it when he presumed — ' She blushed and I wished Clara were present to guide her daughter. There were important things I needed to ask Hetty, however, so I had to persevere. I judged the time was right.

'When did you last see Phineas, Hetty?'

She peeped out at me from under her eyelashes. 'That's just what the policeman asked me.'

'And now I am. It's for Phineas' own sake.'

'Do you mean see him here at Dolly's?'

Ah. Now we were at the heart of it. She was fidgeting with the bows on her sleeve, so I knew she was choosing her words carefully. 'Here or hereabouts, Hetty. Does he come here to see you often?'

'He came here on a Tuesday, in the week before Mr Harcourt died,' she said quickly. 'We went for a walk to Victoria Park.'

'Very pleasant,' I said gravely. 'And when did you *last* meet Phineas?'

Even quicker now. 'He came last Friday. It's my evening off.'

'And before that?' I persevered.

At being trapped, her mouth formed an O, and she looked at me most piteously. 'Late on the afternoon the day Mr Harcourt died.'

'Where did you see him?'

'In Panyer Alley,' she whispered. 'He was staring at the Boy on the wall.'

That was a surprise and one I neither liked nor understood. Was it just chance that took him there? 'Did you know Phineas would be there?' I asked her.

'No. He looked upset to see me. Phineas was *talking* to the Boy,' she added.

That was strange indeed. What could Phineas find of interest in that carving?

'He has his own world sometimes, Hetty. We all do.'

'William doesn't,' she murmured.

I looked at her and realised what she was *really* telling me. 'Only you can choose between them. And that's when that heart of yours is dancing.'

Tears welled up again. 'I've hurt Phineas, Mr Wasp.'

She didn't say anything more, and all I could say was 'It will pass.'

Hurt him though? How? She turned away and so I knew she had not wanted an answer to her question.

*

Staring me in the face was the fact that Phineas hadn't told me that he'd been near the Row on the afternoon of the murder, perhaps because it didn't seem important to him, or perhaps simply because I hadn't asked him. But was it just by chance he was talking to the Boy of Panyer Alley? I remembered the way I had talked to Cockalorum out loud, and so perhaps Phineas also had a problem to solve. I began to have misgivings that I didn't understand Phineas as much as I had thought I did. Did that mean I didn't trust him anymore? No. Sometimes we should have faith, as I did in Phineas.

There must be more to be learned from those gentlemen, the Tarlton Ordinaries, however. They had spent the evening of the murder with

Mr Harcourt. According to them he'd been boasting for some days about an old manuscript, and William Wright had heard them talking about lechery. The latter didn't sound like business talk to me, but as Mr Harcourt had been there himself, they would hardly be discussing his rejection of Mrs Fortescue or his pursuit of Hetty. Yet that same evening he had met his death.

I couldn't pin down what seemed so strange about this missing manuscript. These Tarlton Ordinaries were all in the book trade, rivals or not, so it didn't make sense that they should be so reluctant to discuss it, even if it was only a fragment of Tarlton's work. There could be no self-interest to make any or all of them wish to kill Mr Harcourt over it as his widow would probably inherit both the bookstore and its contents. Even if one of them had stolen this fragment, why would the others lie about it? Only, it occurred to me, if it was more valuable than they claimed and they were hopeful of obtaining it for themselves; perhaps they had entered into a pact to keep it a secret from Mrs Harcourt. Or, it occurred to me, was the pact about the murder?

Random thoughts flitted through my mind. Was Mr Harcourt's murder connected to this manuscript or had William or Jericho followed him from Dolly's to ensure that his pursuit of Hetty ended? Revenge too is a powerful motive, but I couldn't see Mrs Fortescue garrotting her former lover. And then there was Flint, who must be lurking in the shadows of this case, given that Slugger was on the scene. Any of the Ordinaries could have hired Flint through his deputies. Mr Harcourt must have known Lairy John if he traded with Spitalfields dealers, which meant Mrs Fortescue would also have known him.

After I left Dolly's I decided to walk through Panyer Alley. I began to despair over this dark warren, but I stopped to look at the Boy, trying to work out what his attraction was to Phineas. Perhaps it was the mystery about him. What was the lad doing? Just sitting on a panier of bread, so it's thought, since this alley was once where the delivery men for the local bakers gathered for the day's work. The Boy has his foot cocked up ready to examine, so 'Pick-a-toe' is the name some round here give to him, even though Ned believes he's a climbing boy sitting on a roof. The Boy's been here for hundreds of years, and according to Clara, the old chair-mender who sits here daily waiting for custom, Zechariah, sees himself as his guardian.

The carving sits at ground level in a fine brick surround let into the wall between two ancient houses. Below the carving of the Boy himself is a mysterious inscription from the old days when Queen Mary II and her husband William III claimed the throne. It reads:

When you have sought the Citty Round
Yet this is still the highest ground.

The inscription is dated the twenty-seventh of August 1688, but some believe that this might have been carved much later than the Boy himself, so I like to think that Mr Shakespeare once stood here, looking at the Boy. He lived in Shoreditch, not far away, and he would have known this place well. Richard Tarlton, who owned the Castle tavern on the site where Dolly's now is, was a friend of Mr Shakespeare.

'Are you the sweep I saw in Harcourt's Antiquarian Booksellers?' a lady's imperious voice demanded from behind me, taking me by surprise.

I turned to see it was Mrs Fortescue herself. She was a handsome woman save for her hard face, but somehow I couldn't take to her any more than I had to Mrs Harcourt when they were arguing in the bookstore.

'Chimney sweeping's my trade, madam. You'd like my services?' I had no brush with me, but an appointment could be made.

She waved this offer aside. 'I want to talk to you, sweep. Come with me. I'll give you a shilling for your trouble.'

This was an offer I could not turn away, so I meekly followed in her wake towards Newgate Street and her home, which was overlooking the point where St Paul's Churchyard meets Cheapside. She walked in front as befitted her status and me behind as befitted mine. On arrival, she graciously pointed me to the area steps leading down to the kitchen and sailed onwards to her own front door. Shortly afterwards she swept into the kitchen where I was sitting wondering what she wanted of me that would be worthy of a shilling. With me were a grim elderly lady and a young girl who grudgingly vacated the room at her command. Her parlour, I acknowledged, would hardly be suitable for a sweep, even though I had washed last Sunday.

'Mr Splendour,' she began, 'who has kindly offered me a position in his bookstore, tells me that you have some kind of standing with the police.'

'Experience, ma'am. I'm known to Constable Peters of the Detective Department Scotland Yard, who asked me to accompany him yesterday to Mr Splendour's emporium.'

This passed without comment. Mrs Fortescue had other things on her mind.

'I trust the constable is satisfied that this story about a manuscript being missing from Mr Harcourt's premises has nothing to do with me.' She hesitated, then added as though it were of no consequence, 'What is the police's opinion?'

'I couldn't say, ma'am. The police like my help but they don't part with information.'

'Nor you, it seems, Mr Wasp,' she commented drily. 'You also met Mr Timpson and Mr Manley, I understand.'

'At the invitation of Scotland Yard's Detective Department, ma'am.'

'Did their information enable you to reach any conclusions about

81

my late employer's tragic death? One of those mobs one hears about, no doubt, or one of the servants at Dolly's.'

I considered what I might say as she was looking very eager to hear my answer. 'No conclusions, ma'am, save for the gentlemen's opinion that this missing manuscript would have been worth very little, even if it were by Tarlton himself.'

'Indeed?' Her expression was hard to read, but it seemed to register relief.

'Would that be your opinion too, Mrs Fortescue, should the manuscript appear?'

'It would,' she snapped. 'But that it is in my possession is a mere fantasy dreamed up by a jealous woman of whose existence I had no prior knowledge before she attacked me in Harcourt's Antiquarian Bookstore.'

Clara and I had agreed that it seemed unlikely that Mrs Fortescue had been unaware that Mr Harcourt was married, given that she had worked for him and paid private visits to his home as well.

'Mr Harcourt was not a likeable person,' Mrs Fortescue continued coldly, 'and others share my opinion. An excellent employer of course, and a most erudite and worthy gentleman. I am naturally sorry to have lost my position there owing to his death, and no doubt Mrs Harcourt will greatly miss my services.'

A sage nod from me. 'She will indeed, ma'am.' I noticed she was looking at me expectantly, however I've found that when ladies — and sometimes gentlemen, although they mask it better — proclaim their own value, it is a sure sign that they are hoping for reassurance. Until now, Mrs Fortescue had not appeared a lady who doubted her own worth, but now I wondered if that was the case. Losing Mr Harcourt as an employer was a blow, but his dismissal of her from his private life was a bigger one, and for a moment she looked a lonely figure. I decided to strengthen my flattery.

'Not many ladies or gentlemen would have your depth of knowledge of the bookselling trade,' I added.

She inclined her head graciously. 'What time do the police believe Mr Harcourt to have died?' she enquired. I thought I detected a quiver in her voice.

'Not long after midnight, ma'am.'

'By which time fortunately I was at home with my maid, who will testify to that. I entreated Mr Harcourt to escort me home and I was most distressed when he abandoned me a few minutes later. Had it not been for the kindness of a gentleman and his wife driving along Newgate Street in a carriage, who stopped and then brought me to my home, I should have been even more distressed.'

To me, her willingness to impress this story on a mere sweep only made it seem more likely that there might be more to what had happened than she was telling me. From what I had seen of her maid she would loyally back her mistress' story, whether true or false. Nevertheless, I could not believe that Mrs Fortescue herself could have garrotted Mr Harcourt. If she had hired Flint, however, that would be another matter. Mr Harcourt had made it clear he no longer desired her presence in his life well before his death, which would have given her plenty of time to plot her revenge.

Telling me her story must have steadied her for she added grandly: 'That is all, my good man. You may go.'

Having indicated the door by which I should leave, she swept out of the kitchen. And I duly departed — without my shilling, on the grounds, she said, that I had given her no information.

*

As I reached King William IV Street on my journey home, it began to rain heavily and the pavements were a sea of bobbing umbrellas. This street is always noisy and always crowded no matter the time of day, because it leads to London Bridge, the great gateway to the far side of the Thames which is always a-hum with traffic and pedestrians. I tried to dodge between carriages and vans to reach the far side of the street as traffic clattered past me on all sides, but had to wait for a time; I was a puppet in a busy world that pulls the strings of so many. There was noise coming at me from all sides, from the clattering of horses' hooves and the shouts and comments of pedestrians, but one voice momentarily rose above it from crowd milling around me.

'You take care, Wasp. Keep out of my business.'

The voice was smooth and caressing, but I could not mistake its sinister undertone — nor its message. This was no Slugger warning me. This was Flint himself.

I spun round, hunting for its source, but the moving mob swirling around me, an umbrella jabbing at my face, the impassive faces of unknown people pushing past me, all made it impossible to do so.

I was left shivering. Worse than the warning, worse than the fear it had struck into me, was one nagging terror.

I knew that voice.

CHAPTER SIX

The Soot Gathers

It had been a bad morning for business. Those who live on the Ratcliffe Highway aren't known for their cleanliness or for parting with sixpence for chimney sweeping, but usually there is work enough. I had tried to put the fright of yesterday evening behind me, but it sneaked up all too often. Whose voice had it been? I could hear it still ringing through my head, but I could not give it an identity.

Ned and I had been up for an hour or two this Wednesday calling the streets before dawn, but only one maidservant came rushing out to secure our services. I saw Ned looking at her quite grown up like, as he followed her eagerly into the house.

We were deciding where to go next when I heard in the distance a mournful cry that I recognised: 'Murder, 'orrible murder.' Coming round a bend in the Highway I saw old Enoch the patterer, who sells broadsheets by calling the streets like Ned and me. Sometimes he has his daughter with him as a chaunter singer, but today he was alone.

Murders aren't that rare in London's docklands, so his cry didn't make me gasp with horror, but the next one had my full attention.

'Toff's dastardly murderer arrested,' he called. 'Blood everywhere. Desperate struggle.'

A fearsome thought curled itself up inside my stomach. Toff? Could that be Mr Harcourt? *Who* had been arrested?

Ned had the same fright as I had. 'Do you think it's Phineas, guvnor?'

'Let's find out, lad.' Already I was hurrying towards Enoch.

Enoch must be as old as Methuselah. He's been walking these streets with his lugubrious face and straggly beard since I was a nipper and he looked old then. These patterers do a good job in passing on news especially to those that can't read. You don't have to buy his broadsheets, you can just listen to his patter to find out what's happening in the world and slip him a farthing. Enoch invents half his news if it's a dull day and by the time you've bought his broadsheet and found out the truth he's moved on. He once told a crowd of twenty or more that Her Majesty had topped herself through grief at her husband's passing. That had been a patter too far and no one bought a broadsheet from Enoch for many a long day.

'Is this true about the toff's murderer, Enoch? I said, not being able to afford a broadsheet.

'As true as Moses and the tablets of stone,' he assured me, being of a religious bent.

'Has Phineas Snook been copped?' I asked with dread, although to my astonishment I saw Ned handing over a penny to Enoch for a broadsheet of our own.

Enoch's old eyes gleamed with satisfaction but then he spotted another potential customer. 'Local murderer topped,' he cried out eagerly.

'Enoch,' I said sharply. 'If it's Phineas Snook, he ain't yet been tried at the Old Bailey.'

'He's been cuffed,' Enoch replied crossly. 'They don't let no one go.

Not till they walk through the Newgate passage to meet hangman Jack Ketch. Then they goes up to their Maker, who knows where to send them. Right back down again into hellfire.'

'Not Phineas,' I howled. 'Hear that, Enoch? *Not Phineas*. You call out, "Innocent man pinched for toff's murder" instead.'

Enoch was doubtful about this. 'If you say so, Mr Wasp,' he muttered grudgingly. He shuffled off, crying out, 'Toff's murderer wrongly nabbed.'

I seized the broadsheet from Ned. There it was: 'Mr Arnold Harcourt's murderer arrested.' For once, Enoch had not been exaggerating.

'I'm sorry you paid good money for this bad news, Ned,' I said heavily.

'I didn't, guvnor. Enoch paid for it. I nabbed the penny out of his pocket.'

I tried hard to look disapproving. Ned knows I don't like his ways of augmenting our income and never does it when I'm around. Today was different. We were both upset. I'd make it up to Enoch next time I saw him.

'What does it say, guvnor?' Ned pretends to struggle with reading in case he's asked to do more. I didn't force him but just read it out to him, wondering where to go from here. Phineas had been arrested last night not long after we had left him.

'What about Cockalorum?' Ned asked anxiously. 'He won't have anything to eat.'

The way I saw it, Cockalorum was quite capable of foraging for himself, but the least we could do would be to check he was safe. Then I would try to see Constable Peters, but I'd pay that trip alone in case it was really bad news. The good Lord must have approved this plan because there was a fish stall on the Highway on the way to Mrs Tutman's lodging house, and we found some stale fish from yesterday that the fishmonger was anxious to get rid of for nothing. Cockalorum wouldn't mind a bit of smell. I tucked it on to our handcart with the brushes and cloths.

When we reached John's Hill there was Mrs Tutman standing outside her front door, telling anyone passing about the murderer she'd been harbouring in her bosom.

'I always knew something was wrong with that man,' I heard her say. 'Wanting a room to himself indeed. Don't he know that rooms are scarce to come by? Three to a room is my usual. I don't like to crowd them in, more money or not. And who's going to pay me now for that room he kept all to himself? Not him, for sure.'

'I will, Mrs Tutman,' I declared, aware of Ned fidgeting at my side with shock. 'You keep that room just for him and I'll pay for it.'

'Rent's due Friday,' she told me smartly. 'Two shillings a week, and I'll have it in advance if it's all the same to you.'

It wasn't, but I had to keep Phineas' room for him. 'Here's some now and the rest Friday.'

Ned's eyes grew round with horror as he saw me take out one whole shilling which we both knew had emptied our money box.

'What about Cockalorum?' I then asked. 'Have you fed him?'

'Not my job.' She gave a triumphant grin. 'Cats indeed. I keep a high-class residence here.'

Not by the look of the matelots and villains I'd seen here, but I decided not to argue the point. 'Then I'll make it *my* job,' I said grandly. Mrs Tutman sniggered.

When we walked round the back of the lodging house, there was Cockalorum waiting for us, or so it seemed, at the top of those steps. A small window had been left open for his convenience perhaps, as the door was closed. He wasn't sitting as he normally was but pacing around, perhaps hungry or perhaps missing Phineas. He studied us

carefully as we went up but made no objection as we entered Phineas'
room. Perhaps he could smell the fish Ned had brought.

'Let's take him home,' he pleaded.

'He wouldn't like that, Ned. He'll want to be here when Phineas
comes home, so it's our job to make sure that's very soon.'

It was a small room, but it did have a chimney and hearth of its
own for cooking. I saw Phineas' fool's cap and costume hanging from
a hook, and there was a bookcase with a few books in it. One or two
I recognised from my childhood after I'd learned to read, thanks to
a kindly lady after I had landed mistakenly on her hearth during my
climbing boy days.

There was a small table by Phineas' bed, and on it were two piles
of paper lying on what looked like an open cover. It wasn't a printed
book, more like a collection of old letters, for the yellowing pages were
of different sizes and had handwriting on both sides. I looked at one
of the pages in the middle of the pile and realised it was some kind of
poem. Ned was feeding Cockalorum so I studied it more closely at it,
and down towards the bottom of the page on the left I saw the word
'Cat'. Was that what had caught Phineas' eye? I was getting the gist of
this handwriting now and could make out what it said. The first two
lines were:

For I will consider my Cat Jeoffry
For he is the servant of the Living God duly and daily serving him

I looked down at Cockalorum who was busily attacking that smelly
fish, and wondered whether he considered himself a servant of the
Living God. He seemed to have accepted my presence, thanks to Ned
and the fish. I read on further about this cat Jeoffry and his way of life,
trying to think why Phineas had chosen to have this poetry by his bed.
It must be because he thought this cat Jeoffry was like Cockalorum.

Then a dark thought struck me. I quickly turned the pile of papers over to see if there were a name on the leather cover — and there was. I read the two words *Jubilate Agno*. I did not know what they meant, but I remembered Mrs Fortescue using them. I went very cold inside, realising with dismay where this might be leading.

I was very much afeard that this was the poetry folder for which the thief at Harcourt's Antiquarian Bookstore had paid his tuppence, and if so that meant Phineas could have been the thief who had broken in at the dead of night. Surely that couldn't be the case — and yet here I stood, staring at the name *Jubilate Agno*. Even if this wasn't the manuscript that Mrs Harcourt claimed was missing, it showed that Phineas had been in the bookstore.

Cockalorum growled and I addressed him sadly: 'You may be a servant of the Living God, Cockalorum, but we're all in trouble, you and us alike.'

His eyes twitched. He was alert, ears pricking, listening but not to me. Something else had his attention. Footsteps were coming up those steps, and they must be a stranger's, because he'd know Phineas' and not be on guard as he was now.

It was a warning to me too, and something made me slam the folder shut, so that the handwriting inside could not be seen. Then I hurried to the door leaving Ned with Cockalorum, who had leapt up on to the table by the side of the folder, crouching and still growling.

'It's something bad, guvnor,' Ned whispered. 'He knows it.'

It was worse than bad news. As I pulled the door open, I saw Slugger Joe. His face was grim and it grew even grimmer when he saw me.

'What you doing here, Wasp?' he rasped. 'You poke your nose in everywhere. Clear off. *Now.*'

'What are *you* doing here?' I asked bravely. He'd reached the top of the steps and was towering over me as I stood blocking the doorway.

'Where's that stuff, Wasp? His dear old mother wants it,' Slugger leered.

'Wait till Phineas returns,' I said mildly. 'He can give it to her then, whatever it is,' I added hastily.

'Out of my way, Wasp. I'll find it myself. Well, well.' His tone changed as he peered past me. 'If it isn't little Ned. So you're here too. Here to nab all you can while poor Phineas is banged up in the clink waiting for the rope?' Slugger's eyes were darting everywhere — and then they fell on the *Jubilate Agno*.

Fear leaves you when you don't have time to attend to it because you're busy trying to hang on to your life. What to do next?

I stood in front of the *Jubilate*. Slugger made a move to shove his way past me. I moved left to stop him. Then he moved to his left to shove again so I moved right. I could smell his funk. I could feel his hot rancid breath as his beefy hand clutched my shoulder and forced me off balance into the middle of the room where I collapsed on to the floor. Slugger was after that folder and he'd nab it. Ned was in his way and he ran at Slugger Joe, only to be tossed on top of me. There'd be no stopping Slugger now.

There *was* a way. I was forgetting Cockalorum, who came flying at Slugger with a high-pitched screech of a *miaow* that would put all the banshees in Ireland to shame; he had launched himself from the top of the table, and was clinging on to Slugger's ragged clothing, twisting, wriggling and clawing at his enemy's hands, wrists and face as Slugger tried to free himself. Blood was running fast as Slugger cursed. At last he managed to throw the cat off, although a new onslaught sent him staggering backwards outside the open door. Cockalorum was hissing and crouching ready to pounce again as Slugger began to regain his balance. Then the cat hurled himself once more against the enemy and Slugger was propelled back two or three steps as Cockalorum made contact.

By now Ned and I were on our feet again — in time to see Slugger lose his balance, tumbling down the steps into the yard and leaving the victorious Cockalorum hissing from the top of them.

Slugger picked himself up and limped away. 'I'll be back,' he croaked. 'I'll wring that blasted cat's neck if it's the last thing I do.' And then he left.

Ned was whimpering and I felt like doing that myself. 'There's something going on that we don't understand, Ned,' I said heavily. 'Are you hurt?'

'Not much. Guvnor, we'll have to take Cockalorum home with us now, won't we?' He looked at me defiantly.

I was thinking how little I wanted to look after that cat, but knowing how much we owed to him, I knew Ned was right. 'We'll take that poetry with us too.'

Ned wasn't interested in poetry. 'Why?'

'That must be what Slugger's after, and what the thief paid tuppence for,' I said unthinkingly.

'You mean Phineas was the cracksman, guvnor?' Ned looked impressed.

'He *paid* for it,' I added hastily. 'When he saw something in the poetry about a cat he thought of Cockalorum.'

Ned looked puzzled. 'Why do a bust at Harcourt's place if he wanted to *buy* it?'

'I don't know,' I admitted. Should I say more? Yes. Ned was old enough to understand. 'What worries me is that Phineas might know more about Mr Harcourt's murder than we thought, Ned.'

It was possible that Phineas had seen the *Jubilate* at his mother's home, if he'd visited her since last week, but I discounted this. Slugger

Joe wouldn't have left it lying around if he'd been the cracksman and paid tuppence for it. He'd have given it straight to Flint, or rather, his fellow deputy Lairy John. That, after all, is where Mr Harcourt seemed to have obtained it in the first place. It must have been stolen property.

Ned was aghast. 'But he didn't kill that bloke, guvnor. Not Phineas. You said the pigmen had nabbed him by mistake and he'd be back soon.'

'Let's hope, Ned. Now let's get going. Cockalorum can ride on the handcart.'

Ned saw the sense of speed, and promptly carried Cockalorum down the steps to the cart, and I tucked the leather folder beneath my arm and we set off. Or tried to. Cockalorum wasn't happy and jumped off the cart, ready to resume his place at the top of the steps. None of our blandishments worked.

'We'll have to bring a box back,' I said in the end. 'If we make haste we can be home and back within the half-hour.'

'All right,' Ned agreed, rather to my surprise. It took but fifteen minutes to reach Hairbrine Court trundling our cart. Our landlady Mrs Scrimshaw was in the court as we arrived and looked surprised, looking back past us to the entry.

'What's that cat doing?' she asked suspiciously.

I glanced round as Ned laughed. There was Cockalorum, following us down the street. This, I decided, was an independent cat indeed. No ignominious cart-riding for him. I began to respect him more and more.

'Looks like we've another lodger temporarily,' I explained to her hopefully.

'We don't like cats round here.'

'Cockalorum isn't just a cat,' I said, remembering that poetry I'd read about Jeoffry. 'He is of the tribe of Tiger.'

'Then you keep him tied up, Mr Wasp,' she snorted. 'I saw tigers in Jamrach's Menagerie. Nasty, fierce animals, they are.'

'It just shows,' I said to Ned as Cockalorum followed us up the stairs as though he had lived there all his life. 'He seems fond of me now, having followed us of his own free will.'

Ned grinned. 'I stuck the rest of that old fish in your pocket, guvnor.'

*

Ned and I had already discussed arrangements for the new arrival. 'He can sleep in my room,' he had pleaded.

I wasn't sure how Kwan-yin, Ned's much loved linnet, would take to this, but she is a placid bird and the situation could at least be tried. Fortunately, her residence is by the window in our main room where I sleep. Thanks to an improvement in our fortunes a year or two back, we are able to rent two rooms, one for Ned and one for me and our table. Our privy is in the basement and shared of course; there's even a washroom there, courtesy of the same financial improvement. It has a tap all of its own that runs water four times a week if we're lucky, twice if not. To the great pleasure of my landlady, this washroom makes us the envy of the neighbourhood, and so she obliges me in small matters, such as turning a blind eye to Cockalorum and policemen.

I had little time to spend on Cockalorum though, now that he'd been introduced to his temporary home. I had to talk to Constable Peters about Phineas urgently. If he had been arrested at his lodgings then the Metropolitan Police would have been present as well as the City of London force. What was worrying me about this *Jubilate Agno* folder I'd brought back with me was that it might provide damning evidence against Phineas for implicating him in Mr Harcourt's murder, as well as for his being the thief. If I didn't tell Constable Peters about it, though, I might end up making things worse for Phineas — and for me.

Phineas would be in Newgate, where all poor souls go before they are tried at the Old Bailey, but for those on remand no visitors are allowed there for ten days. That meant I might not be able to ask him yet about the *Jubilate Agno*. But I was going to do my best to do so. I'd pay a visit to Scotland Yard straight away.

'All in all, it's a conundrum, Cockalorum,' I informed him. The cat seemed to have accepted me as a decent sort of person who not only carried fish in his pocket but might light the fire for him to lie in front of. 'Not yet, Cockalorum,' I told him. 'Constable Peters first. Think of Phineas.'

Cockalorum cast a glance at me, as though he now realised I was a mere appendage to Ned. At least I wasn't regarded as a target like Slugger Joe. I reminded the cat, who was peacefully licking his paws, that he was a servant of the Living God and just for the moment I was standing in for our Lord as far as he was concerned. And that meant his keeping away from Kwan-yin too. To do him justice, so far he hadn't even glanced the bird's way.

'What am I going to do about this book and Constable Peters?' I asked Cockalorum, as Ned seemed to have disappeared about his own business.

I felt foolish talking to a cat, but Cockalorum glanced up at me, looking very wise, so before I left I read him one last line about Jeoffry: *For he keeps the Lord's watch in the night against the adversary.*

'You did that this morning, Cockalorum. For that you shall be treasured,' I told him. Cockalorum purred and went to sleep.

*

Scotland Yard in Whitehall Place is always busy, and for a sweep it's harder to have an urgent request taken seriously. This afternoon Mr

Harcourt's funeral would take place and I was anxious to join Clara to see the cortege pass. It was some time before I was permitted even to sit in the waiting area at Scotland Yard, however, despite the fact that my business was with the Detective Department, which is now held in growing regard. I resisted several well-meant attempts to direct me to the boiler rooms and was relieved when Constable Peters finally arrived, looking most worried. He suggested we took a walk to St James' Park, it being a fine day. This is but a short distance away, through Horseguards, where mounted cavalry soldiers stand sentry each side of the entrance.

At last, surrounded by governesses out with their charges and many other Londoners eager to breathe the fresh air of trees and grass, Constable Peters felt free to talk. Passers-by probably assumed I was under arrest, we chimney sweeps having a bad reputation for aiding and abetting criminals, owing to our knowledge of the interiors of wealthy houses.

'You've heard the news about Phineas Snook, Mr Wasp? Do you believe him guilty?'

'No.'

'The City of London police are quite sure they have their man. It fits well. They're convinced Flint wasn't just hired to murder Harcourt but was the main player in this murder case, and that Slugger Joe carried it out on his behalf, using Phineas as a willing tool.'

'What evidence do they have against Phineas?' I asked in desperation.

'He was there in Paternoster Row the day Mr Harcourt was killed and expressed harsh feelings towards him on account of his treatment of Miss Hetty. You know about that, Mr Wasp.'

I did, and it was depressing to hear that the police were already aware of Phineas' presence in the Row that day. It was strange though that Phineas had asked me to warn Clara about Mr Harcourt if he was going to the Row himself. I did my best to defend him. 'He was there in the late afternoon but it's a long time from then to midnight, which is about when Mr Harcourt was killed,' I pointed out.

'He also went to Dolly's Chop House.'

'When?' I asked. Phineas hadn't answered my question about his visit and I'd assumed it was only to the alley where Hetty had seen him. 'Who claims that?'

Constable Peters consulted his notepad. 'Mr Jericho Mason, a cook at Dolly's. It seems Phineas was demanding to know if Mr Harcourt was to be present that night at the Tarlton Ordinaries' dinner. Mr Mason confirmed he was, whereupon Phineas insisted on seeing Miss Pomfret. When Mason said she was not there he became very aggressive and accused Mason of falsehood. He stated that Mr Harcourt was a villain and said he would kill him if he refused to stop making advances to her. He then punched Mr Mason and again demanded to see Miss Pomfret.'

My horror grew. I could not believe this of Phineas. He wasn't a violent man. Far from it. But Jericho Mason was a man of mystery and I would not take his word for it alone.

'Jericho's the only witness?'

'No. Mr William Wright supports him.'

William too? This sounded most ominous and I tried to disentangle it. If — and I could not believe it — such a scene had taken place, then Phineas' motive for killing Mr Harcourt must have been a very personal one. Yet I held evidence that he might be involved in the robbery. I had to speak out now, and reluctantly told the constable about the *Jubilate Agno*.

He was as surprised as I and together we considered this information and its relevance carefully. 'A burglary,' the constable said at last, 'yet nothing was stolen as this poetry folder was paid for, and we've no proof that anything else was taken. There can't be two poetry manuscripts called

Jubilate Agno, so it's almost certain Phineas took it from Harcourt's store — unless someone gave it to him afterwards, which is highly unlikely. And we don't know whether it has any connection to Mr Harcourt's murder. In any case — ' He brightened up — 'it's not *evidence* of murder and Phineas has been charged with murder, not robbery. Shall we put this information aside until we see things more clearly?'

'You said *we*, constable.'

'I did.' He grinned. 'That should give both of us time to investigate further. Now that Phineas has been arrested, the case is one for the City of London police, so I can't go nosing into it any further. But you can, Mr Wasp.'

CHAPTER SEVEN

Tolling Bells

I doffed my hat in respect as the funeral procession slowly passed along Paternoster Row. Being on the short side, I found it hard to see, as it seemed every single one of the Row's workers was gathered here to pay tribute to Mr Arnold Harcourt as his coffin made its way from St Martin's in Ludgate to the City of London burial grounds for the burial. Unusually, the service had taken place in church rather than in the late Mr Harcourt's home, Hart House. Clara stood beside me in her funeral black and Ned had joined us too. He plucked at my sleeve anxiously.

'Cockalorum's all on his own,' he whispered.

'If he wants to stay with us, he will,' I comforted him. We'd provided him with a box of soot for his convenience and some food and water that we scraped together. With Cockalorum to feed it had been hard to persuade Ned it was time to get moving so I counted it a privilege that he was here at all. Cockalorum had agreed with me judging by the plaintive *miaow* he had given Ned as we left — and the baleful look I received.

The funeral procession was not a very grand affair for all its black horses pulling the hearse, adorned with their black ribbons and plumes. The front carriages bore the clergyman and the pallbearers. I recognised one of these as being the gentleman selling biblical tracts in St Paul's Churchyard, who had invited me to consider where I should like to spend eternity, and wondered whether Mr Harcourt had also been interrogated on this matter. After these carriages came the hearse and behind it the carriages bearing the mourners. These included several with familiar faces, and among them were the Tarlton Ordinaries, not just the three I had met with Constable Peters that day, but all seven looking most solemn in their black frock coats and black-banded top hats and gloves. Behind them were half a dozen or so other gentlemen, whom I did not recognise.

Much to Clara's disapproval, Mrs Harcourt had broken with convention and had sent out invitations to what she termed 'a business reception' later that day at Hart House.

'She's sent me an invitation asking me to attend,' Clara had told me. 'I have to say, Tom, I'm quite bewildered. Business indeed. She has only just been widowed and shouldn't be receiving *any* guests yet awhile. Does business excuse that?'

'Perhaps murder does. She might have her own ideas on who killed her husband,' I said soberly.

'In that case, I'll forget about convention,' Clara had announced with a searching look; I picked up her meaning.

'I'd greatly appreciate it, Clara, if I could escort you,' I replied, straight-faced. This might not please Mrs Harcourt, but it was an opportunity I should grasp and Constable Peters would agree with me.

Clara had looked relieved. 'Just what I was going to suggest, and Hetty may insist on coming, too.'

Once the procession had passed, Paternoster Row began returning to business and carriage traffic resumed. Ned chose to return to Hairbrine Court, but Clara and I walked back to Queen's Head Passage and Dolly's until it was time for the reception.

'There's more to be learned at Dolly's about this murder, isn't there?' she said on the way. 'The police may think they have their man, but we know they don't. They came to Dolly's several times. I thought it was only the Tarlton Ordinaries who interested them, but there's more to it than that, isn't there? Is that why Phineas is in gaol?'

'It could be, Clara.' For all they were concentrating on the Flint angle and Mr Harcourt's dealings with Lairy John, they'd taken evidence from Jericho and William too.

'Find out quickly what really happened, Tom. Dolly's is a happy place and I never want it thought otherwise. Look at all the people who have come here in times past. I walk in history there. I can hear their laughter sometimes, Dr Johnson pontificating over this and that, his friend Mr Boswell busy making notes, that composer Handel, Gainsborough who painted Dolly for us. Then there was that American president Jefferson staggering out of here well pleased and well drunk. "One among our many follies/Was calling in for steaks at Dolly's" — that's what he wrote afterwards. He'd had such a good time that he'd forgotten to go to the dinner he'd promised to attend.'

'A fine history, Clara.'

'Sometimes I think I can hear Shakespeare and his Shoreditch pals singing and boozing here when Tarlton owned the old Castle tavern. I can't lose all that happiness, Tom. It's in Dolly's woodwork. But I will lose it if this trouble isn't cleared up quickly. And I don't want —'

She stopped, but I knew what she was going to say. 'You don't want Hetty to suffer,' I finished for her and she nodded.

I understood. Dolly's had been a contented and peaceful place before

Mr Harcourt began his pursuit of Hetty. That was the worm that had gnawed its way like a cancer into Dolly's woodwork, and if Phineas was unwittingly trapped by it, I needed to know quickly, both for his sake and for Dolly's. I was fearful that Hetty herself might even have played a role, judging by the mysterious confession she half made to me. Clara was chiefly concerned with Hetty's distress, but I wondered whether there was more going on than she realised. She was right to be worried for when the foundations of an establishment like Dolly's are threatened, it doesn't take long for customers to begin running away like lemmings at the hint of real trouble.

We were approaching Dolly's now and I wondered whether to press Clara about Hetty, but I had no need as she was eager to talk. 'She's still crying her eyes out, Tom. I never realised she liked Phineas so much, what with all the goings on with Harcourt. I thought it was William Wright she was sweet on.'

'And that's led to more going amiss at Dolly's,' I told Clara soberly. 'What's this about a rumpus on the Wednesday afternoon before Mr Harcourt was murdered?'

'I might have guessed you'd hear. It meant nothing, Tom. Truly. I never saw Phineas here that afternoon. Hetty did, but that set-to was all over nothing, she said. And anyway, that was in the afternoon, not in the evening. The police told me he punched Jericho. And then punched William too. That doesn't sound like Phineas, does it? I don't believe it and nor could Hetty.'

I was even more dismayed that Hetty had said nothing to me about this set-to at Dolly's. 'Was it only Jericho and William who gave evidence?' I asked.

'No. Several customers also heard something going on. And before you ask, it wasn't the Tarlton Ordinaries stirring up trouble.'

For all Clara said it wasn't serious, it sounded it to me. 'The rumpus must have been about Hetty if both Jericho and William were involved,' I said, 'so I'll talk to them if I may.' There was still that twist in the flue, though, as to why Phineas had asked me to warn Clara about Mr Harcourt's behaviour on the same day. Why do that if he was coming to Dolly's himself? He could only have had one mission, and that would have been to see Hetty. So why hadn't Hetty told me that?

Clara looked me straight in the face and I could see she was struggling, but she's a brave lady. 'Go ahead, Tom. We have to know the truth and I'll tell Jericho and William you want to see them. You can have the greeting room.'

*

Jericho looked even more formidable than usual today. I looked at his brawny arms as he marched into the room flourishing a chopper and I swallowed hard. His chef's cap and big apron did nothing to allay the fear that he was about to swing the chopper my way and doubtless that was exactly why he had brought it.

He glared. 'What you want with me, Wasp?'

'Much the same as last time we chatted. I want to find out who topped Mr Harcourt?'

'The bloke in Newgate, that's who,' he growled. 'Ain't nothing you can do about that, sweepie.'

'You told the peelers he hit you. *You?*' I looked at this mountain of a man meaningfully.

'Yeah. *Me,*' he snarled. He seemed slow of movement and thinking, but he was watching me very closely. I was watching the chopper. 'And Will Wright,' he added.

It still seemed unlikely to me and he must have seen the doubt in my face because he added, 'You ask him. And don't come bothering me no more. I've got my chops to broil.' He raised the chopper to emphasise his point.

'Just a moment,' I said mildly. 'How did you get into this fight with Phineas Snook?'

Jericho stared at me as though I was a leg of pork he was thinking of boning. 'He said I was leching after Hetty.'

'And then *he* hit you. Not you hit him?' Punches are usually courtesy of the accused, not the accuser.

'You ask Will.'

'I'm asking you, first. Mrs Pomfret is getting most upset.'

The look on his face turned into fear. A job at Dolly's was worth a lot to a cook like Jericho.

'Look you here,' he said nervously, 'I don't hold nothing against you except you're a blasted nuisance. Here's my advice. You'll do no good here, not now, not with *him* around, and you'll be minced beef if you're not careful. There's people got their eye on you, so *clear out.*'

'Not yet.' I sounded braver than my stomach suggested. First Flint warns me off, now Jericho.

At this his eyes bulged and the chopper was raised once more. Even though I knew he wouldn't dare use it now, I couldn't tell what might crawl out of the woodwork when darkness fell. So I decided to take his advice. I would clear out — at least out of his sight — and think this through even if the mysterious *him* was around. And this *him* could well be Flint, who as I knew all too well had his eye on me. The familiar voice ran through my head again, but still I had not placed it. Flint's warning meant there must be some link between him, Mr Harcourt's death and Dolly's, which was an ugly situation for Clara, for Hetty — and for me.

William was even less delighted to see me than Jericho, but he hid it better. No choppers were in sight, anyway. When he hadn't appeared as expected, I had waylaid him as he rushed by into the kitchens. I assured him that I would still be there when he came for the next plate of steaks and chops and he'd have to talk to me before collecting them. All this food speeding by me was beginning to make me very hungry and my thoughts flew to Ned, hoping that by now he had found some supper for both of us at Hairbrine Court.

William seemed resigned to talking to me when he next appeared and we retired to Clara's greeting room to escape the perpetual motion that was Dolly's at all times of day.

'How can I help?' he said in his best waiter's voice. 'Such terrible news about Mr Snook.'

I couldn't believe in his sincerity, as he had given evidence against Phineas, even though he must have been the junior partner in the set-to. 'Most unfortunate he hit you and Jericho so badly.'

'Yes,' he agreed eagerly. 'Phineas is usually a placid man, but that day he was a raging bull.'

'What brought on this attack of his?' I asked sympathetically, as if I fully believed his every word.

William wavered. 'Some things just happen,' he informed me.

'Not of their own accord. Did Phineas strike the first blow?'

The answer was prompt. 'Snook got it into his head that Hetty adores him; he wanted us to know that and keep clear of her. It's nonsense of course, but where Jericho's concerned, that's dangerous. Phineas punched him hard, shouting and screaming at him to leave Hetty alone. I was trying to stop him before Jericho really became upset. Jericho lightly pushed him away and Phineas then punched me.'

I had the impression he was reciting a prepared account, as if Jericho had been tutoring him. 'Phineas just marched in, announced that Miss

Hetty loved him and punched Jericho, then you. Nothing either of you said to upset him?'

'Not a word.' William spoke uneasily.

'Most restrained of you,' I said approvingly. 'Did *you* lightly push him away, too?'

'Of course.' He was even more uneasy now.

'Understandably,' I observed. 'Was Miss Hetty present during this fight?'

He took his time over this one. 'She came in after a while and was upset when she found out what Snook had done to us. Then Snook left.'

'What time did he attack you?' I asked, bearing in mind that Hetty later saw Phineas at Panyer Alley. I was beginning to sound like Constable Peters, but I was by no means sure I was getting to the heart of things as well as he does.

'About four o'clock, I'd say.' William was shifting his feet as though about to dash away. 'Is that all, Mr Wasp? I've got customers to serve.'

I ignored this. 'But Mr Harcourt wasn't killed until nearly midnight? Why did they charge Phineas for that?'

William looked pleased that he had an answer for this. 'Because Snook was shouting at us that he was going to kill Mr Harcourt. He must have hung around in the Row getting tipsy somewhere and come back to kill Mr Harcourt later.'

That set the tinderbox alight. If that's what happened and that's what they told the police it was little wonder that they had arrested Phineas, but I found it even harder to believe they were talking about the Phineas I knew. 'Did Miss Hetty hear him say that?'

'Jericho did,' he muttered.

I was even more shaken. There was a lot I didn't understand here. Could it be that I had been mistaken about the kind of man Phineas was? Surely not. And yet even if Jericho was lying, I couldn't believe William was.

'You'd best get back to your customers, Mr Wright,' I said heavily.

That brought a smile to his face. 'Yes, I'm saving up to marry Hetty.'

With a heavy heart, I asked Clara's permission to speak to her daughter. I had to get this chimney swept clean somehow.

'Come up to my parlour, Tom,' Clara suggested.

Dolly's has always been known for its pretty lady waiters and Hetty was usually the prettiest. Today, however, with flushed cheeks and downcast expression, she looked weary when she arrived and as nervous as though I were a peeler, not a friendly sweep.

'Hetty, you told me you saw Phineas in Panyer Alley in the late afternoon, but you didn't tell me you'd seen him at Dolly's earlier,' I said as gently as I could.

'I didn't really *see* him earlier,' she answered indignantly. 'He was just there, that's all. I heard a lot of shouting, so I went in and William said it was all about me. Jericho was very cross — he frightens me sometimes. Phineas was sitting on the floor, so I asked him why,' she continued. 'He didn't answer and William said it was a misunderstanding, but all was well, so I went away.'

'And Phineas still didn't say anything as you left?' Why would he have remained silent on the floor if he valued Hetty's good opinion of him? At the very least he'd have risen to greet her.

'No. So that doesn't count as my seeing him. That's why I didn't mention it earlier.' She managed to give me one of her little smiles but this time I wasn't thinking how lovely she looked. I was wondering what else there was to this story.

*

'My word, you look a stunner, Clara.' Still dressed in black, but in her afternoon dress now with wide skirts swept back into that becoming bustle, she did indeed. With her warm welcoming face, she was a picture of sympathy and dignity, ready to face Mrs Harcourt's business reception. 'And you too, Hetty,' I added, though it wasn't strictly as true for her. She was looking even more dejected in her dark clothing than she had earlier.

I'd done my best with Dolly's laundry room washing facilities to look like a gentleman should at a business reception, though that couldn't do much to disguise the engrained soot on my face and hands. At least that was black too, and knowing I was coming here today I'd worn my best black jacket. Clara had lent me a proper silk topper, one she keeps in case customers need one after getting tipsy and mislaying their own. She had also set aside two mutton chops for me to take home to Ned for supper that evening and presented me with a muffin to eat in the meantime.

'Mrs Harcourt won't like a sweep coming, Clara, however good a topper I have,' I warned her.

'It's respectful,' she replied firmly. 'We're thinking of the dead, not the living. What's of more help to Mr Harcourt now: you trying your best to find out who caused his death, or a grasping wife who only cares about what he bequeathed to her?'

Clara was right. Furthermore, St Peter doesn't make distinctions at the Gate of Heaven between a sooty face and a pallid white one, so the same should apply at funerals. We set off for the business reception, seeing the carriages ahead of us stopping at Hart House. Mrs Harcourt's butler, Mr Parker, was somewhat to Clara's relief ushering guests through the open door of the bookstore, not the private door leading upstairs. The blinds were now closed in the rooms above and the usual black crepe and wreath adorned the door to the private part of the house.

'At least she's showing some respect now,' Clara muttered.

There were few ladies here amongst the gentlemen, and the former were gathered in the rear room of the bookstore. I was surprised to see Mrs Fortescue amongst them and she came to greet Clara and Hetty, perhaps thinking that in Clara's company Mrs Harcourt would not raise any objection to her presence. I doubted whether she would have received a formal invitation. Mrs Fortescue did not greet me, even though I swept her a lordly bow. We made a strange quartet for a business gathering; three ladies and a chimney sweep who for all his scrubbing could not disguise his trade.

With both rooms crowded, I could see not only the seven Tarlton Ordinaries, but a great number of other booksellers from the Row, including, so Clara whispered to me, religious publishers for which trade the Row was once famous. Many of these guests were examining the shelves rather than partaking of the tea and sponge cakes that were available in this rear room, where I spotted the now repaired window. It was a quiet scene for a while as befitted the day — until Mrs Fortescue and Mrs Harcourt once again came face to face. Clara tried her best to prevent this, but we became mere bystanders in the battle.

Mrs Harcourt bristled in her black as she loudly proclaimed for all to hear, 'If this were not the day of my beloved husband's funeral, I would ask you to leave, Mrs Fortescue, just as *he* did the day he died.'

'If this were not the day of my dear employer and friend's funeral,' Mrs Fortescue retorted even more loudly, 'I would be delighted to do so. However, he would have wished me to be present at such a business reception.'

'You may not remain unless you disclose where my manuscript is,' replied Mrs Harcourt adding a shriller tone to the shouting, which reduced any remaining conversation in the room to shocked silence.

'It was either stolen that night or you already have it yourself,' Mrs Fortescue screeched.

'Stolen by *you*. *You* are the thief,' boomed Mrs Harcourt.

Guests' cups were suspended in mid-air at this immoderate language, and then hurriedly replaced on saucers as though it were unseemly to drink tea while convention was being so flagrantly ignored. 'Such anger between them, where once there was the voice of harmony,' murmured an Ordinary, the plump Pickwickian gentleman whom I had seen sitting at the far side of the table at their luncheon meeting.

'Upon my word, Mrs Harcourt, you choose inappropriate words for a lady in mourning,' Mrs Fortescue replied to her adversary's challenge — less volume was required, as an appalled silence now reigned in both rooms. 'Would I demean myself by breaking into this bookstore at night? Why not ask the Tarlton Ordinaries where the manuscript is, if you're so sure it existed?' That set those gentlemen bristling.

'Be certain that I will,' Mrs Harcourt replied, 'and I shall once again inform the City of London police that you are responsible for the theft of my property.'

By this time, many of the guests considered that etiquette, if not their private wishes, demanded their withdrawal from the gathering and were quietly leaving the building. Our little party remained, however, augmented by one or two gentlemen publishers and all the Tarlton Ordinaries — judging by their discreetly worn badges carrying the Tarlton image. Mr Splendour, Mr Timpson and Mr Manley in particular seemed eager to continue the discussion about this missing manuscript.

'Mr Harcourt definitely said he had it, Mrs Fortescue,' Mr Manley said, bravely speaking out. 'And I can assure you that I do not have it. Perhaps one of my friends among the other Ordinaries has it?'

He must have realised too late that this was not likely to endear him to his friends, all six of whom broke into immediate cries of denial. Mr Timpson was the loudest in his protestations.

'I most certainly do not,' he cried indignantly.

Mr Splendour had a different approach. 'Nor I,' he said stiffly. 'Harcourt was an odd fish. It's my opinion he was giving us gammon that evening. Of course he didn't have the manuscript. We were wise not to believe him.'

There was some surprise when he uttered these words, but a hasty, 'We were indeed' from Mr Timpson set the tone — until Mrs Harcourt had her say.

'Nonsense,' she said briskly. 'He received it as expected on Wednesday afternoon. I received a telegram to that effect in the evening, instructing me to come to London the following morning as arranged. Given the news I then received of his death, I could not have turned to business matters immediately, but now I do. My husband would not have given *me* gammon, gentlemen. So *where is the manuscript*, and which of *you*?' she demanded yet again of the Ordinaries, 'was the cracksman?'

The Ordinaries understandably stiffened at this insult, which had aroused great interest amongst the other publishing gentlemen, while I contemplated my own fears that Phineas was probably the cracksman — and yet would Phineas have known how to break glass in that way? He must surely have had someone with him. Someone like Slugger Joe. But here I returned to the nub of it. If he had been with Phineas, Slugger would surely have walked off with anything he'd taken at Flint's behest, not given it to Phineas, so why was he so anxious to search Phineas' rooms? It was a puzzle indeed.

Another puzzle was why this manuscript should be of such importance that it was outweighing the occasion, mourning the violent murder of

Mr Harcourt. That would hardly be a subject of open discussion in the presence of his widow, and so was the dissension over this manuscript masking a deeper rift amongst them? Did each of them have his own suspicions as to who had garrotted Mr Harcourt?

The argument over the manuscript was still in progress. 'Has a thorough search of these premises been made?' Mr George Timpson asked pompously, looking round at the bookshelves now refilled with books crammed in at random.

'It has,' Mrs Harcourt snapped and I believed her. 'My late husband's safe, every drawer and every bookshelf in this establishment has been searched in vain. It has gone, and *you* have it, Mrs Fortescue.'

'I could hardly have removed this script without Mr Harcourt noticing,' Mrs Fortescue retaliated.

'You returned to remove it the following evening then, no doubt with the help of these gentlemen.'

The gentlemen concerned, increasingly annoyed at being cast as cracksmen, burst into furious denials regardless of funeral convention. As the noise died down, Hetty's sweet voice rose above it:

'What *is* this missing manuscript?' she enquired.

The silence that followed was eventually broken by Mr Splendour. 'Nothing of great importance, Miss Pomfret. It's only of interest to clubs such as our own.'

Hetty tried to be helpful. 'We could all help search this shop again, Mrs Harcourt.'

'No!' the Tarlton Ordinaries cried almost in unison. United they might now appear, I thought, but if there was an opportunity for any one of them to obtain this mysterious manuscript for himself then comradely feelings would not get in the way.

Mrs Harcourt was equally unfriendly. 'Kindly leave this matter to me,

Miss Pomfret,' she snapped. 'I have long been aware you were spooning with my husband, upsetting not only him but myself.'

Mr Splendour tried to calm the deteriorating situation with a loud: 'We don't know what this manuscript might look like so hunting for it here would avail us nothing. We only know what the content would have been.'

'And what is that?' Clara demanded, her arm round Hetty, who was in tears. The glint in Clara's eye suggested she was holding back with difficulty.

No one rushed to enlighten her; the Ordinaries looked very grim, as did Mrs Harcourt and Mrs Fortescue.

It was Mrs Fortescue who broke the tense silence. 'Tell them, Algernon,' she said to her new employer, Mr Splendour. '*Tell* them.'

He cleared his throat and said unhappily: 'Richard Tarlton's lost play of the *Seven Deadly Sins*.

CHAPTER EIGHT

Where is It?

I watched the Tarlton Ordinaries, to see how they would react to this revelation. Their expressions ranged from anger to horror, but it was clearly no surprise to any of them. Mrs Harcourt was the first to speak.

'Of course the manuscript is lost,' she snapped back at Mr Splendour. 'It was stolen last Thursday night by that woman.' A lace-gloved finger pointed at Mrs Fortescue.

For once Mrs Fortescue failed to rise to the challenge. 'The old miser. He told me he was expecting only what he called a small fragment of Tarlton's work and therefore of interest but no great importance.'

Mrs Harcourt instantly dismissed this. 'Nonsense. You knew full well what it was, where it was *and* its worth. Where is it?'

This puzzled one of the publishing gentlemen, not of the Tarlton Ordinaries. 'A missing play by this fellow Tarlton can hardly be said to be a catastrophe,' he remarked. 'I've heard of Tarlton of course, but there were a great many playwrights around in Elizabethan times. I can't see that this Tarlton play is any great loss to literature or of great value.'

'Hear, hear. Certainly nothing to do with our friend Harcourt's death,' George Timpson said hastily, waistcoat buttons straining in his effort to appear calm.

'I do so agree,' Thomas Manley remarked feebly. He gave a nervous smile, which was quickly repressed as he must have remembered where he was.

'Indeed,' Mr Splendour rapidly agreed. 'It is of interest only to the Ordinaries.'

'Unless of course —' the plump Pickwickian Ordinary began, but I could hear no more as his voice could not be heard owing to a sudden outburst of loud conversation from his fellow members.

'Mr Chalcot,' Clara whispered to me.

'Unfortunately the play was lost, Miss Pomfret,' Mr Timpson boomed in reply to Hetty, with no regard for Mr Chalcot's intervention. 'Nevertheless, you will be wondering how we know it ever existed.'

Hetty looked surprised, and I doubted very much whether such a thought had entered her mind. Nevertheless, the Tarlton Ordinaries were all suddenly anxious to inform Hetty of every detail on this subject.

'Because the poet Gabriel Harvey, scholarly adviser to Sir Philip Sidney, saw the play performed in Oxford in the 1580s, no doubt with Tarlton performing as the fool. There are other references to it —' offered Mr Timpson.

'By no means is Tarlton's play to be confused with that of the same name performed in the following decade —' Mr Manley interrupted him.

'The plot of which was discovered last century,' Mr Splendour couldn't wait to let us know. 'Comedy or tragedy however? Of that we cannot be sure just as we cannot be sure whether it was later performed by Lord Strange's Men or the Lord Chamberlain's, of which Shakespeare —'

That name brought a gasp from his audience, which set me thinking.

'Dear Tarlton,' Mr Manley blurted out. 'Such an incomparable comedian. I wonder whether you have heard the jest he made about Sir Walter Raleigh before Her Majesty Queen Elizabeth —'

'— Not now, Manley,' Mr Timpson loudly reprimanded him. 'Today of all days we should dwell on life's tragedies.'

It seemed that none of the Ordinaries wished to join in this discussion of life's tragedies, at least as far as Mr Harcourt's murder was concerned. I wondered again whether that or this play loomed largest in their minds. The name of Richard Tarlton and that of his play, however, disappeared from the conversation. They were so markedly absent that I wondered what Mr Chalcot would have said about the play's relevance for the modern book world, if he had been allowed to continue. As it was, I saw several more of the company edging their way towards the door into the street. Clara too seemed anxious to leave, but loyally stayed as I showed no signs of leaving. I was all too aware that amongst this diminishing group there could be a murderer, and that was what loomed in my own mind, with Phineas' life at stake.

Mrs Fortescue and Mrs Harcourt needed very little encouragement to resume hostilities.

'How much would this Tarlton play be worth?' Mrs Harcourt asked Mr Timpson with less than genteel eagerness.

'As has been indicated, dear lady, very little, save to us, the Ordinaries. Pray do not concern yourself.'

'I *do* concern myself,' she retorted. 'It belongs to me, now that Mr Harcourt is no longer with us, and if it is of any value to you, gentlemen, you will naturally wish to acquire it. *At a suitable price.*'

Glancing at his fellow Ordinaries, Mr Timpson took up the challenge. 'If the play is found, we would of course evaluate it, although I fear it would bring you but scant monetary rewards, Mrs Harcourt;

you would however have the honour of knowing you had contributed to the legacy of Richard Tarlton.' He could contain himself no longer, however. 'But I find it hard to believe it has completely disappeared. Where is it, Mrs Harcourt?' he burst out.

'Where is it, Mrs Fortescue?' she demanded in turn, skirts rustling in indignation.

'Where is it?' Mrs Fortescue demanded of the assembled Ordinaries.

I almost cried 'where is it?' myself, as this play that was apparently of little value was so much in demand.

'This is like running around the Crystal Palace lakes,' murmured Clara.

I agreed with her and was about to suggest we left after paying our respects to Mrs Harcourt (not that she would welcome them) when the conversation took an interesting turn. Mr 'Pickwick' Chalcot spoke again.

'What puzzles me, Mrs Harcourt, is why Mr Harcourt was so sure that manuscript was indeed the lost play. As we have just heard, there was at least one other play of the name *Seven Deadly Sins* in the sixteenth century and no plays were treated with the respect we give them in these modern times. Old stories were revived and used time after time, collaboration on scripts by playwrights was commonplace.'

Mr Timpson was becoming agitated and clearly wishing to change the subject, but Mr Chalcot was warming to his theme. 'Fortunately, as Mr Timpson has explained, we know that Tarlton did indeed write a play on the seven deadly sins. But if the script is genuine, how did Mr Harcourt find it?'

'That is immaterial,' Mrs Harcourt snapped.

'I gathered,' Mr Splendour said airily, 'that he was keeping that a secret because it was undoubtedly genuine — or worthless.' His last two words were accompanied by a laugh that fell short of its objective in this tense gathering.

'There are other reasons for keeping silent,' Mr Manley said shrilly. 'We all know Mr Harcourt had connections.'

'*What* connections?' Mrs Harcourt asked stonily, as no one else spoke and the tension in the room grew. Even Mrs Fortescue remained silent.

'Fences?' Mr Chalcot enquired blandly, voicing what most of us already knew.

Mr Timpson did his best to look shocked. 'No, indeed. The Spitalfields dealer from whom Mr Harcourt obtained his stock was a reputable London trader, with access to private libraries.'

No one queried what means of access this dealer had, but Mrs Harcourt naturally seized on this. 'I have told you that is immaterial. My husband undoubtedly bought the Tarlton manuscript direct from such a collection and not from any such dealer.'

'Whose library, however?' Mr Timpson asked. 'Madam, we Tarlton Ordinaries have spent much time in pursuing this question. Tarlton's associates were hardly possessors of vast estates. Apart from the so-called adopted son referred to in his jest book, Tarlton had only one son, legitimate or otherwise, of whom there are no further records because it's probable he died at the hands of a crooked lawyer. It is therefore clear that the manuscript came into the hands of some private gentleman after Tarlton's death in 1588.'

'And what is also clear,' Mr Splendour quickly added, 'is that this matter has no relevance to Mr Harcourt's shocking murder, still under investigation by the police. No doubt the perpetrator will soon be found; he is probably one of the staff at Dolly's, as we saw no sign of any ruffians when we left Mr Harcourt.' I could see Clara stifling a furious response, judging by her flushed cheeks and tightly-set lips, and Hetty looked near to tears.

Mrs Harcourt, however, seemed determined not to let go of her current grievance. 'The thief — for whom we need not look as far as Dolly's — took advantage of my poor husband's death to steal this manuscript.'

This made it sound as though she thought the theft and the murder might not necessarily be linked, but even so where did that take me on this journey to prove Phineas' innocence? Was the real killer present now, or was he William or Jericho? And over all these possibilities lay the shadow of Flint. I was not aware of having heard that distinctive voice here today, but the conversation was so loud and confused there had been little chance of doing so. But whatever his means, Flint would be following my every movement.

*

Newgate does its best to frighten you away from crime from the very moment you arrive. That great door with its formidable spikes above the huge knocker strikes fear into both innocent and guilty alike, and it's a relief to be allowed inside, at least as far as the lodge-keeper's office.

Since little in the way of food is provided for those committed for trial, Clara had been sending food from Dolly's to Phineas daily. This was not to Jericho's pleasure, I'm sure. Hetty faithfully carried it to Newgate each day, although she had to leave it with the warders, as he was allowed no visitors yet. She's inherited her mother's kind heart.

Even though I had a special authorisation from Constable Peters, the lodgekeeper was not disposed to let me in when I called on Thursday morning, but knowing me of old he relented. Even lawyers for the accused are not permitted in for the first ten days of imprisonment, let alone other visitors, so this was a great favour.

Newgate has had modernisations in recent years and not much of the old prison still exists, when prisoners had to sleep head to toe like slaves on a ship. Now, the men's side has four galleries full of cells, much better I have been told, where the prisoners sentenced to penal servitude can pick their oakum. But Phineas, as someone committed for trial, was on the ground floor in block A. I felt my heart thumping as I followed the warder down the long silent corridors, the only sound being the clang of the iron gates every so often as he locked them after us along the way. *Silence.* Not a word can pass in prisons amongst its inmates whether awaiting trial or on penal servitude.

My special treatment continued as I was not taken to a cell but to one of two boxes with glass doors and windows used for lawyers to communicate with their unhappy clients. Only a wired square grille allowed me to see even Phineas' head. I had seen through the door that he had a warder with him, but my own warder escort remained outside, grimly peering in at me from time to time. Phineas had not yet seen me and my heart thumped again at the sight of his shorn hair and forlorn face. He looked like a wind-up toy that had run down.

'Phineas Snook,' I said softly and he raised his head.

At first he merely stared at me. 'Hey nonny, Tom Wasp,' he managed to whisper at last.

I wanted to say it wouldn't be long before he was freed, but I decided to go carefully. Something that might have been a smile came to his face, obviously thinking I'd come with good news of his release.

'Today?' he asked.

'Not yet, Phineas.'

HeHe looked at me in alarm. 'Cockalorum?'

'He's being looked after.' That was an understatement. Ned watched over that cat so closely I had a feeling Cockalorum was getting more of our supper than Ned and I were. Cockalorum did some close watching of his own — he watched Kwan-yin, though fortunately not because he fancied her for supper.

The news about Cockalorum seemed to cheer Phineas up. 'What am I doing here, Tom?' he asked. 'I didn't kill Mr Harcourt.'

'There's a mistake been made, but we're going to put it right,' I said more cheerily than I felt. 'You have to tell me what happened that day though.' Could I risk going further with the warders listening to every word? I'd no choice. 'You didn't tell me you'd been to Dolly's that Wednesday afternoon.'

He frowned. 'Did you ask me?'

From anyone but Phineas I'd have thought this a charley pitcher's trick, but with Phineas it was different. You asked him a question and he replied with the truth, no more, no less. He seldom bothered with details. He was preoccupied with his own world — save where Hetty was concerned.

'Why did you go to Dolly's on the day that Mr Harcourt died?'

'That was in the afternoon. I wanted to see Hetty but they stopped me.'

'Who? Mr Mason and Mr Wright?' He nodded so I added, 'Stopped you how?'

'Mr Mason snatched the flowers I had picked for her and threw them to Mr Wright. I tried to get them but Mr Mason knocked me down and wouldn't let me get up. They were laughing, and I shouted that I wanted those flowers back.'

So that was behind the yelling and shouting that Clara's customers had heard. I believed Phineas but I didn't know how much he had told the police. Not that I didn't trust what he said, but I didn't want to add to their 'evidence'. 'Did you talk about Mr Harcourt too?'

'Yes. I tried to convince them that Hetty needed our help because Mr Harcourt was planning to seduce her, but they wouldn't believe me. Mr Harcourt wouldn't go that far, they said. He *will*,' I shouted.

At last I was beginning to understand. Either accidentally or on purpose, his 'will' had been turned into 'kill' in the testimony given by Jericho and William. It was going to be hard to convince the City of London police of that though.

'What happened after that, Phineas? Hetty saw you later in Panyer Alley. What were you doing there?'

He looked surprised. 'I like the Panyer Boy.'

I thought of Ned and his different reaction. 'Why's that, Phineas?'

'I like the way he looks at you with his foot stuck up. He'd have made a good fool when he grew up.'

'And then you walked home?'

'Yes.' But Phineas was getting impatient. 'How's Hetty? When can I see her?'

'Visitors aren't allowed, Phineas. I had to have special permission.'

I had a warning glance from the warder, and had to be quick about my questions. 'There was a folder of poetry in your lodgings, Phineas, some of it about a cat.'

He managed a grin. 'My Cat Jeoffry. He's just like Cockalorum.'

'You took that book from Mr Harcourt's bookstore, didn't you?'

'I paid for it,' he told me indignantly, as my heart sank. This was looking bleak.

'When did you go to the bookstore?' I asked, dreading the answer.

'After it had shut,' he replied blithely. 'About eleven o'clock on Thursday night last week.'

This was indeed black news, but I had to force myself on. 'Did you break in?'

'No. I stayed in the Row and Joe said he could get in round the back of the house. Then he let me in.'

Slugger Joe? My worst fears confirmed. Only Phineas could have presented such a story so disastrously. He could well have given the police the impression he was Mr Harcourt's killer as well as a thief.

I was groping my way slowly to what I hoped was the truth about his murder. Even with this bad news, I felt I had begun to clean the chimney. Now I had to let the machine do its job.

'How did you come to be with Joe, Phineas?'

'He asked me to go with him to get the manuscript he wanted,' he replied readily.

'Why you? You'd left your mother's home by then.'

This raised another smile. 'Joe often stayed with my mother and Cockalorum bit him. I was scared that Joe might poison him, so I decided to find lodgings elsewhere and take Cockalorum.'

Now for the all-important question, but to my frustration my warder had had enough; the door had been thrust open and I received an unceremonious order to leave. 'Out! *Now.*'

All I had time for was to throw a last question at Phineas: 'Did Joe get what he wanted that night?'

'No.'

This was worse. Phineas hadn't asked me what this manuscript was. He knew.

The last thing I saw through the grille was his anxious face. But as I left I heard one last plea from him: 'Look after the cat!'

As I walked along in front of the warder, I could hear Phineas singing one of his songs:

When that I was and a little tiny boy
With hey, ho, the wind and the rain …

I vowed I'd make it my job to make the sun shine again on Phineas Snook. As I went out of the first of the many iron gates, it clanged behind me and I could hear no more of his song. All I heard now floating back from Block A was the warder's shout to the inmates:

'*Silence*!'

CHAPTER NINE

Entering the Den

I've walked into the notorious Paddy's Goose tavern after a ship's come into dock, I've walked down Nightingale Lane after the watchman's called midnight, and I'd even survived an encounter with Flint, but I had to brace myself before facing Mrs Tutman again. There she stood, arms akimbo, regarding me as though I were the Spanish Armada come to visit Phineas' room on a rainy Thursday evening before returning to Hairbrine Court.

'Where's that rent then?' she demanded.

'I paid a shilling yesterday and you'll get the same tomorrow when it's due. And Mr Snook sends his regards,' I added meaningfully. 'He'll be back shortly.'

She snorted. 'A fine thing for murderers to be renting my rooms. How am I going to rent it out after he's been strung up? I'll have to fumigate it.'

I had to work hard to be genial. 'You'll make a fortune, Mrs Tutman. Everyone will want to live here once they've heard the story.'

She brightened up and the arms went down to her hips. 'That being the case, the rent's four shillings a week, not two.'

'Less two bob for you not keeping an eye on the place.'

I knew from the way she coloured up that I was right. Phineas' room had received another visit since I left. Slugger must have been back for another hunt.

The delicate matter of rent now settled, I went round to Phineas' room expecting something bad and I found it. It wasn't that things weren't left tidily. They were. Everything from his bed to saucepan and kettle was piled in the middle of the room. Even Cockalorum's basket had been balanced neatly on top of the pile, together with a broken Toby jug that Phineas used to fetch beer. Slugger had obviously helped himself to the contents.

Tom, I told myself, as I surveyed the wreckage, this has to stop. I put everything back tidily, although probably not in the same state or place as before. The tidiness of the pile he'd left suggested he must have found what he was looking for, or that he was in a good mood. Unlikely though that was, I couldn't see that the first could be true. If the Tarlton manuscript had been in the room I would already have found it.

I stood for a while, trying to make sense of the situation. I could be sure of one brick in this wobbly chimney. If Tarlton's *Seven Deadly Sins* play had been in Harcourt's Antiquarian Bookstore that Thursday night it must have been what Slugger was hunting for there; it couldn't have been the *Jubilate Agno* as he wouldn't have let Phineas walk off with it. So why didn't he find it (assuming Phineas was right about that) and why hadn't it been found since? Slugger was obviously still looking for it.

I took another look at Phineas' room, and my eye fell on Cockalorum's basket, which I'd replaced near the small hearth. Could the manuscript have been hidden there? I didn't think so, but it did jab me into realising that I ought to put the *Jubilate Agno* folder somewhere safer than where it was in case Slugger was confused between the two manuscripts. At present the *Jubilate* was at Hairbrine Court underneath the old box that Ned had provided for Cockalorum; this boasted an old blanket to keep him warm which helped hide the folder from the likes of Slugger — and therefore Flint.

Being the faceless power behind the underworld, Flint brought more fear in his wake then the threat of Jack Ketch, the hangman. There was no escaping Flint though; if Slugger was involved in Mr Harcourt's murder and any links it had to the Tarlton manuscript, then Flint was involved too. Whether I liked it or not — and I didn't — I had to work out where I'd heard that voice before.

*

I felt no better the next morning. Tom Wasp, I told myself, you're climbing a crooked chimney with no sign of the light above. Assuming the voice had been Flint's, I could at least rule out the possibility that Flint was a woman. That said, I've known of many gangs with women in them and they're not all molls, leaving the dirty work to their menfolk. Many play their part in the crimes with gusto.

It was hard to tear Ned away from Cockalorum, but it was going to be a busy Friday. After our usual quota of chimneys to clean, I duly paid my shilling's rent to Mrs Tutman, who received it almost with disappointment; then we still needed to clean one or two more chimneys to meet our budget. After that, I knew what my next step must be: tracking down Lairy John. Slugger did the slugging but Lairy John would have been involved over the manuscript. I went alone for this task; I wasn't going to risk having Ned with me.

And so I made my way to Spitalfields, which is a most interesting area of London. When the silk weavers first gathered there after being forced to leave their native land in France many years ago, Spitalfields became poor but honest, like the lady up from the country in the music hall song. Now there are far fewer weavers and of the other residents most are poor and many downright evil. That's because amongst them are the hordes turned out of the Nichol rookery by well-meaning folk who want to give a helping hand to the East End by clearing slums.

The narrow streets and tumbledown houses in Spitalfields have made it a den in which few would choose to live if life had treated them less harshly. Some of the former weavers' cottages hover on the brink of respectability, which makes them a halfway house for likes of Lairy John, who needs to keep a foot both in east and west with his aspirations to high class crime. That would bring him (and Flint) the higher class takings to provide a rolling income for Flint's other ventures. In the past I have run into gangs further east in London, Wapping way, like that of the great Dabeno, not to mention the Rat Mob which is now lying quieter than once it did. Dabeno however understands a deal between gentlemen, but I doubted whether Flint bothered with such details.

I walked through the hubbub of the market, where stallholders of all sorts cried their wares. Vegetables, meat and old china vied with the weavers' goods of every colour in the rainbow. I asked around in vain for a trader in antique objects called John, but all I received were shakes of the head.

With each step I felt a hundred eyes watching me, though, and I was glad I had not brought Ned with me. Climbing boys are highly prized for their skill in getting through small places, and although Ned is getting to be on the old side for that, he still has a few of his former tricks that find favour with the Sluggers of this world. No one came forward to ask for my services, though. Nobody came forward for anything. In desperation I picked on a young weaver dressed more smartly than his competitors and tried a bold approach.

'Tell Lairy I'm here about Phineas Snook.'

That aroused some interest. 'The bloke that did for that gent?'

The details of the law aren't appreciated round here and so to save time I said yes. The youth disappeared into the interior of a nearby shop and an individual came out to eye me up and down. It certainly wasn't Lairy. This was an old man with rheumy eyes and a difficulty in walking, so he beckoned me over.

This was going to take courage for I'd be entering the den. I swallowed and said in a lordly voice, 'I need to speak to Lairy.'

The old man spat on the ground in front of me, but perhaps this was a goodwill gesture for he said: 'Behind the pub. Alley on the left. First right.'

I didn't trust my informant, but I did trust in the good Lord to keep me safe as I was trying to help Phineas. I picked my way through the Cock and Sparrow's yard — the pile of dead rats must have been the product of the last fight, and made me quicken my step. The alley was dark for all it was not yet noon, so I was glad it was first right for me. A large figure loomed up, blocking my path.

'What's yer business?'

'Lairy John,' I said more bravely than I felt.

He sized me up — not a difficult job. 'What for?'

'Business. Phineas Snook.' That name seemed to work some magic charm like Aladdin and his lamp. He stood aside and I turned right into a terrace of two or three houses of surprisingly well-maintained weavers' cottages. One door was open and with a deep breath I entered it. Behind a desk sat as lordly a young gentleman as I have ever seen, almost as plump as Mr Chalcot and wearing a flower in his buttonhole. If it hadn't been for his guard who had followed me in and was breathing heavily down my neck, I might have thought he was off to Buckingham Palace.

This was no cheap pawnbroking dolly-shop, though. There were several works of art displayed and even a dainty harpsichord. There were, I noted, several ancient-looking books too.

'My dear sir,' the youth — clearly the great Lairy John himself — addressed me languidly, 'am I to understand you have news of our good friend Mr Snook?'

I was ready for this. 'Someone made a hash of his room and I'm paying good rent for that.'

Lairy John looked shocked. 'Most distressing, most unfortunate. Does that affect me, however?'

I took a further step in these negotiations: 'Something's missing.'

'That cat of his, perhaps.'

If he knew about Cockalorum we were playing for high stakes. I sent up a swift prayer to our Lord, hoping He could see me down here. 'No,' I said. 'A play by Richard Tarlton.'

Lairy was watching me like Cockalorum himself, probably assessing the best means of attack. His podgy fingers played with a quill on the desk.

'Pray tell me more,' he said politely.

'This Mr Harcourt who was rubbed out last week, he was a regular customer of yours, eh?'

Lairy's face darkened. 'You'd best forget that, Tom Wasp.'

He knew who I was, which was bad, but I'd won a modest victory.

Lairy wouldn't risk Flint's finding out about any private side deals. Emboldened I went further. 'Tell your Mr Flint that I'm not interested in manuscripts, I'm after whoever killed Arnold Harcourt.'

I saw the fingers tighten round the quill. Then I noticed it wasn't a quill at all — it was a stiletto dagger.

'Snook admits stealing this Tarlton play,' Lairy lied idly, as though he couldn't have cared less, 'and so he can hardly complain if it's stolen from *him*. And it seems that it has been — but not by us.'

'That's gammon,' I said firmly. 'He doesn't have it and as for who does, I don't know the ins and outs of that, nor the rights and wrongs.'

'Which of us does? That's hardly the point,' the aristocratic blister remarked.

'I know the rights and wrongs of whether Phineas Snook should be in Newgate. It's wrong.'

'Mr Wasp, take care you avoid us.' Lairy's fingers shot open, the dagger lay exposed on the palm of his hand, and the mask of the benign face switched to the real Lairy; cold, ruthless and as sharp as the stiletto itself.

I'm not a brave man, but sometimes it's wise to look brave even if you are not. This was one of those times. 'Tell Mr Flint I called,' I said, trying to keep the squeak out of my voice. Then I picked up my hat and quickly left the great Lairy's presence.

What had I achieved? I asked myself that as I made my way back through the crowds of the Spitalfields market. It seemed Flint didn't have this Tarlton script either. But nor did I, nor did Phineas. Nor could Slugger have it, as he would not have dared to double-cross Flint by holding on to it himself. Therefore if he and Phineas had missed it in Mr Harcourt's store, either Mrs Harcourt or Mrs Fortescue would have found it during their frantic searches.

Had Mrs Fortescue stolen it as Mrs Harcourt had so often accused her of doing?

*

'I call him Mr Pickwick,' Clara laughed, when I asked her that afternoon where Mr Chalcot lived, and I was amused that we shared the same impression of him. I was still intrigued as to how he would have continued his observation on the value of the missing Tarlton play at Mrs Harcourt's 'business reception'. Judging by the sudden burst of conversation that interrupted him it seemed that no one had wished him to finish his sentence — or to be heard, if he did. There might lie not only the secret of the script but the key to the murder of Mr Harcourt, as it seemed to me there was a disproportionate amount of interest in this supposedly valueless manuscript. These gentlemen of Paternoster Row did not convince me that passionate concern for the contents would overrule that which they had for their pockets.

'Mr Chalcot lives and works in the Churchyard,' Clara told me. 'You've probably seen his store. He sells old and new books, especially children's, under the name of Chalcot Books.'

'Is he as convivial and jolly as Mr Pickwick?' I asked.

'He is indeed. Like Mr Timpson, only shorter and plumper.'

I was not sure that Mr Timpson was at all jolly, although he tried to appear so. I set out for Mr Chalcot's premises, confident that I might be a step further along in my hunt. I found the bookstore with some difficulty as it did not boast its presence, but it had a pleasing display in its bow window. As I entered, I saw him at once, waving his arms enthusiastically while his high-pitched voice was excitedly engaged in persuading a lady of the virtues of Mr Kingsley's *The Water Babies*.

'A fine book, madam,' he was saying. 'A most worthy story for your children.'

He caught sight of me at that point and beamed. 'It is,' he continued to his customer, 'a little hard on chimney sweeps, but they are not all as evil as Mr Grimes in Mr Kingsley's splendid novel.'

'Indeed we are not, madam, though he is quite right to draw attention to the appalling treatment of children still being forced to climb chimneys.' I thought I should add my contribution here, as the lady was viewing me with some trepidation. Caught with the book in her hand she had little choice but to purchase it, and then she hurried past me on her way back to a world where sweeps keep to the kitchen quarters, boiler rooms and chimneys.

I was much gratified that Mr Chalcot had recognised me.

'My dear sir, pray take a seat,' he invited me. 'I cannot leave the premises as my wife is indisposed and cannot tend the counter. But if you would take tea with me I would be most appreciative.'

I replied in kind. 'I'd be much obliged, sir.' I took the armchair that he had bustled round the counter to indicate, then he paid a brief visit to the inner part of the house, and a maid duly appeared with a tray of tea and sponge-cake, which she deposited on the counter; she then curtseyed and left us.

'Now, my dear friend, how can I assist you?' he asked me anxiously. 'Mrs Pomfret tells me you are aiding the poor man in Newgate whom you believe is innocent. Indeed the talk of the Row is that you are assisting the police in this matter.'

'Both statements are true, sir,' I explained. 'There are those in Scotland Yard's Detective Department who believe Mr Snook is innocent of the murder of Mr Harcourt.'

'Why do you so believe, Mr Wasp?'

'He is a man of peace, he brings joy to this world of ours.'

'Joy,' he repeated thoughtfully. 'Too many seek to reform the world with most Christian-like charity but will not speak of its joys. Our police are seldom interested in joys, nor are our preachers and publishers of religious books and tracts. What other evidence is there, Mr Wasp, that Mr Snook is innocent?'

'False witness, sir,' I replied, thinking that this choice of words would please a literary bookseller.

'The ninth commandment. Very well, Mr Wasp, let us assume Mr Snook is innocent. What do you require of me?'

'This Richard Tarlton —' I began.

'Ah yes.' Mr Chalcot beamed. 'Richard Tarlton did indeed bring joy. A great deal of it, both to the common folk and to the court. A hundred years later he was still known as the king of mirth.'

'And this play, sir, about the seven deadly sins. Was that joyous?'

'Who can tell? It was reputed to be a comic drama and certainly for the greatest jester in English history to write a play without a fool's part would be strange indeed. Fools have their role in Shakespeare's *Othello* and *King Lear*, for example. It was the custom of the day that comedy lived alongside tragedy.'

'As it does in life,' I added sagely.

'Indeed, but our modern taste is far different. As I may have mentioned at Mr Harcourt's funeral gathering, in Tarlton's day the players wrote plays as well as acted in them, playwrights would act as well as write, and it was taken not as an insult but as a tribute to add to another's work. In short, English drama is a merry mixture, my dear Mr Wasp.'

That was all most educational, but I was here for a purpose. 'At the late Mr Harcourt's gathering, Mr Chalcot, you said —'

'A shocking affair, shocking.' He shook his head gravely.

'When speaking of the manuscript's value —'

'— Ah, the lost play. But who can tell when something is truly lost. It can, like sheep, be lost and found again, and —'

My turn to interrupt as gently as I could. 'You spoke of the value of this manuscript, which Mr Splendour thought so low, and —'

'— That fellow,' Mr Chalcot said disparagingly. 'I am inclined to think that he had his own interests at heart and not those of literature.'

I pressed on. 'You began a sentence with *unless of course* but I did not hear the end of it.'

'A frequent problem with provisos. Yes, indeed. Tarlton's play of the *Seven Deadly Sins* is your concern, is it not? Why then, my point on the merry mixture of English drama is proven, as there were other plays of the same name.'

'Is there no copy of Mr Tarlton's play other than this missing manuscript?'

'Alas, no. When he was writing in the 1580s, very few plays found their way into print. Richard Tarlton died in 1588 and his play, although it had been performed by the Queen's Men about 1585, was then lost, although a few of his other works still exist at least in fragments. Ah yes. I recall —'

I tried again. 'You spoke of the lost manuscript's value —'

'— Indeed. *Seven Deadly Sins*. Which of us has not sinned to one degree or another? Tarlton, as you may know, once claimed his favourite sin was lechery. Of that I fear he was often guilty. It is said he died in Shoreditch in a fallen woman's arms. Her name was Em Ball, if I remember a'right.'

I saw my opportunity. 'Lechery was a sin committed by Mr Harcourt, I'm told.'

I thought Mr Chalcot might not wish to speak ill of the dead, but I was mistaken.

'Unfortunately, yes. You refer to his partiality for young ladies and one in particular. And there is Mrs Fortescue, of course. Dear me, what a subject when his death is so recent. She and Mrs Harcourt were undoubtedly both troubled by his lecherous nature, seeking comfort from the Bible. As did Adam and Eve in the book of Genesis — they were comforted by the voice of the Lord God as they walked together in the garden. Until Mr Harcourt's terrible murder divided them of course. Mrs Fortescue and Mrs Harcourt, that is. But I digress,' he added in alarm. 'You tell me that you believe Mr Snook is innocent of that and yet is to stand trial, and so it is my duty to impart anything that might be of help. I considered Mr Harcourt's behaviour to Miss Pomfret alarming and that to Mrs Fortescue disgusting. Miss Pomfret had confided some interesting news to Mr Harcourt, so he told me, only a week or so before his death.'

'Of a personal nature?' I asked in horror. A cold dread crept over me as to what this might have been.

'Dear me, no,' he replied to my relief. 'Had it been so he would not have mentioned it at all. He did not tell me what the news was and indeed there were other items he shared with us about that time.'

This needed consideration, but I had to remember my reason for being here. 'You began to speak of the value of Tarlton's play,' I tried once more.

He looked at me in mild surprise. 'Indeed, but what of it? I merely observed the low valuation Mr Splendour was placing on it was justified.'

'But you added a proviso,' I almost howled at him.

He gazed at me in mild reproof. 'My dear sir, there is no need for excitement. I no doubt added that the valuation would of course have been much, *much* higher had the script included additions from the hand of William Shakespeare.'

*

I am a great admirer of the plays of Mr Shakespeare, even though I suspect that the performances I see at the penny gaffs are not the best of his work. I have seen his plays in the pleasure gardens at the Eagle tavern too and very gripping they are. I was beginning to think that if this Tarlton play *did* include additions by Mr Shakespeare, as Mr Chalcot suggested, it could indeed have been a reason for Mr Harcourt's death. Could all the Ordinaries have known of its possible value? If so, it would explain their reluctance to talk about it, hoping to confine the secret within their own circle, while in the meantime each of them might be planning to buy or otherwise acquire it at the cheapest possible price.

I was still considering this as I walked along the Row to Queen's Head Passage and Dolly's. I was just passing Dolly's front entrance on the way to the rear yard when Mr Manley came out of the door. To my surprise, he rushed to greet me with a cry of pleasure, which is not my usual experience of a gentleman's reaction to my presence.

'My dear man,' he cried. 'The very man.'

'For what, Mr Manley?' I asked cautiously.

'I believe you have seen Mr Snook. Is there any news?'

If Mr Chalcot was Mr Pickwick, then Manley was Mr Snodgrass, and the look of pleasure on his face did not entirely disguise his usual soulful expression.

'None,' I told him.

'But has he not confessed?' he asked anxiously.

'Why would he? I believe he is innocent.'

'Yet it was a crime of passion, was it not?'

'Not yet known,' I said correctly, as I had to bear in mind that the manuscript might have nothing to do with Mr Harcourt's murder, and my job was to secure Phineas' release from prison.. I still had to challenge William and Jericho, as their stories about that afternoon were so different to Phineas', and bearing in mind that they had ample reason to wish Mr Harcourt dead. 'Do you know Mr Snook, sir?' I added. 'Is that why you are concerned for his wellbeing?'

He flushed. 'I saw him once performing at the Tower. Very fine, very fine. He was singing *When That I Was and a Little Tiny Boy*. Such poetry. Shakespeare's song of course, but it is thought he wrote it for Tarlton.'

'Did Mr Shakespeare know Tarlton well?' I asked, in view of my conversation with Mr Chalcot.

'Tarlton was his hero. A father figure. Shakespeare's fools are based on him. And of course in *Hamlet*, Shakespeare wrote a lyrical tribute to Tarlton when Hamlet picks up Yorick the fool's skull. "Alas, poor Yorick," he writes so movingly. "He hath borne me on his back a thousand times," he tells us. Such poetry.'

'*Did* Tarlton carry Shakespeare on his shoulders?'

Mr Manley was only too eager to enlighten me. 'It is possible. In Shakespeare's youth many troupes visited Stratford and some say Tarlton, before he came to fame, joined Lord Leicester's Men who visited Stratford when Shakespeare would have been seven and again three years later. Indeed there is a story that when Shakespeare was a lad of eleven his father took him to Kenilworth, Lord Leicester's castle, where the Queen herself was staying and Tarlton himself might even have been one of the players who entertained her.' My informant paused for breath, awarding me a nervous smile.

'Shakespeare undoubtedly knew him well,' he continued, filled with renewed enthusiasm. 'It is generally accepted that he probably joined the Queen's Men, to which Tarlton belonged, in 1587, but many believe, including myself, that he was with them much earlier. Tarlton died in 1588 so how could Shakespeare have built up such a close relationship with him if he'd joined only a year earlier?'

'And might he have helped Mr Tarlton with his playwriting?' I asked innocently.

His face was suddenly ashen. 'Quite ridiculous. Tarlton needed no such assistance. No, no.'

'But if Mr Shakespeare did contribute to the play,' I continued earnestly, 'and if it were valuable, that could be why the cracksman was so eager to break into Mr Harcourt's bookstore. It's my belief the police should be told,' I finished virtuously.

'There is nothing to tell,' he snapped. I just looked at him and he flushed again. 'I've not seen the manuscript,' he added feebly, 'so how can I know what's in it? My colleagues Mr Timpson and Mr Splendour may know more of it.'

'Perhaps Mr Harcourt's murderer might have known too.'

His expression changed. 'Be careful, Mr Wasp. I plead with you. It is true we owe it to literature to find this manuscript. It is true Mr Harcourt boasted about having bought it that afternoon, but its theft was not dependent on his death. That was indeed a crime of passion — of that I am sure. Mrs Fortescue had reason enough to commit such a crime. Or indeed Mr Snook or others who were angry at his treatment of Miss Pomfret.' He glanced at me as he added hopefully, 'Perhaps the fence Mr Harcourt dealt with committed the crime.'

He hurried away, leaving me glad that I was a chimney sweep and working in a trade that is black and white. I'm not suggesting that our life is other than a hard one in this crowded world where everyone fights for their own and the seven deadly sins are all too much with us, but we can play our part in making things better. Is that how Mr Tarlton saw it too? I wondered. He made people laugh, and yet he wrote a play about the seven deadly sins. Perhaps that was his way of dealing with the soot in life.

CHAPTER TEN

The Chimney Darkens

I still could put no name to the voice I had heard, save that I was certain it must have been Flint's. Danger does its work best when it's unrecognised, as fear strikes tenfold when it taps you on the shoulder. Was Flint behind me in the crowds that flock around the Row and the Churchyard? Would he be waiting to pounce on me when I reached Hairbrine Court this evening? Was he in the carriage that had clattered past or already inside Dolly's enjoying one of Jericho's mutton chops?

Tom Wasp, you're losing your grip, I told myself. Choose a different chimney. There was a play by Mr Shakespeare I'd seen at the penny gaff about one of our kings called Henry who won a big battle in France at Agincourt. He hadn't merely relied on his generals' plans for the fight ahead; he'd gone out the night before wrapped in a cloak so that he wasn't recognised and had a word with some of his foot soldiers, listening to what they had to say. Did Flint do that? He left all his violent evil deeds to Slugger and more delicate matters to Lairy John, so how did he know what was going on? Sometimes he would need to see for himself, not just sit in a tavern or swell coffee house counting up his money.

Like King Henry, Flint must be very near me. He was also likely to be close to whoever had paid him for the job, which brought the unwelcome thought that he might be connected to Dolly's or, more likely, to the Tarlton Ordinaries. I might have been chatting to him unknowingly. Assuming the manuscript was the reason for Mr Harcourt's murder, could Mr Harcourt have come to know Flint himself during his dealings with Lairy John?

I wondered whether I might have stepped half an inch nearer to the truth, but if so in which direction was I stepping? Towards the Ordinaries? Or Jericho and William? I looked up at Dolly's welcoming façade that still beckoned all comers, despite the violent murder in its yard. Nevertheless, I still had to talk to Clara, however hard it was, given that one of Dolly's staff or customers was almost certainly guilty of it.

Clara looked worried to see me here so unexpectedly after my visit to Mr Chalcot, and even more concerned when I asked if I might have a word with her daughter. 'The girl's not herself, Tom. She's blaming herself for Phineas being in prison. Every day she insists on taking his food up herself, even though she knows she won't be allowed to see him. Cruel it is, cruel, the way they treat those prisoners. And Phineas not even had his trial yet.'

'She could be upset because there's more she hasn't told us, Clara.' I saw fear in her face. There was no answer she could give but she took me upstairs to the coffee-room where we saw Hetty clearing plates away. She looked frightened to see both of us together.

'Tell him everything you've been holding back, my pet,' Clara said gently — and bravely, considering she had no idea what the everything might be.

Hetty looked fearfully from her mother to me and back again. 'I can't tell you, Mr Wasp. It would make things worse for Phineas, and I have harmed him enough already.'

142

The poor girl was trembling and Clara put her arms round her. 'How would it be if you just whispered it to your mother?' I suggested. 'She'll know whether I need to hear it too.'

Clara was not happy about this, but Hetty wavered. At last she did whisper to her mother and I saw Clara's face change. She darted a warning look at me as though I were about to clamp handcuffs on her daughter. 'Tell him, Hetty,' Clara said.

'That missing Tarlton manuscript everyone's talking about,' Hetty blurted out. 'I didn't realise at first what it was. Then I did. It came from Phineas.'

So that was why Clara's face had turned white with shock and mine would have followed suit if it could. I summoned up my courage.

'When did he tell you that, Hetty?' I said. I made it sound of little importance, but that wasn't the case. I was flabbergasted. After the talk of Mr Harcourt's dealings with fences, I'd assumed that Mr Harcourt had obtained the script through Lairy John, so how did Phineas come into the picture? 'You're sure this was the manuscript of the Tarlton play, *Seven Deadly Sins*?'

'Yes,' she said miserably. 'I told Mr Harcourt that Phineas had it and Mr Harcourt went to see him to tell him he might like to buy it. Phineas took the manuscript to him on the afternoon of the day he died. That's why Phineas came to the Row. He doesn't know it was me who told Mr Harcourt about it.'

I had to try even harder to pretend this was of little importance because Hetty was looking so upset. 'Don't worry, Hetty. It's good news for Phineas. From what you told me, he had no reason to want to kill Mr Harcourt, did he?'

She looked up hopefully. 'No.'

I held my breath. 'Did Phineas say who had given it to him?' Could it possibly be Lairy or Slugger? I couldn't see how — but then I couldn't see any other explanation.

'His father, I think.'

My face must have looked as startled as a mole in the sunlight. 'Phineas *owned* it?' It seemed to me very unlikely that Phineas' father would be a collector of old scripts.

Hetty nodded happily, unaware what a shock she'd presented. 'Yes. Mr Harcourt told Phineas that he would pay him some money for it when Phineas brought it to him and more after he had sold it to one of his customers. That would mean we could then get married.' She blushed.

I began to see why Phineas had asked *me* to warn Clara about Mr Harcourt's conduct. Expecting Mr Harcourt to pay him immediately, he would naturally be reluctant to reproach him that same day for his behaviour to Hetty and risk not receiving the money. Then a happier thought came to me. If Phineas owned the Tarlton play, didn't that mean that he was merely stealing his own property back?

My hopes were doomed. 'Only Mr Harcourt didn't pay him any money. He said he'd have to wait,' Hetty blithely continued.

Which gave Phineas a reason to want his script back — a request which Harcourt would have refused. What might have been good news for Phineas now looked bleak — and doubtless the City of London police would agree. They would see it as a motive for his murdering Mr Harcourt.

I did my best to reassure Hetty, however, and to thank her for telling me all this.

'Will it help Phineas?' she asked dolefully.

'It might well do so,' I said, although I secretly thought that it might well do the opposite. Then I saw a gleam of light at the top of the chimney. 'What would help even more, Hetty,' I continued, 'would be for you to persuade Jericho and William to tell the truth about their encounter with Phineas that Wednesday. Their stories are quite different to Phineas's.'

Hetty looked happier. 'I can do that easily. Let's go now, together. Come with me, Mr Wasp.'

She leapt up and hurried down the stairs with Clara and me following in her wake. It took her but a moment or two (with me out of sight) for her to bring Jericho and William to join us in Clara's greeting office.

They were both so concerned with not ceding victory to their rival in the race for Hetty's favours that they made no objection to my presence. Jericho sat with folded arms as William glared at him.

'A most unfortunate thing has occurred,' Hetty began demurely, her hands clasped in her lap and looking very proper.

'What's that, Miss Hetty?' Jericho asked, looking ready to leap on the nearest charger to ride off to save his lady fair. Almost simultaneously William followed suit in his readiness to assist.

'It is most distressing but Mr Snook's version of what happened between you last Wednesday afternoon is very different from yours.' Hetty dabbed at her eyes with a handkerchief.

'Of course it would be, Hetty,' William explained. 'He would hardly admit that he attacked us both so viciously.'

Jericho seemed less certain of this approach, perhaps wisely, because Hetty gazed at William in admiration but said, 'Suppose you are wrong, Mr Wright. I could not tolerate poor Mr Snook's death either being due to me or to anyone I might be fortunate enough to marry. I do realise it takes a brave man to admit he has been mistaken.'

William took her point immediately and once she had turned her eyes on Jericho he saw it too. He glared at us all, even Hetty, but especially me.

'Tell him, Will,' he growled, and reluctantly William obeyed.

'We didn't like the way he was presuming with you, Hetty. We thought he was pestering you and that had to be stopped,' he explained earnestly. 'We saw him coming through the Passage entry, so I went to tell him to come round the back because you'd like a word with him. But it was us who wanted the words.'

'And none of these words had punches accompanying them?' I asked.

'Just a push,' William muttered.

There was a silence, but by the time I departed it had been agreed that this new version of events should be passed on to Constable Peters, who would know what to do next.

I left Dolly's downcast, however. Getting Phineas released would take more than the change to Jericho's and William's account of what had happened, as the shadow of the new information about Tarlton's play would overlay it. Phineas was undoubtedly part of that story, but how big a part wasn't clear. For a start it could rule out both Lairy John's and Flint's roles in it. What was worse was that it would prove a weighty weapon at Phineas' trial.

To have murdered Mr Harcourt either in Dolly's yard or so close to it that the body could have been dragged in, Phineas would have had to remain in the area for some hours after Hetty had seen him in Panyer Alley late that afternoon. That would have been possible, had I not believed his story that he was at home alone. He must have known that the Ordinaries would be meeting at Dolly's that evening, but I'd heard of no evidence that he'd been seen during that time.

What was clear was that I had to find out more about that manuscript. Mrs Fortescue said she had left the bookstore before Mr Harcourt received it; she might not be telling the truth about that but it had certainly arrived according to Hetty's account, so where was it now? I contemplated this interesting matter as I walked along the Row to Mr Splendour's bookstore, hoping to find Mrs Fortescue alone. I was beginning to feel at home in the Row now, with coming here so frequently and getting to know all these people.

Both Mrs Fortescue and Mr Splendour were in his shop when I arrived, however, and she looked at me suspiciously when I said I had come with news of Mr Phineas Snook. Mr Splendour, in contrast, seemed pleased when I told them solemnly and not altogether truthfully that Phineas could be released very soon.

'That is good news indeed for his friends,' Mr Splendour answered warmly, 'I have always been of the opinion that Harcourt was set upon by one of the fences he traded with.'

Mrs Fortescue looked at him indignantly. 'It may be that on rare occasions Mr Harcourt was tempted to deal with such villains but it was hardly his usual practice. It is true that Mr Harcourt did acquire at an advantageous price what he described as a job lot from the respectable Spitalfields dealer I mentioned earlier. It included the *Jubilate Agno*, which the dealer considered of little interest. Mr Harcourt thought otherwise.'

Mr Splendour had been considering Mrs Fortescue's words. 'Most interesting. This surely suggests that this dealer — fence or not — might also have been the source of the *Seven Deadly Sins* manuscript; he had told us of its imminent arrival some days before our meeting that night. As you must know, Mr Wasp, in our trade we frequently have offers from questionable sources.'

I did not comment — or mention that both manuscripts were the property of Phineas Snook. What interested me was that the Ordinaries would have had plenty of time to hire Flint's services, whether the Tarlton play belonged to Phineas or had been acquired through Lairy

John. Why was it suddenly so important for Slugger to steal it back so promptly after the murder? Or was that just because Phineas had not been paid? Something was still very smoky here.

I decided on a touch of humility. 'These are deep waters, sir. And I'm glad that folk like yourselves are aware of them.'

'We have to be in our trade, Mr Wasp.' Mr Splendour shook his head gravely. 'This Phineas Snook is part of a gang as well as — if I understand correctly — being smitten by Miss Pomfret's charms.'

'That hussy. Poor Mr Harcourt was deluded by her too.' Mrs Fortescue sniffed. 'I pitied his poor wife.'

Neither I nor Mr Splendour commented on her sudden concern for Mrs Harcourt's feelings. Instead he continued, 'If the Tarlton manuscript was delivered as Mr Harcourt claimed on the afternoon of his tragic death, and Mrs Harcourt wishes to sell, you may be sure that we would deal only with a manuscript whose origins and ownership are clear.'

Mrs Fortescue did not look impressed by this virtuous statement.

'And, Mr Wasp, if you should happen to hear of its whereabouts,' Mr Splendour continued, 'we can of course advise you as to the best course. The problem for us honest brokers is that we don't always recognise dishonesty amongst our own circle. Of course I usually trust my fellow Ordinaries completely,' he explained blandly, 'but if that faith were misplaced, as I fear it may have been, one of them might have carried out that vile murder, reluctant though I am to consider such a thing.'

This shook me, and a thought scuttled across my mind like a cockroach. I knew little of these gentlemen beyond their polite exteriors, and yet the Ordinaries were beginning to fight amongst themselves. I had not yet recognised Flint's voice amongst them, but I recognised his shadow.

*

As I walked back to Hairbrine Court, I looked down on the majestic Tower and thought of how often I'd seen Phineas dancing on Great Tower Hill. He would be up for trial very soon and if convicted, would shortly be hanged. Instead of inching to the end of this sorry matter, I felt as if I was walking round and round an impenetrable tower just like this great fortress, that resisted every attempt at entrance.

I reasoned that even if Phineas hadn't been paid by Mr Harcourt for the manuscript, he would have had every expectation of receiving the money at some point. He wouldn't just go out and murder Mr Harcourt — although he might, I conceded with sinking heart, have thought he could reclaim it after he knew Mr Harcourt was dead. I was sure that wouldn't have occurred to Phineas himself, but Slugger could well have threatened Phineas into coming with him to break into the bookstore. I was also sure that Phineas wasn't capable of organising a cracksman's job himself and so he must have had Slugger Joe with him. It was far more likely that Slugger insisted on his presence as Slugger wouldn't know an Elizabethan manuscript from a pile of Enoch's old newspapers.

Whichever way I turned, however, the puzzle of why Slugger was still looking for the manuscript remained, and if Flint had been hired, was that primarily for Mr Harcourt's murder or for the manuscript? I could not decide. Our minds produce their own phantasmagoria when the light grows dim.

*

It was dark by the time I reached home, the time when danger begins to lurk in the unlit corners of the Ratcliffe Highway. As the highway is near the docks, footpads and other villains are there in plenty to prey on matelots from all nations as they lurch along it. As a sweep I walk in comparative safety — what riches would I have to steal? My riches lie in Ned and our home, but tonight they too had been threatened.

I found Ned crying on the stairs leading up to our door. I've only seen him sobbing aloud once in the years he's been with me and that was over the death of Jack, the linnet he had before Kwan-yin. I sat down on the stairs next to him and waited for him to tell me what was wrong.

'He's gone, guvnor.'

'Who?' I asked in alarm.

'Cockalorum.'

Phineas' words shot back at me. *Look after the cat.* I'd taken his words to heart, but now I'd failed him.

'He's just gone … for … e'll be back, Ned. Just out for a stroll,' I said, thinking to comfort him. 'He'll be back.'

He lifted a woebegone face to me. 'They took him. Slugger and another man. They threw Cockalorum in a sack and tied it up to drown him.'

There are times in life when you feel sick to the stomach. There's enough trouble in this world without the likes of Slugger creating it when it isn't necessary. 'Did they threaten you, lad?'

'No.'

'Tell me the truth, Ned.'

He squirmed sheepishly. 'They said they'd be back for me if they didn't get what they wanted.'

'And what was that?' I asked sharply.

'Dunno, guvnor.'

I heaved myself upright and went up to our rooms, bracing myself to face what I might find. I surveyed what they'd left of our home. No neat pile for us. The wreckage was everywhere, turned over, upside down, smashed and torn. Ned's birdcage was upright but Kwan-yin had gone.

He loved that bird just as he loved Cockalorum. Cockalorum seemed to have had a lot of respect for Kwan-yin too.

But then I saw her and for that at least I rejoiced. She was perched outside on the window ledge. I opened the window and brought her in and Ned looked just a little bit happier.

'They didn't find the sixpenny box though.' Ned's voice was wobbly.

'What about Phineas' cat book?' I asked, not seeing it anywhere.

'Didn't get that either. I'd already moved it and put it in my pillow.'

That was fine thinking on Ned's part. His pillow is made from an old soot bag with a sprinkling of soot still in it and he never lets me near it to clean it — so it was clever of Ned to think of putting it there. If the *Jubilate Agno* had already suffered from Ned's using it as a pillow, it might as well stay where it was.

'Keep it in there, Ned. They may be back.'

He considered this. 'I don't think so. They think they've done a thorough job. Amateurs,' he added scathingly. His lips were trembling though.

I had an idea. 'Suppose we get that poetry out of your pillow, Ned, and read some lines as a sort of prayer for Cockalorum.'

Ned bit his lip and I could see he was trying not to cry again. 'All right, guvnor.'

And so we did, once we'd put the rooms to right and mended what we could. Then Ned fished the *Jubilate* out. He'd wrapped it snugly in one of Enoch's old broadsheets and given it a clean bag of its own so the soot wouldn't get at it. He took it out of its bag, gave it a good blow, then took off the newspaper and found the right two pages in the folder for the lines about my cat Jeoffry. Then I read some of them aloud (with a little adjustment of my own):

For I will consider my Cat Cockalorum

For he is the servant of the Living God duly and daily serving him …

I was feeling tearful myself by the time I reached

For he keeps the Lord's watch in the night against the adversary …

For he purrs in thankfulness when God tells him he is a good Cat.

'Cockalorum was a good cat, Ned,' I said as I finished.

'They'll pay for this, guvnor,' was his reply.

'We'll make sure of that, Ned.' What had happened here made my mind up. 'I'll get Phineas free and then we'll smash them.'

'Soon?'

I made a promise to him and myself. 'It'll all be done by the time you're Jack-in-the-Green, Ned.'

The first of May. *Nine days away.* It wasn't long.

*

There had to be an end to this, and I set off on Saturday morning to discuss it with Clara. I took Ned with me after our chimney sweeping was done, so that he wouldn't have a go at Slugger Joe or Lairy John himself.

When we reached the Row though, there was a rumpus afoot. I could see the Row was blocked further along, with what looked like every bookseller and tradesman in the City of London. I sent Ned to Dolly's in the hope that Clara would settle him with a pie and hurried up to see what this was all about. As I drew nearer, I could see peelers and a Black Maria.

A sweep can always manage to work his way through a crowd as his smell goes before him and the crowd parts like the Red Sea for Moses. I easily worked my way through and saw that the peelers were standing outside Mr Splendour's shop.

What's all this about? I wondered fearfully. Another cracksman had a go? No, all these people wouldn't be gathered just for that.

Once at the front of the crowd I could see Constable Peters through the window of Mr Splendour's shop. He was with Inspector Harvey, whom I remembered from the start of this case, and they were talking most earnestly.

'I've business in there,' I said to the guardian of the door, making it sound important.

'Not today, you haven't,' was the answer. 'No sweeps needed. There's a stiff in there. Murdered. Blood everywhere.'

'Mr Splendour?' I asked in horror, but without reply.

Constable Peters saw me while the peeler was still intent on stopping me, and so I managed to get inside the doorway. There were police everywhere, but no blood that I could see. No Mr Splendour though, which looked ominous. Then I saw two legs jutting out from behind the counter, and nerved myself to go further in. It was a grisly sight, and there was no sign of life.

Mrs Fortescue was undoubtedly dead.

CHAPTER ELEVEN

Stories of Yore

'Mr Wasp!' Constable Peters came to join me. I'd feared that with the City of London Police present I would quickly be shown the door, but the constable's presence here ensured that I could stay. Mrs Fortescue lay there on her side, her tongue bulging out between purple lips, and grooves in the angry red neck, where a leather razor strop that had been used to strangle her had bitten deeply. The strop was lying at her side and her eyes were staring out as if demanding to know why this was happening to her. Grotesquely, her hat remained pinned to her hair, squashed by the fall of her body. He has a tender heart, does Constable Peters, and seeing that poor woman must have been hard for him, as it was for me.

'You were acquainted with the lady, weren't you?' he asked me.

'I was.' I thought of the unfortunate encounters I had with her and put their memory aside. 'Is Mr Splendour here?' I asked.

'Upstairs. He's suffering from the shock. He came down at his usual time of eight o'clock and found the door to the street open and Mrs Fortescue dead. It looks as if when she arrived this morning someone followed her into the shop, thinking to rob the money till or perhaps snatch her purse. She resisted and she's dead as a result.' Constable Peters was looking at me hard as though he wasn't at all sure that was what had happened.

'That's how it looks to you, constable?'

He gave a sidelong look to see if Inspector Harvey was listening. He wasn't, so Constable Peters whispered, 'No. Another murder so soon after Mr Harcourt's seems too much of a coincidence. There was a witness, though.'

'Who?' I asked.

'Mrs Harcourt. She wasn't on good terms with Mrs Fortescue. She found the body. While having breakfast at her parlour window, she saw Mrs Fortescue arrive about a quarter past seven and decided to go across and have a word with her, as she was still convinced that Mrs Fortescue had stolen that manuscript from her. She delayed doing so for about twenty minutes as in the meantime she had noted a smartly dressed gentleman here in the bookstore whom she assumed to be either Mr Splendour himself or a customer. By the time she had finished breakfast there was no sign of him, so she came across the road and found just what you see here, Mr Wasp.'

Two constables were taking the body away now, and I looked with sadness at the way Mrs Fortescue's life had ended. She hadn't been an attractive lady, but she must have had her own hopes and dreams that perhaps could have been realised. Now, they never would be. To be widowed and then cast off so brutally by Mr Harcourt must have been very hard for her.

'Why did she come early to work?' I wondered aloud. 'Eight o'clock would be more normal.'

'Mr Splendour said she liked nosing around,' the constable said, 'and of course she hadn't worked there long, so perhaps she was eager to make a good impression.'

'Or she might have been looking for something — such as the *Seven Deadly Sins* manuscript,' I said. It wasn't a charitable thought to express, but charity doesn't always explain the truth of things.

'And that would connect her death to Mr Harcourt's.' The constable looked impressed. 'Plenty of smart gentlemen would fit that theory. All of the Ordinaries, for example.'

'And the Swell Mob,' I pointed out. 'Or Flint.'

It was hard for me to mention his name, conscious as I was that he could well be outside in the crowds now. I thought of Mr Harcourt, I thought of Mrs Fortescue, and I thought of Cockalorum. Three deaths that might have a common source in Flint. I couldn't answer for Mr Harcourt, but the other two deaths were needless; only obstacles in Flint's path to be swept aside.

At that moment, Mrs Harcourt swept in, her mourning black making her face look sallow and bitter. 'I trust the poor woman has now been removed. Is Mr Splendour under arrest?'

'No one is yet, ma'am,' Constable Peters said politely.

She looked astonished. 'He should be.'

'Why would that be, ma'am?' I asked.

I was accorded a look of disdain. 'I see no reason to be interrogated by a chimney sweep,' she informed the constable.

'Very well. *I'll* ask you, ma'am. Why would that be?' Constable Peters asked. 'I'm told you saw the probable murderer.'

'Yes. It's quite obvious what happened. That woman stole a valuable manuscript from me, as is recorded in your records. Mr Splendour lured her into working for him, killed that woman and purloined my property.'

'Was Mr Splendour the man you saw in here?'

'Certainly. Who else could it have been?'

'You once thought it might have been a customer,' the constable pointed out.

'Rubbish. I'm quite sure it was Mr Splendour. Where is the Tarlton play? Either she or Mr Splendour had it. I trust you are looking for it as a matter of urgency.'

'Not yet, ma'am,' the constable answered blandly. 'Even if she were the thief, the late Mrs Fortescue is unlikely to have brought a stolen manuscript to her place of work and Mr Splendour is unlikely to have killed her in his own bookstore.'

'Really, constable. Even if Mr Splendour did not commit the murder himself, he could have hired some criminal to murder Mrs Fortescue just as she did herself when she wished to kill my husband. She hired that fellow Phineas Snook to carry out the murder.'

Seeing this flight of fancy had floored Constable Peters, I tried a question of my own. 'Was your husband excited that tragic evening, ma'am, because he thought Mr Shakespeare had a hand in writing this play?'

Mrs Harcourt, taken unawares by this unexpected turn, made a credible attempt at looking amazed at this very idea, while Constable Peters looked most impressed.

'How,' she managed to say, 'could I possibly answer that? A most foolish question. The manuscript had only just arrived when he sent me the confirming telegram. I advise you to keep to sweeping chimneys, Mr Wasp.'

*

'Maria?' Clara was horrified at hearing the news. 'Well I never did.'

The Saturday luncheon rush was on but the news brought her to a standstill. 'Poor woman. Poor foolish woman.'

'Why foolish, Clara?'

'To believe that old goat Harcourt loved her. Easy to do, Tom. Inside ourselves we remain as comely and enchanting as we were when young and I expect you feel the same. But to others, the outside has worn harshly.'

'Not you, Clara. True beauty is of the soul and that shines through you.'

I saw a tear in her eye as she replied, 'Thank you, my dear. Maria was useful to Harcourt, no doubt, when he had no fallen woman at hand or no young lady to seduce, but no more than that. I suppose he had his attractions. He could not have been a successful ageing Don Juan without them. I knew Maria from her youth, Tom. She was a stunner, but life did not treat her well. Widowed young with two small children, left a pauper and forced to work. She has done well, but now this. Dead at the hands of some hustler, you believe.'

'I believe no such thing, Clara.'

I eyed the scones she was removing from the oven and she brought one over to me. 'You need someone to look after you Tom. You're half starved.'

For a moment I thought of a life in Clara's loving arms, but I pushed the thought away.

'I've Ned to think of,' I said gently. He needed the only home he'd ever known, Hairbrine Court. In any case, how could I, a sweep, live in a place like Dolly's, with its high class clientele?

'He'll meet a girl soon — and he's already thinking that way,' she warned me.

I knew that. I'd seen the signs, but it was too early. 'He's not thirteen yet.'

Clara sighed and changed the subject. 'What if Maria were Mr Harcourt's murderer? She'd reason enough.'

'She wouldn't have had the strength, but she might have used Flint.' I heard that voice again in my mind, and still its owner eluded me.

'Best find him quickly, Tom. It could be she knew who killed Mr Harcourt. She was murdered because she threatened to tell the coppers.'

'Or she might have had her own plans for the Tarlton play. I could be wrong. Perhaps it was she who stole it, tried to raise a price on it and dealt with the wrong people. She'd have known about Lairy John.'

Clara shivered. 'Books. Everything comes back to books. It's all so refined and scholarly in Paternoster Row, religious booksellers, ancient histories, books of poetry, all looking so learned and readable — yet underneath, there's something vicious.'

'Like Lairy John and Flint.'

'If so, they did a poor job in ridding themselves of both Mr Harcourt and Maria and *still* no one knows where this dratted manuscript is.' She frowned. 'Suppose Slugger did find it in Phineas' lodgings once he knew the cat was no longer there.'

'He and Flint would have gone quiet but they haven't. It seems they're still looking for it. Ned's and my home was turned into a pile of rubbish last night. They didn't take Ned, but they took Cockalorum and drowned him.'

Clara exclaimed. 'And Phineas so fond of him! They're louses. No need for that. You've *got* to find them, Tom.'

I knew that. The question was where. That manuscript surely had to be the key. 'How much do you know about William Shakespeare, Clara?'

She blinked at my sudden literary turn. 'I never met him. Before my time.'

I grinned. 'Pity. He'd have been a good customer.'

'He would have come to the Castle, Tarlton's pub.'

'Who took that over after Tarlton died?' The thought occurred to me that the *Seven Deadly Sins* manuscript had been left behind.

'Can't say, Tom. I had it from the Ordinaries that there was some skulduggery going on and he had to plead with Sir Francis Walsingham to look after his family, Sir Francis being in charge of the Queen's Men, the troupe Tarlton and Shakespeare belonged to. Stories, eh? Most of them get lost in time.'

'Like the carving of the Boy in Panyer Alley,' I remarked, thinking of Phineas. 'No one knows who he is.'

Clara was startled. 'Fancy your mentioning him. There's an old story that Zechariah — that chairmaker in the Alley — tells about that Boy being an inn sign outside the Castle in the olden days. You ask him.'

I pricked up my ears. This sounded a tasty morsel of information.

'I will. Ned doesn't like the Boy, Clara, because it reminds him of his climbing boy days. The strange thing is that Hetty told me Phineas was interested in the Boy, too.'

It was Clara's turn to look puzzled. 'I can't see why that should be. Most folk look at the Boy without thinking much about it. Pity really, all those people in the past, vanishing away and leaving mysteries behind them. Sometime I think old Tarlton himself haunts this place, maybe because he's afraid I'm not running it as I should. And now we've *two* murders to worry about. There's evil at work, Tom, and Dolly's being swept into it.'

'It's like one of your scones,' I told her, accepting another one. 'We're the butter in the middle; on the top are the Ordinaries and Flint and the underside is —'

I'd tripped up, but she guessed what I was going to say as she pushed the butter towards me:

'Jericho and William. Don't worry, Tom. If you're going to get to the bottom of this nightmare, you have to think that way. With murder on our premises we're bound to be under suspicion. Jericho is a strange fellow, but he's the best broiler of chops in the City, and as for William, well, I don't see him murdering anyone and he fair dotes on Hetty. As for killing Maria, that's right off his beat.'

'Unless someone knew he killed Mr Harcourt, I thought to myself, but hadn't the heart to voice it.

*

I doffed my hat as Zechariah looked up at me, removing a long nail from his mouth. Oblivious to what was happening in the Row, he was working on an old Windsor chair that looked as if one tap from a hammer might result in its total collapse.

'You're doing splendid work, Zechariah,' I told him.

He nodded graciously. 'This little beauty comes from a noble household come down in the world. I always say you never know whose bum has been sitting on a chair, so every one of these darlings deserves respect.'

I looked at the broken chair and thought of all the silent histories of the world, of the chairs that had seated kings and emperors, of the beds that had cradled lovers like Abelard and Heloise, of the plates that could tell tales of last meals. And that brought me back to the Boy of Panyer Alley. I'd like to know why Phineas had been so interested in him.

'I heard you've a tale about the Panyer Boy, Zechariah,' I began.

'*My* boy,' he grumbled.

'Yours?' I mistook his meaning.

'What do you think I sit here for?' he asked indignantly. 'I looks after him day in, day out, and no one ever cares who he is.'

'I do. Tell me who he is, Zechariah.'

'Why?' he asked, his tone not rancorous, just curious.

'Phineas was here on the day he died and they've arrested him for the murder at Dolly's.'

'He'll swing for it. Friend of mine,' he muttered.

'I don't believe he's guilty.'

He thought about this and finally said grudgingly, ''Tis a long time ago. A bloke called Tarlton kept an alehouse nearby here, and my pa said the Boy was outside his alehouse.'

This was a start at least. 'How did it get here then? And what about that verse? It reads, *this is still the highest ground* and there's a date on it of 1688. It doesn't seem that high here.'

He looked at me as though as I was the local peeler come to give him his walking orders. 'What's it matter to you, mister? That old alehouse was the Castle, weren't it, and castles be built on hills. That high enough for you?'

Zechariah turned his attention to his chair again. 'Put your hand on the wood, mister.'

I obliged, wishing I'd gone more gently with him.

'Feel it,' he said. 'The living wood. Yew and elm it is. Crying out they are for a drink. You wouldn't starve your old woman of water, why starve the wood?'

I felt the wood myself and then watched his hands as he did the same, lovingly, eyes closed, and I wondered what other stories lay behind them.

*

Mr Chalcot looked delighted to see me as I walked into his store after leaving Zechariah. 'My dear sir, pray take a coffee with me.' He was sitting by the counter, hands folded peacefully across his belly. 'I wished particularly to see you and good fortune has sent you my way.' He rose from his chair and hurried into the inner sanctum to ask for another coffee.

This was grandeur indeed. I thought about the old Chapter Coffee House on a corner partway along Paternoster Row; that was another place where the notables in the literary world met for refreshment and conversation. Mr Chalcot's bookstore, despite being so much smaller, seemed to work on the same principle. For all I knew, amongst the gentlemen visiting his establishment there might be another Shakespeare. Fortunately today it was only myself visiting.

'This is terrible news concerning poor Mrs Fortescue.' Mr Chalcot shook his head gravely. 'I knew her through her work for Mr Harcourt, who was most impolite to her on the day of his death and now she too has met her death. Murder at the hands of a scoundrel who sought money, I'm told by Mr Splendour.'

'We hope the City of London police believe that, sir.'

'Do you believe it?'

'I'm a sweep, sir.'

He smiled. 'With friends in our great Metropolitan police force I understand. Well, Mr Wasp, this is a fine thing. Are we all to be murdered one by one in the name of Richard Tarlton? The seven deadly sins do not expressly include murder, but I am sure the ancient originators of the list would not condone it.'

'It could be regarded as the result of wrath, sir.'

'Or greed,' he added thoughtfully. 'Certainly not sloth. Two murders in ten days could be said to be extreme.'

'If by the same hand, Mr Chalcot.'

'Come, come. Can we doubt that? A mere passing scoundrel as is suggested for Mrs Fortescue's attacker is hardly probable when a manuscript by Richard Tarlton — very probably written with the help of a youthful William Shakespeare — suddenly appears in our midst, and there is likely to be keen competition to acquire it.'

'Could any of it be proven to be by Mr Shakespeare?'

'Mr Harcourt must have been reasonably sure of there being some evidence of that, as he had seen the manuscript. I cannot recall Harcourt's precise words, but he did mention a comic song or two, a turn of phrase, a speech here and there. One can usually detect a change when the rhythm of the poetry alters. All such things are indications. And there is little doubt that Shakespeare not only knew Tarlton but was very fond of him. Mr Manley and I are as one in our conviction that the sheer affection for Tarlton in Shakespeare's work makes it clear that it's unlikely their friendship began as late as 1587, only a year before Tarlton's death. My dear Mr Wasp, consider the "Alas, poor Yorick" speech — full of tenderness.'

Mr Chalcot was so impassioned that I did indeed consider it once again, having heard Mr Manley on the same subject. 'But, Mr Chalcot —'

'— Making it highly likely Shakespeare wrote an earlier version of *Hamlet* and then rewrote it — as he did other plays — years later for the Lord Chamberlain's Men.'

'But I —' Again, Mr Chalcot seemed not to have heard me for he swept on enthusiastically, hands folded once again across his belly with a smile of pleasure as he spoke of his beloved Mr Shakespeare. 'I have many other observations on this subject —'

I seized my opportunity. 'As does Zechariah the chairmaker.' I recounted the story of the Boy and the Castle alehouse.

'Ah, yes,' he commented happily, 'the reference to the highest ground in the inscription underneath the Boy might indeed support your story that the monument originally stood outside the Castle inn, castles being built on hills in early times, and yet —'

'— It seems to me, Mr Chalcot, that there are too many unknowns in our theories,' I said firmly, liking to keep my feet on solid ground (whether highest or lowest). 'And,' I felt bold enough to point out, 'we're straying from the fact that Mr Harcourt and now Mrs Fortescue have been murdered, possibly on account of Mr Tarlton's play.'

'You are right, my dear sir.' He looked crestfallen. 'We must continue to look further. However, we might agree that fanciful theory and scholarship blend well together on occasion? One can be as true or as false as the other.'

'But the written word cannot be changed,' I said, my interest at this turn in the conversation growing.

'Yet was it true in the first place?' he countered, and we were both well satisfied.

I felt myself quite an antiquarian, but all this did seem a long way from the task before me. Freeing Phineas by finding out who murdered Mr Harcourt and Mrs Fortescue was not going to be greatly advanced by my newfound knowledge. Or was it? It had taught me that there were depths of passion that would make gentlemen stop at nothing — even murder — to gain what they were after: be it money, a script by Richard Tarlton or a girl like Hetty.

CHAPTER TWELVE

When Night Falls

'Wasp!' he roared.

I blinked. The one person I least expected to see at our door, especially on a Saturday evening, was my old 'friend' — if I could call Inspector Wiley that — formerly of the Thames River Police and now of the Metropolitan. We had never seen eye to eye and not just because he is a whole lot taller than I am. We had come to an understanding, however: I helped him where I could, and he tolerated me. This arrangement seemed to have broken down, judging by the tone of his voice and the glare on his face when I opened the door after his thunderous knock.

'I bid you good evening, inspector,' I said courteously. 'What can I do for you?' I decided to be very cautious.

'You can come with me.' His tone of voice did not make this suggestion sound welcoming, nor did he look impressed that I already knew his improved status from sergeant to inspector.

Ned had informed me he would be late back tonight on one of his missions that I don't enquire into, and so there was nothing to stop me from going anywhere with Inspector Wiley — except a healthy dislike of his ordering me around.

'Where might that be?' I enquired.

'You'll find out.'

'Under arrest, am I?'

'No.' This being too gracious he quickly amended it to, 'Not yet,' and a suspicious 'What you done to be arrested?'

I pretended not to understand as I locked my door behind me (a useless process since if Slugger returned he would simply break his way in as before), but I counted on a short respite before he might try this again. He'd have to report to Flint first.

Once through the entry into Blue Anchor Yard, I saw a growler waiting for us, into which I was beckoned (at least I wasn't being frogmarched) to sit in state next to the inspector. The horses seemed eager to get out of this area for they picked their way enthusiastically over the filth and stones of the roadways as they headed west towards the Tower of London. Fortunately, we didn't stop there, which meant the inspector couldn't have had any plans to escort me through Traitor's Gate. Instead, as I began to suspect, late as it was, we were bound for Scotland Yard, where the cabbie set us down outside the police headquarters.

Five minutes later we were in an interview room with not only Inspector Harvey of the City of London Police but also (to my relief) Constable Peters and the popular Sergeant Williamson. He was a merry gentleman, and on the one occasion I had met him before he had been most polite to me, despite his somewhat awesome appearance; he had paid great attention to my every word. Here he was again with a flower in the buttonhole of his black jacket; he is well-known for this, and picks one daily from his own garden, of which he is very fond.

It had to be a grave matter that called them all together on a Saturday evening and indeed Sergeant Williamson did greet me gravely. For all he was still a sergeant and Wiley an inspector, it was clear to see who was in charge, even though Constable Peters did a lot of the talking. The way he spoke, so assured and confident, made me realise how far he had come in a year or two since he was under Sergeant — my apologies, Inspector — Wiley's command in Thames River Police.

I listened attentively as Constable Peters held the floor. It was his job, so he had whispered to me, to convince his audience that the two police forces needed to work together over the murders of Mr Harcourt and Mrs Fortescue.

'We have to decide whether these two murders,' he began somewhat nervously, 'are linked. We haven't enough evidence to prove whether they are or not.' He cast a look at Sergeant Williamson who nodded encouragement .' If we work on the assumption that the link exists, we've already agreed that these murders cross the boundaries of our two forces. Both murders took place in your territory, Inspector Harvey, but the one suspect you have in custody can only be held for the first murder and he stems from our territory, as do Slugger Joe, Lairy John and Flint.'

'What's the evidence of the murders being linked?' asked Inspector Harvey quietly.

The constable was warming up now. 'That of actions taken by Slugger and possible actions by Lairy John and Flint over a missing manuscript relating to the City. You have evidence of Slugger Joe's activities, don't you, Mr Wasp?'

'Two in person,' I replied promptly, doing my own best to sound important, 'one outside my residence and one at Mr Snook's, and a third when he wrecked my home in search of this missing property. He also—'

Inspector Wiley's eyes gleamed as he broke in with, 'Snook, eh? That means he's guilty — working with Slugger. Hear that, Inspector Harvey?'

Sergeant Williamson fortunately intervened. 'Snook would hardly be working with Slugger if Slugger had cracked into his home — that's what you were about to add, isn't it, Mr Wasp?'

I agreed it was, and thankfully this theory of Inspector Wiley's was given no more attention. I listened while they talked of boundaries and co-operation, until Inspector Harvey decided to turn to me again.

'This Flint connection. Any further forward, Mr Wasp?'

This was a question I could answer. 'He's on to me. He's warned me off in person.'

That held their attention all right and I told them what had happened. 'You'd know him again?' Sergeant Williamson asked.

'By his voice only.'

'Not worth a tinker's cuss,' snorted Inspector Wiley.

I was inclined to agree with him for once, but I wasn't going to admit it. 'Flint doesn't favour murder alone; it's a means to an end for him, so this missing manuscript is what he's after.'

'Thus involving both Slugger and Lairy John,' Constable Peters contributed.

'I'll clear 'em both out,' offered Inspector Wiley eagerly, seeing which way the wind was blowing after Sergeant Williamson gave a nod of agreement.

Constable Peters must have seen my warning glance because he promptly replied, 'Not yet.'

'Not your place, constable,' roared Inspector Wiley.

Luckily Sergeant Williamson again intervened to calm down the inspector's enthusiasm. 'We need them undisturbed until we get further along the line. If we nab Lairy and Slugger now, we'll never get Flint. They're our guides for getting to him — that and his voice which you heard, Mr Wasp,' he added courteously.

While Inspector Wiley was still debating whether to fight this battle or not, I wanted my say. 'What about Phineas Snook?' I enquired. 'When's he to be released?'

That loosened some of the soot in the chimney and they began talking quite sensibly. I let them meander around the point for a while, and then said, 'If there's a link between the murders, what about Mrs Fortescue's? Who did that? It can't have been Mr Snook. He was in Newgate at the time.'

'He's charged with the first murder, though. And while there's no direct evidence for that, there's the question of this robbery at the bookstore,' Sergeant Williamson said, to my dismay.

Constable Peters had had to come clean about Phineas' role in that of course. And the sergeant was right. If the Tarlton manuscript was central to the case, then Phineas' part in the burglary must count at least as indirect evidence. My spirits plummeted like a goose down a chimney. I've never tried that old method of chimney sweeping myself as it's far too outdated now we have machines, but I knew in my youth of a sweep who did — and remember the helplessness I felt at the thought of the poor goose's suffering. I was as helpless now as I had been then, because in this current chimney *I* was the goose.

'It's my opinion,' Inspector Wiley said darkly, 'that Snook could have been working with Wright and Mason — they all wanted Harcourt dead because of that Pomfret girl, but they left Snook to do the job. Now he's mouldering away in Newgate, like he should be.'

Inspector Harvey's turn: 'I still have my doubts as to whether the cases are linked. Snook killed Harcourt for personal reasons, and one of those booksellers, with or without Flint's involvement, killed Mrs Fortescue over this missing play.'

I was beginning to be fearful. One police force was looking at personal motives for wanting Mr Harcourt removed; the other at the Tarlton play. And Phineas was involved on both counts.

Nevertheless, the meeting ended with agreement that the forces should indeed collaborate, in the expectation that evidence would emerge to prove that the cases were indeed linked. To my surprise Inspector Wiley then gave me a ride in a growler back to Hairbrine Court — well, nearly there. The cabbie having refused to go down Glasshouse Street, I walked the rest of the way and reached home with relief. Ned was still not back from his mission elsewhere, which gave me a chance for some reflection.

Neither Flint nor Slugger Joe would give up their hunt for the manuscript easily. Slugger hadn't found the *Jubilate Agno* when he wrecked my home and that was good, because he might have mistaken it for the *Seven Deadly Sins* manuscript that they were really seeking. However, it was important to keep the *Jubilate Agno* with its precious cat poetry safe for Phineas' sake — even though Lairy had sold it in a job lot. Its true ownership would at some point have to be settled, since it had probably been stolen.

That gave me an idea. I went to Ned's pillow and carefully drew out the sack with the *Jubilate Agno* in it. I took out the bundle and unwrapped the newspaper to make sure its precious contents were still safe; they were and it again fell open at the pages with the My Cat Jeoffry lines on them. It was quite a fat packet, but even after I had rewrapped it in the newspaper I managed to fit it into an old bag with handles that I'd found thrown out in the rubbish when I was cleaning a Wapping chimney once. The newspaper was the *Morning Post* which I thought a most impressive broadsheet, well worthy of protecting the Christopher Smart poetry.

I half expected Slugger Joe or one of his minions to be waiting with a cosh as I set off on Sunday afternoon to Dolly's, but to my relief no one appeared. All the same, it felt as if he was peering around every corner as I walked past the Tower of London, with the contents of the bag I was clutching burning into my mind. Ned had returned late last night and I'd told him my plans for the *Jubilate* which he rather reluctantly agreed might be better elsewhere. I think it had pleased him to be sleeping on My Cat Jeoffry.

When I reached Dolly's, business was slack. As there was no sign of Hetty downstairs, I asked William Wright where she was, but he looked as anxious as though I was planning to steal her affections from him. I need not have worried because she came down the stairs, wearing her bonnet and shawl.

'Dear Mr Wasp,' she greeted me. 'I'm going for a walk in the Churchyard. There is a pavement artist there on Sundays whose work I admire.'

'I'll escort you, Hetty.' I could not leave my precious bag here without explaining my mission, and I couldn't do that in William's presence. 'I've an errand there myself.' This was true, although my errand would be merely to talk to Hetty. Off we went, she clinging to one of my arms, which made me most proud, while I was clinging to my bag with the other.

'How is Phineas?' she asked me, as soon as we were away from Dolly's. 'I take food to him every day but they never let me see him. When will they release him?'

'Not yet, Hetty,' I said sadly. 'They want to keep him safe while they hunt down Slugger Joe. Phineas might help them do that.'

Her face fell. 'But how can he help? Phineas has told me about him; he doesn't like him. He was horrible to poor little Cockalorum and now he's killed him.'

'Did Phineas ever talk to you about someone called Flint?'

'No. Only Joe because he is a friend of Phineas' mother. Who is Flint?'

'He's a master criminal that the police want to trace.'

Hetty looked alarmed. 'Why do they think Phineas knows where he is?'

I explained about Flint and his being Slugger Joe's employer as best I could without worrying her even more. We were at the Churchyard now, which, with Paul's Chain across the road to stop carriages entering, was less noisy but still crowded with one or two flower and tract sellers busy at their trade and with families out walking. The sound of Evensong greeted us, hundreds of voices uplifted in song, and I sent up a brief prayer for Phineas as we passed the entrance to the cathedral.

'Would you do something for Phineas, Hetty?'

'Of course.' She looked surprised that I should ask.

'It's this. He bought a very special old manuscript about cats and I want him still to have it when he returns home. But I'm worried that Slugger Joe might go back to his lodgings hoping to steal it or come to mine and find it. Could you take it and hide it, Hetty — and tell nobody?'

'Even Mama?' Hetty smiled.

'Even her, and certainly not William or Jericho. Nobody.'

'I like secrets. I promise I won't tell anybody.'

'When we know Phineas is coming home, he won't have Cockalorum but at least his cat manuscript will be safe,' I said. 'This is it.'

Her pretty face clouded over. 'Not the one he took to Mr Harcourt?'

'No. But although you told me a little about that one, is there anything more you know about it?'

She looked scared and I was afraid that she wouldn't answer. But at last she did. 'He said he'd been given this wonderful manuscript about the seven deadly sins, which was very old, and how much he liked it. Then I thought that Mr Harcourt might be interested in it, so I told him.'

She looked at me piteously, but I had to continue.

'You said you thought his father had given Phineas the playscript, Hetty. Did he say anything more than that? Where his father had got it from? Or whether Slugger Joe wanted it?'

She shook her head.

'When you saw him in Panyer Alley only a few hours before Mr Harcourt died, what did Phineas say about the play? He must have delivered it by then.'

'I told you. That Mr Harcourt was very interested and kept it, but didn't give Phineas any money as he'd promised.'

This was looking very dark for Phineas. 'Do you want to marry him, Hetty? You said you didn't know.'

'Oh *yes*,' she said immediately. 'I don't want to marry Jericho, because he scares me. But as for William, I don't know. Mama says William has a good career in front of him, so perhaps I should marry him, not Phineas.'

We walked slowly through the gardens and out of the far side to where the pavement artist she had wanted to see was working. He was very talented. Two marvellously coloured drawings displayed a sky with birds flying in it and a tree on a hill. Such beauty, but the sadness was that the rain would wash it all away. Perhaps the artist didn't mind that. Perhaps he just wanted to create something beautiful. And he had. Hetty gazed at both the drawings, especially the blue sky one. She gave him a threepenny piece and then turned to me, bursting out with:

'I love Dolly's of course, I've known it so long. But oh, Mr Wasp, I read books about wonderful things, and look, you see that sky the artist's drawn? You see the grass and the tree? And there's the seaside — I saw it once on an excursion train. Sometimes I just want to go away with Phineas and see all these things. Is that wrong?'

'I don't see William dancing,' I said gravely. 'Dancing doesn't earn much money though — do you mind that?'

'Not if I'm with Phineas.'

We walked back through the gardens paying our respects to the statue of Her Majesty Queen Anne and made our way to the string of the Churchyard, as it's called, the other side being the bow. People were beginning to emerge from Evensong, and for no apparent reason it seemed to me there was something sinister here, even threatening.

'Miss Pomfret, how pleasant to see you.' Mr Timpson had loomed up in front of us, looking most smart in his Sunday best frock coat and topper. He lifted his hat to Hetty, ignoring me. 'Permit me to escort you home to Dolly's.'

This posed a problem. Hetty could hardly refuse, and I could not leave them as I was still carrying Phineas' precious cat poem; I therefore had to walk behind them, much to my discomfort and, indeed, Hetty's.

'A terrible business, poor Mrs Fortescue,' Mr Timpson boomed.

'Yes,' I heard Hetty agree crossly.

'Mrs Fortescue only had herself to blame, however. Mr Harcourt was a married man and yet she lured him into regrettable paths, a situation bound to end in disaster.'

As far as I could see Mrs Fortescue had done nothing to deserve a terrible death, save to break a few social rules in the form of loving Mr Harcourt and expressing her emotions too publicly. Perhaps Hetty thought so too as she spoke out most strongly. 'Mrs Fortescue was not aware that Mr Harcourt was married. His wife seldom, if ever, came to London.'

'My dear Miss Pomfret, indeed she knew. You are inexperienced in the ways of this world. It was almost certainly she who stole the Tarlton manuscript — she no doubt knew very well it would be arriving and could arrange for its disappearance before Mrs Harcourt arrived in London the next morning.'

I decided to speak up from behind them. 'Mrs Fortescue claimed she had already left the bookstore when it was delivered.'

Mr Timpson's back stiffened. 'One moment, Miss Pomfret.' He disengaged himself from her arm and turned on me. 'Let me explain this to you, my man. She hired a ruffian to steal the Tarlton script the evening after Mr Harcourt's death. He would know how to gain entry to the shop.'

'Not many ruffians would recognise the *Seven Deadly Sins* manuscript, sir,' I answered him. 'Few ruffians can read.'

He dismissed this with: 'Mrs Fortescue obviously accompanied the robber. Now kindly let Miss Pomfret and myself continue on our way.'

'Certainly, sir,' I replied promptly, taking note that he hadn't heard of Phineas' presence on the scene. 'I hadn't thought of that. It might even have been Flint himself after this play, having killed Mr Harcourt.'

I've never seen a gentleman's back look so shaken. He threw a dismissive 'Highly unlikely,' towards Hetty and myself, forgot all about escorting Hetty home, lifted his hat in great agitation and stalked away.

That meant that at last I was able to pass the bag over to Hetty once we reached Dolly's, which she chose to enter by its front entrance, thus evading Jericho. 'I'll keep it safe for Phineas,' she whispered.

I began the walk home, greatly perturbed. The mention of Flint had shaken Mr Timpson. Why? Was it even possible that Flint was one of the Ordinaries, who all looked so respectable, probably with wives and families? Mr Timpson, Mr Splendour and Mr Manley were the three who could most easily have killed Mr Harcourt that night — and any of them might also have killed Mrs Fortescue.

I wondered if I had done the right thing in handing over the *Jubilate* to Hetty. I tried to feel glad that I had done so and could now return to Hairbrine Court with one problem temporarily solved. I was beginning to feel lost without My Cat Jeoffry, however. It seemed almost as bad as losing Cockalorum.

I climbed the stairs at Hairbrine Court feeling weary and low. The first inkling I had that something was wrong was that the door was locked and a sudden fear struck me as I unlocked it.

I went inside and straightaway sensed the emptiness of the room. I was alone, save for a silent Kwan-yin. And then I knew. I wasn't going to find Ned at Phineas' lodgings this time, or anywhere else. It wasn't a matter of his simply being late again.

He had gone.

CHAPTER THIRTEEN

Climbing the Chimney

I tried hard to tell myself there was no reason to think anything was amiss. I reasoned that Ned had been late plenty of times before. It had happened only a few days ago. Ten to one he'd stopped at Rosemary Lane to cadge a pie for supper and been told to wait awhile.

Inside me, though, I knew he wasn't going to come bursting through that door whistling *Jack Robinson, the Dogs' Meat Man* as he so often does. He was gone like Cockalorum, a thought that put me a-shiver. Cockalorum had been drowned in a sack. Was that what happened to Ned?

Stop that, Tom Wasp, I cried aloud. You just take hold of the sense God gave you! I swallowed, lighting a candle with a lucifer as though that might guide him home. Our Lord would shed His light on the situation when he chose. But please Lord, make that *now*!

Instead He was saying, 'Come on, Tom. Think straight. Make a plan.' That was difficult to do when my stomach was churning with fear.

A plan, Lord. Send me one, I prayed. But He was waiting for me to think for myself. Usually the evening begins with lighting the fire to warm up our supper, but not tonight. A plan, I repeated to myself. I must have a plan.

I tried to push all my fears to one side. Ned's absence might be nothing. It might be that the peelers had nabbed him, if he'd been caught dipping. Even that would be better than the fate my fears were conjuring up and I clutched at the idea of his being safe in a police station. Or he might have had an accident and some kind person had taken him to hospital. Guy's, most likely. I seized on this, sure I had found the truth of it. Ned wasn't one for gangs of youths parading the Highway. He could be at that hospital now, crying out for me, and here I was wasting time.

It was already dark, but I rammed on my hat and set off once more. I'd take Doshie and the cart, so that I could bring Ned home safe and sound. It's Ned's job to feed him so just in case Doshie hadn't been fed today I took some hay with me.

Doshie was pleased to see me when he saw it in my arms, but not so pleased to find he was expected to come out. He was hungry, though, no doubt about it, and that set my stomach churning again. Don't worry, I told myself. Ned's had an accident, and couldn't get here.

Once we'd begun the journey, Doshie seemed to be sharing my worries for he did his best to clop along at a smart pace, and we were at London Bridge and paying our toll money in no time. It's said these toll charges are being done away with and that can't happen too soon for me. Tonight, those precious minutes handing it over felt like an hour.

By the time I'd crossed the river to Tooley Street I was almost cheerful, convinced I would find Ned in the hospital. If he was well enough to come home, we'd get some nice liver and cook it in our home for a quiet supper. These hospitals are wonderful places, I thought, as I tied Doshie to a post and entered Guy's. I took my hat off to the brass statue of the founder in the courtyard where clerks were busily running around, and the sight reassured me that Ned was just waiting for me to come. Ned, I'd cry, what are you doing here, lad? I've come to take you home.

Inside I found a young gentleman who listened to me most sympathetically. He led me to a table where they record all those who are currently in the hospital and showed me a ledger of those who had come in that day.

Ned's name wasn't amongst them.

'Perhaps,' I ventured, trying to overcome both fear and tears, 'he wasn't conscious when he came in.'

He looked again. 'No children of that age.' When he saw my expression he added kindly, 'You could try looking in our waiting room. That's where people sit before being treated.'

'Yes, sir.' I clutched at this hope and was directed to a large waiting hall. It was a room of misery and noise, where young children screeched in pain, mothers wept and hardened criminals and opium eaters groaned together, all awaiting the great miracle that would make them better. My hopes rose when I saw a lad hunched up in the corner of a large chair.

I hurried over to him. 'Ned,' I whispered. He stirred and turned to me, but it wasn't Ned.

Another hospital? I could try St Bartholomew's, but I knew I was deluding myself. I'd try the peelers first.

'Come on, Doshie,' I said as I untied him. 'We've got to find Ned.'

He must have understood because he pricked up his ears and we set off back across the river and along the Highway to Wapping. The Thames River police are stationed by the steps to the river bank and I knew the place of old. At night it's a busy place, being near both the river and the docks. It was not yet eleven o'clock though, and it wasn't too crowded. As children are disappearing every day in London there wouldn't be much they could do for me officially, but some of the policemen know me and might help. They greeted me jovially — until they saw my face.

'What's up, Waspie?' one asked me anxiously.

'My Ned's missing. Have you got him dubbed up?' I asked, trying to keep panic at bay.

I failed, for they gathered round me in concern. 'Not here. He's too smart for us,'

I swallowed. 'Then he's been nabbed for sure. Flint's mob. They threatened me.'

That sobered them. 'Slugger Joe?' one asked.

'More like Lairy John's side of things,' I said heavily, wondering whether I'd ever see Ned again.

'He's been busy recently. We'll keep an eye open for him. Best be nippy, Waspie.'

I knew that only too well. Where to nip off *to* was the next question.

I tried St Bartholomew's, but with the same result as Guy's. With a heavy heart I set off home, patting Doshie for his help and giving him an extra dollop of hay. I walked back in the darkness down Blue Anchor Yard which only boasts two gas lamps, one each end. That's because the lamplighters don't care to venture far into the street itself. I usually carry my own lantern, but in my haste I'd forgotten it. The light of the moon graciously appeared to guide me back to Hairbrine Court and perhaps that was the Lord telling me to get in touch with Him.

Ned might have returned in my absence, I told myself, but as I climbed the steps to our door there was a desolation about the place that made me fear otherwise. Our rooms were just as I had left them; still, silent and empty. Kwan-yin was asleep, and even the fire I had lit had gone out.

I took up the Lord's offer. 'What's the plan, now?' I whispered. He took pity on me, because I realised what it had to be. I had to tackle not Slugger, but Lairy John, who must have known what was afoot. But this time I had nothing to bargain with.

*

I had to eat, though my stomach went up and down like a swing at Bartholomew Fair, churning at the thought of food. I'd be no use to Ned if I didn't eat something.

'Where you off to?' the muffin lady asked when I turned up on Monday morning after an all but sleepless night. 'You've a face like you dropped sixpence in the nightsoil.'

I couldn't speak. The words stuck in my throat, but I managed a grin, then hurried on my way to Spitalfields.

There's a good side to Spitalfields too, for all its name came from the spittles which were leper homes. Those lepers have gone now, and the villains have taken their place as outcasts, crawling like maggots on a dead man. But there are plenty of good folk there too and every year a special sermon is preached outside Christchurch. I went once, but it took three and a half hours and it's my belief that our Lord himself tired of listening to it, especially as He's so much else to do. Today, He and I would have to work hard together if we were to find Ned.

I walked through the market with bright coloured scarves and kerchiefs everywhere, probably mostly stolen, and I picked my way through to where I'd met Lairy. The same huge guardian at the end of the smelly alley stared at me, but didn't stop me. That suggested I was expected, which made me cold inside, as though the devil himself had said to me, 'You come here, Tom Wasp. You're mine now.'

Don't be crack-brained, Tom, I quickly scolded myself. This is your chance to find Ned. Nevertheless my knees were knocking together as

I went through the door, with the guard treading at my heels. Lairy was there, lounging in a chair and looking as cocky as before, with a smug smile on his face.

'Thought you'd find your way here again, Wasp. Took your time, didn't you? I've been waiting for you.'

'Most kind,' I said churlishly.

'After your lad, are you?'

No pleading here, I warned myself. He'd enjoy that.

'What's your game?' I asked briskly. I made it brisk so that I could ignore my heart which was beating like a drummer at the Victoria Park bandstand.

'The game's called Three Players, Wasp,' he sneered. 'Me, you and young Ned.'

'Four,' I corrected him. 'There's Flint.'

His eyes narrowed. '*I* do the bargaining.'

'I'll only deal with Flint.'

'Going to let the kid croak, are you?'

I'd put a foot wrong. Two feet perhaps. I did my best to withdraw a step or two. 'I've seen your face, Lairy. If he dies, you're for the rope.'

His eye narrowed. 'It's *you* who'll be the stiff, Wasp.'

Checkmate. 'Let's talk.' I added a touch of briskness again. 'What's the price and where is he?'

I had to know where Ned was or I'd never get him out alive. But I also knew that they'd most likely kill him even if I did what they wanted.

'Price is that Tarlton play, Wasp. You know where it is. All of it.'

'What's that mean, *all* of it?'

'All what Flint wants he gets. Me too.'

I decided to be clear on this point. 'What Flint wanted was the *Seven Deadly Sins* manuscript and that's what he's got. Slugger Joe stole it from the bookstore after getting Phineas Snook to look for it.'

'Not what Flint says. He ain't got it and he wants it. He's a customer waiting.'

If that was so, then I still couldn't understand the situation. Slugger Joe wouldn't have let Phineas keep the Tarlton script after they raided the bookstore and I couldn't see Slugger wanting to keep it for himself. Or even Lairy. Too much at stake for them not to play by Flint's rules. But I was getting desperate. Ned's life depended on Flint having that script.

'You tell Flint I ain't got the script either,' I said. 'He must know that. Slugger turned over my place and Phineas'. It wasn't there in either of them.'

'Oh yes it was, or you know where it is.'

'If I did,' I howled, 'why wouldn't I have given it to its rightful owner or sold it on? I wouldn't have held on to swag like that. Too dangerous.'

'Rightful owner, eh?' he jeered. 'And who's that, in your opinion?' He was watching me most carefully.

'How should I know? Mrs Harcourt perhaps, but then her husband never paid for it, so it still belongs to Phineas Snook.'

His eyes glinted. 'Get it for Flint, Wasp, and the kid goes free.'

'Where is he? How do I know you've not —' I could barely say the words — 'killed him already?'

'You'll have to take that chance, pal.'

'I'm no pal to Flint's clever-boots.'

His eyes flared fury. 'Clear off!' he roared, 'and get that script back here.'

I staggered out of the shop into the air — not clean air round here, but as clean as it ever gets in this part of smoky old London. I pushed my way through the crowds not knowing where I was going or what to think. The noise of the street cries, traffic and general hub-bub swallowed me up in their own chaos. I knew no one and no one cared about me and Ned.

And then I saw Jericho Mason, of all people, pushing his way through the market crowds. I gawped at him. There he suddenly was, and in my daze I'd nearly run straight into him. What was he doing here on a working morning? He wasn't too pleased to see me and tried to shove me out of his way. I wasn't having that, so I clung on to his jerkin.

'I've got things to do, sweep,' he said, trying to tear himself free, but I wasn't going to let him go.

'You tell Mrs Pomfret and Miss Pomfret too that my Ned's been taken,' I yelled at him, clutching hard. 'Kidnapped by Flint's mob. But you know that, don't you? You're one of them.'

He gazed at me as if the words meant nothing, then pushed me roughly aside, sending me staggering into a plump lady who looked at me as though I was trying to nab the kippers she'd just bought. Was Jericho on his way to see Lairy John? If so, I'd done no harm in coming here because the more people knew about Ned the better. If he was still alive I wouldn't have much time wherever they were holding him. They would lose patience. Too much trouble to give him food and water. I'd no choice now. I'd have to find Slugger Joe.

And then a golden path opened up before me — in my mind that is, as the streets of London aren't paved with gold, especially not in Spitalfields — and it wasn't Slugger I was thinking of.

At the end of my golden path stood Mrs Snook.

For all she didn't see eye to eye with Phineas and for all she was devoted to Slugger Joe for reasons of her own, she must have some motherly feelings for Phineas and perhaps that might stretch to a maternal spot for young children. Could she be looking after my Ned on Slugger's orders?

The flare of hope waned as I considered the unlikelihood of Mrs

Snook tenderly feeding my Ned pies and puddings. Then it flared up again when it occurred to me that she might at least know about his being kidnapped. Kidnapping children is a popular London trade, sometimes just for their clothing, sometimes to sell them for purposes of chimney sweeping — or worse. For all I knew, my Ned, who had been an 'anybody's child' and sold as a climbing boy, might have been born a duke's son.

On the small chance that Mrs Snook might be able to help, I hurried back to Wellclose Square and on to Pell Street as fast as my legs would carry me, gathering my courage to knock on that familiar door in the yard.

'What do you want?' She granted me her usual welcoming greeting, standing there as formidable as Mr Dickens' Mrs Gamp.

'A word, Mrs Snook.' I tried to keep the trembling out of my voice and I was hoping she'd call me in so I could see if there were any signs of Ned. But it was the doorstep for me again.

'Say it here,' she sneered, 'and one word only.'

'Kidnap,' I promptly replied.

She stared at me looking, as I was sadly aware, genuinely puzzled.

'My Ned,' I continued desperately, 'he's only a lad and he's been kidnapped by the mob. Thought he might be here with Slugger — Phineas' Uncle Joe,' I quickly amended.

'My Joe wouldn't do a thing like that,' she cried indignantly, although not, I thought, convincingly. 'I don't want no boys here. I had enough with Phineas and look what's happened to him after I brought him up so decent.'

I had to speak out for Phineas. 'He's not guilty, Mrs Snook. It's my belief he'll be released soon. I saw him in Newgate.'

'Better not tell Joe that,' she snapped. 'They don't get on.' I could almost see her wrestling with herself and then she blurted out: 'How is he?'

'Missing home cooking.' I thought this might please her, although when I thought of the loving way Clara and Hetty were looking after him, this might not be true.

''E wanted to move out,' she said crossly. 'I didn't push him out. It was all because of that cat Cockalorum. First it makes Joe sneeze and then it attacked poor Joe just because he tried to put it outside where it belongs.'

'The cat's dead now so Phineas might come back here to you. Joe drowned him.'

More indignation. 'My Joe wouldn't do a thing like that either.' A pause. 'Did he?'

'Yes, and now his mob have kidnapped my young Ned. He's only ten.' I knocked off a year or two for effect.

'Ten?' she said and I thought I detected a softening. 'I remember young Phinny at that age. I took him to Bartholomew Fair to see his pappy perform. Both of them real artistes.'

I saw an opportunity. 'I wish my Ned could do something like that. It's no life for him, chimney sweeping and calling the streets.'

'He's not here,' she said abruptly, 'this Ned of yours. I ain't seen him.'

I believed her. 'Could be Joe didn't want to upset you by bringing him here. Somewhere else he might have put him perhaps?'

'He doesn't talk business with me.'

'What *is* his business?' I asked, wondering how he explained killing people to order.

'He runs a high-class prize-fighting team,' she said with pride. 'Might have taken your boy as an apprentice. I'll keep my ears open, Mr Wasp. I don't hold with being unkind to youngsters.' Another pause. 'If you can get Phineas out of Newgate, I'd be obliged. I don't want him hanged. I'll leave a note at his place if I've news of your youngster.'

That evening I went to John's Hill but there was no sign that Mrs Snook had been to Phineas' lodgings. Too soon, I comforted myself. Then I had to face going back to Hairbrine Court, which was worse. Here I was doing nothing with no idea of where to turn next. Ned could be anywhere — on a ship to China or just around the corner. Even Kwan-yin wasn't singing anymore, and without her song the loneliness was even worse.

All I could do was wait, in the hope of Mrs Snook finding a clue to where he was. I'm not good at waiting. I need to sweep a chimney until it's clean. That made me realise I was leaving one flue unswept. The *main* flue leading to getting Ned released. The missing Tarlton play was stuck in it, so I'd have to do my best to climb it.

*

It was nearly two weeks since Mr Harcourt's murder and I couldn't see why Lairy John or Flint appeared still to be hunting for the *Seven Deadly Sins*. Even so I had to fix my mind on its being the key to ending this black nightmare, and dismiss the fear that even if I put the Tarlton play in their hands they might not release him.

My first plan was to talk to Phineas again. I wouldn't be allowed into Newgate without another pass, which meant another visit to Constable Peters early on Tuesday morning. It was up to me to find Ned, and I clung to the hope that visiting Phineas would solve the mystery of where the script was. Had he passed it to a friend or hidden it too carefully for Slugger or me to find in his room? Or would he confirm that he'd given it to Slugger who had sold it elsewhere?

Constable Peters said he'd arrange for a pass, but at first he was uneasy about it, as Newgate is so particular about visits from anyone at all and the City of London police might also object. When I explained about Ned he agreed immediately though. No harm would come of it, I assured him. I wasn't going to take a hacksaw or blunderbuss with me to free Phineas by force. Such passes take time to arrange, however, and several hours went by while I fidgeted, tormented by the thought of Ned all on his own — even dead.

Tuesday evening found me outside Newgate at last, where I then went through the same routine as before. This time, though, I was sitting in my wooden box cabin before Phineas was brought in from his cell.

I was shocked. He looked diminished, smaller and his usually merry face was drawn, as though songs and smiles were forgotten things of the past.

'That play manuscript of yours, Phineas. The one your father gave you. The one you went to collect at Mr Harcourt's bookstore with Joe that night. Where is it?'

At first Phineas didn't seem to know what I was talking about but at last he showed interest. 'Yes. In a cover marked *Seven Deadly Sins*. Mr Harcourt came to see me and I told him I'd take it to him on Wednesday afternoon. Is that what you mean?'

'It is, Phineas,' I said with relief. Now at last I might be on the path to freeing Ned, but first I had to finish cleaning the chimney. 'Hetty's upset, because it was she who told Mr Harcourt about the manuscript.'

'Upset?' Phineas looked astonished. 'Why? She's my darling bud of May.'

That reassured me. 'What happened to the *Seven Deadly Sins*, Phineas?'

'After Mr Harcourt's death, Joe said my mother wanted it back and he would take it to her. It still belonged to me, he said, because Mr Harcourt hadn't paid me for it. I didn't like Mr Harcourt and I knew that he often bought stolen property from one of Joe's friends. That's why I asked you to tell Mrs Pomfret about his behaviour to Hetty. I couldn't complain to Mr Harcourt about that myself because I wanted him to buy the play first. I didn't want to sell it, but I did want to marry Hetty.'

Phineas paused for breath. The words were tumbling out now. 'I had wanted to surprise her by calling at Dolly's with flowers to tell her we could get married. When Mr Harcourt said he wouldn't give me the money until he'd sold the play, I had to tell her immediately — but I met Jericho and William first.'

My hopes sank again. I understood now what had happened with Hetty and Mr Harcourt, but I still didn't know any more about the *Seven Deadly Sins*. Minutes and hours were ticking away while Ned suffered. I had to go on.

'You said you didn't think Joe had what he wanted when you both left the bookstore, so what happened to the *Seven Deadly Sins* folder?'

'I gave it to Joe to give to my mother as he asked. He was delighted when I showed it to him and pointed out the name *Seven Deadly Sins* on the cover. He grabbed it from me.'

'And that's the last you saw of it?'

He nodded, looking pleased that he had helped me. Or so he believed.

I felt I was whirling around in a jig, like Phineas or Tarlton himself. If Slugger did have the Tarlton play, what had happened to it? I was back where I had begun and my only hope for finding Ned with or without the script lay with Mrs Snook.

This soot was getting too hard even for me to scrape off. I decided to go to Phineas' lodgings once again, although I was losing hope that the Widow Snook would prove my saviour. The next morning found me knocking on Mrs Tutman's door to assure her the next rent would be paid on Friday and then I walked round to the steps to Phineas' room, still not knowing where to turn next. Even if I could beard Slugger in his den he wasn't going to tell me anything about the *Seven Deadly Sins,* or, more importantly, about Ned.

My hopes were whittled down even further as there was, as I'd feared, no sign that anyone had visited Phineas' rooms since my last visit — the small window was still open and the door closed. Nevertheless, I hurried inside in case I was wrong and I'd find either Mrs Snook or a note from her. I found neither, but there *was* something waiting for me and my heart lifted.

Perched on Phineas' armchair, glaring at me, was Cockalorum

CHAPTER FOURTEEN

Lost

Cockalorum? His ghost? A twin cat? I blinked twice, had another look and there he was. No doubt about it. I was receiving his special glare. Somehow or other he had escaped from that sack, because compassion for cats wasn't likely to be a quality highly rated by Slugger Joe. Cats and kittens have a hard time of it in this part of London, being pinched for their skins, drowned at birth or even eaten. Cockalorum did not look in fine fettle. It was nearly a week since he had been taken; his fur was standing on end and he looked thinner. The hunter in him was plainly to be seen, the cat that had purred for Phineas and Ned was absent. He must be hungry, even though his hunting instinct would surely have meant that he didn't starve. I'd have to provide something tempting, though.

He watched me carefully and jumped off the table to greet me, yowling loudly. I didn't think I was going to get the same treatment as Slugger Joe and stroked him affectionately, admiring his endurance.

'You and me are stuck in the same chimney, Cockalorum,' I informed him. 'We both want Phineas and Ned back with us. Trouble is, the chimney's toppling fast. What are we going to do about it?'

As he rubbed himself against my trouser legs there was a smell of stale fish, which seemed to come from all over him, as though he'd been lying in it. As I bent down to stroke him again I could sniff it even more strongly. Had Slugger or his men taken him down Billingsgate fish market way, or had he just passed through it to keep himself alive on the way back home? Then a thought came to me: perhaps he was dumped there in the sack. There were plenty of warehouses and wharves around Billingsgate and so …

Could Ned be there?

This notion was like a flue with a right-angle bend, but I'd nothing else to go on, so I grasped at it eagerly.

'Mr Wasp!' A now familiar voice summoned me from outside. It was Mrs Snook herself panting up the steps towards me, skirts rustling with the effort and bonnet askew. She stopped short when she saw what awaited her inside.

'You said Joe had croaked that cat.'

'I thought he had. But here he is.' I was about to add 'stinking of fish', but I stopped, just in case she was in Slugger Joe's pay.

'Billingsgate,' she said grimly. 'Joe were stinking of fish Sunday night. Where you been? I asked him. None of your business, said he. Oh yes, it is, says I. I told him that's my bed you're sleeping in,' — she blushed modestly — 'so it's my business too. And what did he say? Bloke he knows has a couple of warehouses down by Billingsgate. So all I says to him was next time you bring a tidy bit of cod back here, but it set me thinking.'

'And what next?' I pressed her, seeing a glimmer of light at last.

'He says to come 'ere darling, and give me a hug,' she tittered.

Slugger Joe's endearments weren't of interest, but that warehouse was. If Cockalorum had been taken to a warehouse might not my Ned be there too? Slugger did not seem the kind of man to be adventurous in his dealings.

'My thanks to you, Mrs Snook,' I said, seizing my hat.

'Where are you going?' she asked, as I raised it to her and hurried past.

'To find my Ned,' I threw over my shoulder. 'He might be there.'

'I'm coming with you,' she shouted after me. 'I don't hold with kidnapping children. Bad enough pinching their clothes. Ain't right.'

Coming from Slugger Joe's woman this was a screamer, but I solemnly agreed with her.

'And what you doing about that cat?' she threw at me as we hurried down the steps. 'Looks as if he hasn't eaten in a month of Sundays.'

I wasn't so sure about that, but I climbed quickly back to reassure Cockalorum (and Mrs Snook) that he hadn't been forgotten.

'And next time we come,' Mrs Snook said grimly, 'you make sure my Phineas is back too.'

*

Billingsgate is to fish what Smithfield is to meat. Smithfield remains Smithfield for all it's been reborn as the Metropolitan Cattle Market, and Billingsgate will always be Billingsgate. Every fish in the whole wide world must be sold here, some fresh, some dried, some pickled. Every morning at five o'clock sharp it opens for trade with coster-mongers, fishmongers, country dealers and hotel keepers, all yelling their heads off.

Mrs Snook was several inches taller than me and several inches wider too, so we made an odd couple as we struggled our way through the noisy crowds. By this time, I was already tired of her telling me what a gentleman Slugger Joe was and how good at heart. There are many people already past St Peter's Gate to eternal rest who wouldn't agree, but today I needed allies and Mrs Snook was one.

'I'll give Joe a wigging after we find this lad of yours,' she said. 'I don't hold with it. No, I don't.'

On Tower Hill we passed Enoch, who thrust a broadsheet at us but we had no time to stop. 'Later, Enoch,' I shouted at him. 'It's my Ned. He's been nabbed by Slugger and shoved in one of those warehouses Billingsgate way. Know which of them?'

But he just stared at me with his watery eyes and I despaired. I remembered the penny I owed him, found one in my pocket and handed it over. He stared at that, too. 'Toff's murder,' I heard him calling. 'Toff's murder ...' but I was already on my way, catching up with Mrs Snook as she strode ahead.

The smell of fish was all around us outside the market as we passed the Custom House. This is a most respectable establishment and it was hard to believe that Flint's mob was operating anywhere near that. But that's Flint all over. I realised I was still assuming that Ned's kidnapping was tied up with Flint's racket and the murders and not one of Slugger's own ventures, but I had to cling on to my own instinct.

There are so many ships and boats moored near London Bridge and in St Katharine's or London docks that you can hardly see Old Father Thames beneath them. He's there, though, flowing in his stately fashion as he has done for thousands of years. There are ships from all over the world arriving here, all flying their bright flags, only to be greeted by the sight of London's chimneys belching out their smoke. That brought back the fearsome thought that Slugger might have put Ned on one of those ships, just as in the bad old days boys were kidnapped for manning the vessels. I had to be nippy about finding him in case he was about to be shipped off to Australia.

'These warehouses of Joe's — know where they are?' I panted as we hurried along.

Mrs Snook didn't, and so we had to work our way along the wharves — Nicholson's Steam Packet, Cox's Quay, Fresh Wharf — all the time avoiding huge stacks of merchandise and sailors and dockers. They were swarming around us carrying out their daily work, while here we were, a sweep and lady trying to rush by them hunting for one small boy amidst this lot.

The huge warehouses presented a different picture. No one hurried here, everyone walked in stately fashion, being landlubbers who kept the stores and records. Mrs Snook seemed as daunted as I was at the prospect of finding Ned. Had I made a mistake coming here? I took hold of myself. I must not think that way.

We tried Fresh Wharf first for warehouses, this being nearer London Bridge; the first warehouse had a gatekeeper, a most imposing gentleman who eyed us up and down and then asked haughtily: 'Where's your orders?'

Explaining we were in search of a lost boy availed us nothing. 'No one comes in here, especially ladies, without an *order*!'

'Where do we get that?' I asked desperately.

'London Dock House of course. No ladies allowed until after one o'clock.'

Mrs Snook took exception to this. '*I* am,' she said imperiously. 'I'm looking for Joe Higgins.'

That shook even this stately gentleman. 'Not here,' he barked and there was fear in his face.

'Where then?' I barked back.

'Next one along.'

Oddly enough the gatekeeper there said exactly the same thing, and so did the next, and the next. It seemed to me that whether or not we plodded back to the London Dock House for our orders, they had little to do with this matter and much to do with the fact that Mrs Snook mentioned Slugger Joe. Just when I was thinking we didn't stand a chance, however, there was a change in response.

'Never heard of Joe Higgins,' was the answer. There couldn't be a trader this part of London who hadn't heard of Slugger Joe, so I was suspicious right away. That didn't help us to get past this gatekeeper, but the next warehouse presented a different problem. There was no sign of a gatekeeper or anyone else, and the door was locked.

'Here,' I cried out, almost choking with anticipation. 'I *know* he's here!' I had to believe that or hope would vanish for good. I could feel the tears on my cheeks as I tried without success to ram the door. The stink of old fish around this place made me retch but the windows were too small to climb through even if we smashed them.

'Round the back,' cried Mrs Snook. 'There may be another door.'

My respect grew for her; she wasn't going to give up and she was ignoring the smells like a true docker. It was hard even reaching the rear of the building thanks to all the piles of rubbish in the form of old boxes and sacks — and, yes, evidence in the form of fish bones. When we managed to reach the back of the building there was at least a clear path through the piles, but Mrs Snook took a dim view of it.

'This is no place for a lady,' she snorted. 'Look at my shoes. Covered in fish guts. We'd better find your boy here alive, or I'll have words with Joe.'

'There's a door,' I cried, as though this in itself was proof we were on the right track. It was locked, and the windows were just as small. 'I'll try ramming it,' I shouted, but my puny weight got us nowhere.

'I'll give it a wallop,' Mrs Snook offered. 'I've learned a trick or two from Joe.'

The tricks didn't work, and by now I was convinced that Ned was inside. What to do? Only one way now. 'I'll look for a peeler,' I said.

'No, you won't!' she yelled at me. 'Joe would have me guts for garters.'

I wavered but help arrived in an unlikely form; we'd been so intent on the door we hadn't noticed that we had company. Jericho Mason and William Wright were watching us. How or why they were there, I didn't enquire, I didn't care. Such mysteries could wait. I just wanted Ned back — if he wasn't already dead.

'Have you got my boy in there?' I hurled at them.

No answer, but Jericho marched towards me. I thought he was going to wallop me but he pushed me aside, then rammed the door with his sturdy shoulders. I heard the locks give and my spirits rose. One more try, and to my joy it burst open.

He stood aside and motioned us in. William made no move and Mrs Snook and I looked at each other, each suspecting that these men might be Ned's gaolers. Once we were inside we would be in for it. A woman and a puny chimney sweep weren't going to stand a chance. Sometimes decisions are quickly made.

'You stay here,' I told Mrs Snook. 'I'm going in *now*.'

'Don't talk twaddle,' she snapped, then turned to Jericho and William. 'You first,' I heard her say to them grimly. I had already rushed in and was scanning the ground floor by the time I heard the door slam behind her.

The place was dank and dark — and the smell of fish from ages past hit my nostrils. Empty packing boxes piled high filled every space, and I began to push them aside, my arms flailing. Then Jericho seized me by the shoulder and fear struck through me as he pushed me towards an old rickety staircase.

'Up,' he ordered me. Could Ned be up there or was this to be my deathbed? Did he want us conveniently out of sight before he and William croaked us?

'Up!' Jericho shouted again, but this time he must have been calling William as I was halfway up by now.

'You stay there,' I shouted back to Mrs Snook, as her skirts weren't going to like these stairs.

'I'm coming,' she yelled and was up there in a jiffy.

To me this floor too looked full of boxes, which Jericho was already heaving around with William in his wake. I realised now they were *helping* us. I didn't waste time worrying over this, but hurried to the far end of the warehouse to start work there. I had only moved one pile before I thought I could hear scuffling. Was it my imagination? Was it rats? Just as I worked out where it was coming from, William joined me with Jericho hard on his heels.

I saw a movement and heard a grunting sound. Yes, between two piles I could see Ned's head poking out from the sacking into which he was bound. A scarf was tied round his mouth and there was none too pleasant a smell as he must have been tied up for a while. Scraps of old newspaper suggested food of some kind might have been brought.

Mrs Snook promptly pushed William and Jericho aside. 'It's your boy,' she said joyfully, as I whipped the scarf off.

Ned was coughing now, trying to croak with tears on his face — and mine.

'Thanks, guvnor,' he managed to whisper.

I turned to thank Jericho and William but they'd already gone. I didn't have time to worry about that either.

Between us Mrs Snook and I managed to half-carry Ned down the steps once he got a taste of his walking legs again. We had to hurry him in case Jericho and William weren't on our side after all. Perhaps like Mrs Snook they had only thought that boys should not be kidnapped — but even so, what brought them here?

After a brief sit-down we set off for Phineas' lodgings as they were nearer than Hairbrine Court. Mrs Snook then ordered Mrs Tutman to give her a basin of water — this not being a day when the water runs in this part of the world. Mrs Snook is more formidable than Mrs Tutman, so not to my surprise it was easy to arrange this. The other person who didn't get his own way was Ned, who to his fury had all his clothes whipped off for a wash.

I realised that we were missing one from this party however: Cockalorum. He was nowhere to be seen; out hunting perhaps. He must have heard the uproar though, and sure enough he came bounding in, though he didn't seem pleased to see Mrs Snook. But he set Ned's eyes shining again so I blessed that cat.

'Cockalorum!' he shouted in glee.

It was a joyous reunion and Mrs Snook departed well satisfied. I had persuaded her not to reveal her part in Ned's rescue for her own sake, and she saw the sense of this, on condition I got Phineas out of prison quickly. That meant that I had to get Ned back to Hairbrine Court double quick as Slugger would not be far behind us and for both our sakes I felt more secure there than here.

I also had to get Phineas out of prison, and therefore I still had to find out very speedily who had murdered Mr Harcourt and Mrs Fortescue. To do that, I had to return to tracking down the *Seven Deadly Sins* manuscript. It was going to be a ticklish job and no mistake.

Ned had other things on his mind. 'I can still play Jack-in-the-Green, can't I, guvnor?'

'Yes, Ned.'

Only *four days* away, and with the crowds that would be milling around the procession how could I protect him? What other answer could I have given him though?

Where next? With Ned himself, I decided. I wouldn't put it past Flint to nab him again, and if so I wouldn't get him back. I sensed there was more Ned had to tell me, but he had shut up like a clam and I ought to let it be for a while. I'd had time to think about Jericho and William now. Surely they couldn't have been involved in the kidnapping? I thought I knew what must have happened. After I saw Jericho in Spitalfields, he must have told Clara about Ned being kidnapped and she ordered him or both of them to find Ned. That explanation didn't quite add up, though. Had it been coincidence that I had seen Jericho in Spitalfields, or did he have a mission of his own there? Was it his idea to come to Billingsgate and if so how did he know where to come? More likely William forced him to come. It was a puzzle I couldn't solve and there was only one person who might be able to help: Ned. I needed to know more about his ordeal and so I had no choice but to press him to speak.

'Who did this to you, Ned?' I asked gently. 'Slugger Joe must be behind it, but you wouldn't have let him nab you. Was it Jericho?'

'No,' Ned muttered. 'It was at the Churchyard.'

'What were you doing there, Ned?' I remembered I'd been there on Sunday too, and lamented that by chance we must have been there at different times.

'Just *things*,' he answered me defiantly, by which I knew he'd been up to one of his tricks. I'd leave that for a while.

'Who nabbed you?'

'Lairy John saw me. I thought he was being friendly. He pointed out a toff who was busy talking to another cove and looked ripe, so I went over to him but they and Lairy got me. They took me to Slugger.'

The Swell Mob, without a doubt. I sensed there was more that Ned could tell me, but he shut himself off again. And as yet he'd made no mention of Jericho or William.

Once he had been strengthened by a meat pie fetched by Mrs Snook before she left he became more of his old self and felt up to returning to our home. It turned out that all he'd had to eat while he was away was a dried herring or two and a pint of ale.

'What about Cockalorum?' he asked anxiously. 'We can't leave him here.'

Cockalorum was also faring well for food, as Mrs Snook had unbent enough to bring some fish as well as the meat pie for Ned.

'I'll put some fish in my pocket again. See if he follows,' I said.

Ned was wiser than me. 'I think he'll come anyway.'

Our budget was suffering because I hadn't been able to get much sweeping done, but once it was known in Hairbrine Court that Ned was back and needed feeding, food arrived in plenty. Ned was right. Cockalorum had once again thrown in his lot with us and followed us back to our home. He seemed as anxious about Ned as I was, judging by the way he pawed at his trousers and licked his arms affectionately. It's true he did consider Ned's food as his own to share, but that worked out all right because he ate more fish and Ned another meat pie. What did I eat? Nothing much. I was too happy to eat.

Mrs Snook reappeared the next morning to see how Ned was, as Slugger was safely employed elsewhere, and I took the opportunity to ask her about the *Seven Deadly Sins*.

'Phineas told me his father gave it to him,' I said, trying to sound casual.

She snorted. 'His dad was no good at anything but playing the fool, just like my Phinny.'

'Any reason his dad would have a manuscript of an old play to pass on to Phineas?'

'That pile of old paper? That came from his grandpa.'

'Did you read it?'

'Me? No, it wasn't even in proper English, only a few words.'

'How would his grandpa have acquired it? Did you meet him?'

'Met him a few times. *His* dad was a proper actor. Played at Drury Lane. What's all this about, Mr Wasp?'

'Your Joe seems interested in this play.'

Mrs Snook looked at me straight in the eye. 'I see no evil, hear no evil, and I certainly don't speak no evil where Joe's concerned. Not often anyway.'

'Even though Phineas is in prison?'

'You're going to get him out of that place and don't waste time about it. And,' she said meaningfully, 'I can tell you Slugger didn't kill that bloke Harcourt, either. He was snoring beside me. And he don't get up till long after the lamplighter's come round of a morning. Unless he's on a job, that is. So he don't have nothing to do with that woman that got croaked, either.'

*

Now that I knew this missing manuscript had been in Phineas' family for a long time I decided to have another word with Mr Chalcot, though I was worried about leaving Ned on his own. I need not have done. Mrs Snook insisted on staying with him — not to Cockalorum's pleasure,

I'm sure. Mr Chalcot might not be too pleased to have me turning up again, but I couldn't help that if I was to get Phineas freed. *Three days left.*

Mr Chalcot was courteous as ever when I plodded through the bookstore door, despite the fact that he already had customers — or rather guests, as it was Mr Timpson and Mr Manley who were taking coffee with him.

'My dear Mr Wasp,' Mr Chalcot greeted me. 'Do, pray, join us.'

I accepted his offer despite the glowers from Mr Timpson. Mr Manley looked so worried that I must have been the least of his problems. I sensed a tense atmosphere that had little to do with my arrival. I'd walked into a set-to of some sort.

Mr Timpson made an effort at cordiality. 'How is that boy of yours, Wasp?'

News travels quickly in the Row and I realised that Jericho and William must already have spread the story. 'My thanks to you,' I said, as if taking coffee with gentlemen was my normal pattern for passing the day. 'He's safe, thank you kindly. He was taken,' I swept on, delighted to have this opportunity, 'by someone anxious to obtain that manuscript by Mr Tarlton — and that someone believes I know where it is.'

A curious silence fell. 'And *do* you?' Mr Timpson enquired. Mr Chalcot merely looked perplexed and Mr Manley even more anxious.

'No, but I shall find out.'

'We should be *much* obliged,' Mr Chalcot assured me.

Mr Timpson had something to say on this account. 'Our friend Mr Splendour is also making every effort to find the *Seven Deadly Sins* on Mrs Harcourt's behalf, but he has so far failed. Indeed the police seem to believe — quite mistakenly of course — that our friend Mr Splendour already has it. Doubtless he believes that the *Seven Deadly Sins* is as valuable as a whole lost play by Shakespeare.'

'It *is* lost,' I pointed out. 'Even Flint is looking for it.'

Another curious silence, which Mr Timpson once again broke. 'You mentioned that name before. I don't believe I know the gentleman.'

It was then I remembered his being at the Churchyard on Sunday afternoon — where Ned had been nabbed by Flint's men. Coincidence, or was there more to it?

'Moreover,' he continued smoothly, 'even if this Mr Flint is searching for it, there is the question of these two tragic murders. Neither of those can have anything to do with myself, as Mr Manley and Mr Splendour were with Mr Harcourt after I had left.'

'That is not my recollection,' Mr Manley immediately fired up. 'I recall leaving you with Mr Splendour and Mr Harcourt after I decided to take a walk to the riverside.'

'Then you recall wrongly,' Mr Timpson flared up in indignation.

A polite cough from Mr Chalcot. 'My dear Mr Wasp, I'm told this Mr Flint murders people to order. That is quite shocking, the material of penny dreadfuls.'

Mr Timpson seized on this. 'It seems to me entirely possible that is the truth of what happened. I had begun to fear that you were under the impression that one of us was involved in these terrible murders, Mr Wasp, but clearly that is not possible as we had never heard of Flint — although I cannot speak for Mr Splendour.'

'It concerned me,' I said, trying to look concerned as well, 'that only the Tarlton Ordinaries knew that Mr Harcourt had received the script from Mr Snook that afternoon.'

Mr Manley's turn to be shocked. 'Mr Wasp, your implication is offensive.'

I waited to see what Mr Timpson might reply, but it was Mr Chalcot who responded, looking most troubled. 'We cannot deny we all knew about the manuscript. Mr Harcourt was only too pleased to talk of the great fortune it would bring him. However, a great many other people might also have known of it.'

'Naturally, we could hardly believe it,' Mr Timpson cut in smoothly. 'Certainly not myself. Of course, we were all delighted at his news. Irrespective of whether it had value, it was a magnificent find for literature.'

Mr Chalcot blithely chimed in once more. 'Especially as we believe it did have Shakespeare's hand in it. Indeed, we sincerely hope it might have a whole armful.' He waited for a chuckle at this witticism, but none came so he gravely added, 'One can dare to hope too much in such circumstances, of course.'

'A tweak or two during his early days at Stratford, perhaps, but no more,' Mr Timpson swiftly conceded. 'Shakespeare was the pupil, Tarlton the master in those days. Nothing of great *value*.'

'Unless of course Harcourt was right —' Mr Chalcot began.

'— He seldom was,' Mr Timpson cut in loudly.

At this Mr Chalcot grew pink in the cheeks. 'Even so, the possibility of the script being of very great value indeed must be considered. However, I should also point out that Mr Harcourt asked us to keep news of this discovery to ourselves, particularly if the script *was* of great value, something to which we all — with some readiness — agreed. In the circumstances of two murders, however, I believe I should absolve myself from the need for secrecy.'

Judging by their sharp intakes of breath, both Mr Timpson and Mr Manley disagreed with this policy, but there was no stopping Mr Chalcot. 'Furthermore it was our shared common knowledge that Mr Harcourt on occasion dealt with a fence in Spitalfields, I believe. Stolen property is a serious matter.'

By now Mr Timpson was bristling with anger. 'If the Tarlton script was stolen property,' he snapped, 'perhaps it was indeed this Flint who took action in the form of two murders. As for secrecy, for shame, sir. You have betrayed the trust of the Ordinaries.'

Mr Manley in comparison was so shaken that he could only manage a 'Hear, hear, sir.'

Mr Chalcot seemed not a bit dismayed at this rancour. He beamed at both myself and his other guests. 'Take each man's censure but reserve thy judgement' — I believe that was Shakespeare's advice? Now, Mr Wasp, what do you have for us in the way of information?'

Should I speak out now, or would it be wiser to wait? Now, I decided. 'The manuscript, sir. It was not stolen property,' I informed them. 'It belonged to Phineas Snook and was a family heirloom.'

This stirred up the soot all right. Mr Timpson was spluttering with rage and Mr Manley went very pale. Mr Chalcot, however, looked most interested.

'I wonder,' he said brightly, forestalling Mr Timpson's attempts to speak, 'how far this family heritage of Snook's goes back. Most interesting that this Phineas Snook is a fool, just like Richard Tarlton. Whoever in his family acquired the script was probably a fool, too. And yet the *Seven Deadly Sins* is usually considered to have been a tragedy with comic relief.'

'You're talking nonsense, Wasp!' Mr Timpson shouted. 'What would a fool's family be doing with a Shakespearean treasure?'

A gasp of horror from Mr Manley made him aware of this lapse. 'I meant *Tarlton* treasure of course,' he added hastily. But it was too late.

'Mr Timpson,' asked Mr Chalcot mildly, 'do you have more information on the *Seven Deadly Sins* than Mr Harcourt confided to us that evening?'

Mr Timpson's face went very red. 'A mere opinion, given to me in private by Arnold Harcourt when I happened to call in at his store before our meeting that sad evening. A preliminary glance at the manuscript made him sure that Shakespeare's hand was indeed in it and to a great extent. He was to tell me more, but alas the opportunity never came.' He looked round defiantly to see how this was being received.

Mr Manley made no bones about it. 'Sir,' he said, visibly trembling with anger, 'you failed to behave in accordance with the rules of the Tarlton Ordinaries. These decree, if I am not mistaken, that each Ordinary shall behave as a gentleman in business matters, and you, sir, have not. I wonder whether there *is* more you can tell us about Harcourt's death?'

Mr Timpson jumped to his feet in anger, but at this point a lady made a most dramatic entrance from the street.

She was about the same girth and height as Mr Chalcot and was clearly *Mrs* Chalcot, from the way she flew straight to her husband.

'There is news, Mr Chalcot. *News!*'

'My sweetheart, of what?' He was most alarmed. 'Cousin Florence, perhaps?'

We had all risen immediately at the presence of a lady, agog to hear what this news might be.

'There is to be an *arrest*,' she declared. 'For *murder*.'

That set the chimney on fire. Mr Timpson and Mr Manley paled, and Mr Chalcot lost his smile in sheer astonishment.

Mrs Chalcot barely paused for breath. 'I had the news from Mabel — the evening editions — and when I saw the policemen around —'

'— But where, my chuck,' her husband asked in agitation. 'Who?'

'In the *Row* of course. As to who —'

But her audience was vanishing. I almost forgot my hat in the excitement as I was pushed aside by Mr Timpson and Mr Manley. Even Mr Chalcot passed me by in the rush to reach Paternoster Row.

Ahead of me, Mr Timpson and Mr Manley disappeared into the crowd of onlookers attracted by the sight of a Black Maria and police carriages, together with uniformed police from both the City of London and the Metropolitan police forces. By my usual means of parting the crowds, I managed to reach the front with ease. Was it Harcourt's store they were outside? No, Mr Splendour's.

I could see Sergeant Williamson and Constable Peters and with some difficulty managed to reach them. The constable was looking upset. 'Mr Splendour, Tom. Arrested.'

As I had thought — almost feared. Mr Splendour could have reason enough to wish both Mr Harcourt and Mrs Fortescue removed, but the latter surely only if she had been in possession of that much coveted Tarlton manuscript.

'For both murders, constable?' I asked.

'Mrs Fortescue — for the moment, Mr Wasp. It's understandable. He could easily have been in the bookstore earlier than he claims; the razor strop used to kill her would have been at hand. It was the old sort that hangs from a hook, and there's a new one in his rooms. And Mrs Harcourt is still sure that Mr Splendour was the smartly dressed man she witnessed in there with Mrs Fortescue. She's also still convinced that Mrs Fortescue stole the Tarlton play, but Inspector Harvey's opinion is that Splendour did that and Mrs Fortescue was trying a touch of blackmail on him.'

'And what's your opinion, constable?'

He hesitated. 'It's possible. And there's some good news, Mr Wasp —'

But then he had to hurry away, for they were bringing Mr

Splendour out. Gone was his usual jaunty air; instead there was panic, desperation and sobs of denial as he was unceremoniously thrust into the Black Maria.

Constable Peters might be thinking as I did. That they'd arrested the wrong person *again*.

CHAPTER FIFTEEN

One Last Flue

Greatly troubled, I set out for home. I had tried to find Clara to talk this over, but there was no sign of her, and my priority was Ned. The quicker I found out the whereabouts of the *Seven Deadly Sins* script the better.

Three days. That was all I had left before May Day. It was Thursday afternoon and by Sunday morning I had promised Ned that Phineas would be free to come to the procession and see his Jack-in-the-Green. I was passing Billingsgate and remembered I needed food for Cockalorum and ourselves. It was hard to stop there, because I was so eager to reach home again.

When I did, Ned was waiting outside with Cockalorum who gave a yowl of delight as he shook himself and ran up to greet me.

'Smelled the fish in my pocket eh?' I joked.

Ned laughed too, which was good. Mrs Snook had had to leave, he told me, and Ned must have felt safer out here in the court with folk passing every now and then. Cockalorum led the way upstairs and into our rooms, then looked at me expectantly. Once the question of supper had been discussed and Cockalorum satisfied, we settled down for a talk. Cockalorum took my armchair, Ned took his own and I had the broken one we're waiting to take to Zechariah for mending once we have enough sixpences.

'There's more to tell me, isn't there, Ned?' I asked gently. 'You need to spit it out, lad.'

He looked sullen at first but at last he began to talk. 'They threw me in that sack, guvnor. They said they'd drown me, but they didn't. They forced me right inside it for a bit till they threw me into that place.' He stopped, but then wailed, 'It was like being in a chimney again.'

I silently vowed they would pay for that.

'I told 'em I had to get back,' he went on, 'because I was going to be Jack-in-the-Green, but they just laughed. I didn't know where I was except that I could smell the river.' I knew what he meant. Nothing like Old Father Thames for smell. It's my belief the fish are glad to get out of it.

'They tied me up.' His voice was getting croaky now. 'I couldn't even get out to crap.'

I knew that all too well and so did Mrs Snook. I'd make them pay for that, too. 'What about Jericho Mason and William Wright? See anything of them, did you, save for when we picked you up?'

'No, guvnor.'

This was a puzzle. Jericho and William were rivals for Hetty's hand and now it seemed likely that Jericho was mixed up with Slugger Joe's affairs, perhaps even working for him as part of Flint's mob. Could William be the victim here? Had he been caught up in Jericho's private press-gang, and even part of Flint's mob? Certainly William had not looked happy when they were there to help us, when we had needed them at the warehouse.

'I'll have a word with Clara about this,' I told him gravely. 'And the sooner the better. You coming with me?' I asked, not wanting to leave him alone. Seeing his face, I quickly added, 'Tomorrow. You'll feel better then.'

'What about Cockalorum? If they come, they might find him.'

'I'll find a way round that, Ned.'

He looked happier at that, but could I find a way? Now I was truly down in the dumps. Ned was right. *Look after Cockalorum*, Phineas had said, and I hadn't done so. Kwan-yin was looking happier with Cockalorum's return, but Phineas was still in Newgate. Tom Wasp, I ordered myself, *find that way.*

*

'Letter for you, Mr Wasp!' Mrs Scrimshaw called out the next morning, that being her landlady's duty. 'From the pigmen. What's going on? They arresting you?'

I hoped not, but I unfolded it in trepidation until I remembered that Constable Peters had said something about good news. It *was* good news and cheered me greatly. Inspector Harvey had been kind enough to let me know that Phineas was being released on Saturday. Tomorrow! Plenty of time for him to see Ned as Jack-in-the-Green on Sunday.

Mrs Scrimshaw had lingered so I told her the good news. Mrs Snook nipped by to tell *me* the good news. Then Enoch called with one of the morning newspapers for me in case I hadn't heard the good news. I waited for Slugger Joe to toddle in with the good news, but he didn't.

'I'll take Doshie tomorrow,' I told Ned, 'and drive Phineas home in state. Then we'll take Cockalorum back to him and get some fish on the way.'

I'd spoken without thinking and saw Ned's look of distress. Parting with the cat was going to be hard for him. 'We've still got Kwan-yin,' I comforted him.

'She won't like it if Cockalorum goes,' Ned muttered.

'He belongs to Phineas, lad.' Cats don't truly belong to anyone, especially cats like Cockalorum. They make their own choices out of what's available, in my experience, but mine was the easiest way of telling Ned what had to be. 'You're right, though, Ned. When I saw him in Newgate, Phineas shouted after me, *Look after the cat.* I didn't, but I can tell him tomorrow how much *you've* done for him.'

He looked at me in a puzzled way. 'Phineas never called Cockalorum the cat — he thought it was impolite. He always called him Cockalorum.'

'Those were Phineas' very words, Ned. He shouted *look after the cat* as I left.'

Ned still looked doubtful and so I thought about this and then — by gosh — it came to me.

'The cat *poem*!' I cried. 'He meant those lines about Jeoffry in the *Jubilate Agno.* 'Phineas would have known that we would look after Cockalorum, but that cat poetry was different. I might not think of looking after that.'

'But that's just poetry, guvnor. Anyway, you have looked after it. It's still in my pillow.'

'It's not there any longer, Ned. Don't you remember I gave it to Hetty to keep it safe in case Slugger Joe came back here and destroyed it?'

I'd spoken without thinking and Ned went very white. 'I'll ask Hetty for it back when I get to Dolly's today,' I assured him.

'What about work?' Ned asked crossly, seeing me put my boots on.

'Chimneys will have to wait. Getting Phineas' cat book back is more important. Coming with me?'

He wavered. 'Only if I can bring Cockalorum.'

I thought of Cockalorum getting loose in Clara's kitchens and shuddered. 'He won't like it, Ned,' I explained tactfully. 'He'll think he's being given away again when he sees strangers and he's going home tomorrow anyway. He'll be happy enough here alone today.'

He glared at me. 'I'll stay with him.'

I didn't like this idea either, but the chances of Slugger coming here in broad daylight were slim indeed, particularly after he'd had his wigging from Mrs Snook.

*

I still wondered whether I'd done the right thing in leaving Ned, but I had to put this to one side in the interests of getting to the bottom of this matter. The cat poem had to be taken care of for Phineas' sake and the Tarlton script was the key to two murders. They needed sorting out rapidly, if Mr Splendour was not to be wrongly charged as Phineas had been.

It was Clara I needed to talk to first and she seemed just as anxious to talk to me, for all she was as busy as ever.

'I heard the news, Tom,' she said as we sat down in her greeting room. 'I don't know whether to laugh or cry what with Phineas free and Mr Splendour taken away. But you've found Ned, that's the main thing.'

'I've Jericho and William to thank for that.'

She smiled. 'When they told me Ned was missing I told them to do everything they could to help or else I'd beat the living daylights out of them. I'll make William's lost tips up to him. But, Tom, how they came to be there at the right time is a puzzle. They told me they were just passing. That's gammon, but why should they lie about it?'

'I was hoping you'd tell me why, Clara.'

'I can't. They're not pals, Tom. Why were they even together? William's so fond of Hetty that he keeps a suspicious eye on everything Jericho does. But they're both so devoted to her and to Dolly's that I can't see they'd be mixed up themselves in anything criminal.'

At that moment Hetty opened the door and peered in. 'Oh Mr Wasp, isn't it wonderful? Phineas is to be free and I'm to be the Queen of the May on May Day!'

She looked so pretty, she could have stepped right up to her throne this very moment. I could see William standing behind her in the corridor, however, and his face suggested the news wasn't at all wonderful. To have Phineas out and wooing Hetty was the last thing he or Jericho would want. I needed to speak to Hetty alone, but I couldn't do so with William around. I had to act quickly if Phineas was to have his cat poetry back tomorrow.

'And a prettier queen they'll never see,' I assured Hetty, then adding the first thing that came into my head. 'I'd like a few words about the Boy in Panyer Alley, Hetty, if you can spare a minute.'

Hetty giggled and Clara and William looked highly puzzled, which wasn't surprising. It achieved its purpose, though, as William returned unwillingly to his serving duties, with Clara bustling after him.

'Not a word to anyone, Hetty, but I'd like that bag of papers to give back to Phineas tomorrow. He values it highly.'

Hetty looked disappointed. 'I could bring it on Sunday, Mr Wasp. Phineas will be at the procession — isn't that wonderful news?'

I agreed wholeheartedly with the good news, but I wanted My Cat Jeoffry back. 'It's safer for me to give it back to Phineas right away, Hetty,' I said. 'And on Sunday Phineas will have more to say to you than just thanking you for his poetry book. He loves you, Hetty, and he didn't mind your telling Mr Harcourt about the Tarlton manuscript.'

'Oh, Mr Wasp.' She threw her arms around me. '*Thank you*. But this poetry book isn't dangerous, is it?'

I stretched the truth a little. 'Flint might be interested in it. We wouldn't want him getting confused between that and the *Seven Deadly Sins* manuscript he's so determined to get.'

'I don't think Flint exists,' Hetty said crossly. 'It's all Flint here, Flint there, Flint everywhere but he's just a story book character.'

'He exists all right,' I said sadly. Youth will have its way but we older ones know that in life there's always a Flint around somewhere, a devil thrown out of heaven and touching earth on his way down to hell.

Hetty cheered up. 'I'll fetch the poetry book for you, Mr Wasp.'

Within minutes she had returned with the bag I had left with her and seeing it again made me realise that I couldn't wait until I was home to see if my suspicion was right. Instead, I opened it immediately and took out the manuscript.

I wasn't right. When I opened the manuscript to study more closely what lay within, I began at the very first page, not where it had been opened before. The *Jubilate Agno* began with some pages all in the same handwriting as the lines I'd already seen. Then I came to those about My Cat Jeoffry, the servant of the living Lord. There was nothing about the seven deadly sins or Richard Tarlton.

'It's a very long poem,' Hetty said in awe, peering over my shoulder. 'It must have taken a very long time to write.' She lifted a few of the following pages, and then I registered that the paper size and handwriting had changed. Nor did it look like the same poem any more in which each line began with a capital letter. Then I caught sight of a few words that I could read, despite the old language. 'Hey nonny'. That was one of Phineas' songs. And Phineas sang Shakespeare's verses, not Christopher Smart's.

I almost choked in excitement as I turned the pages. This new handwriting continued until nearly the end of the pile, but then the last few pages were written in the earlier style and handwriting. There must have been about thirty pages in all of the earlier style, and in the middle was a great wodge written in the new style. The paper looked different, too.

I hardly dared to look again in case I found out I was wrong. But I *did* look again, and I knew the *Seven Deadly Sins* was before me, even though it had no separate front cover. Flint would have that, perhaps one or two pages of the *Seven Deadly Sins* with it, to fool him at first into thinking this was the manuscript he was after. Whatever else was in it, to give the necessary bulk to satisfy him that he had the whole play after his initial glance, certainly wasn't by Tarlton, because I was holding *that* in my hands.

At first I could not read much of the handwriting in the *Seven Deadly Sins,* but as I lifted the pages I saw: 'Scene II: A room in the Duke's Palace. *Enter the Duke, the fool and musicians*'. Then as my eyes grew more accustomed to it, I grew even more excited: the Duke had the first speech:

Pray, fool, cunningly disclose
The strange variety of things

To this the fool replied:

Why then consider women, sire
Some women are wanton, and hold it no sinne
By tricks and devices to pull a man in

Now I saw the way of it, I stopped trying to read more. My admiration for Phineas grew. He had known Slugger Joe had no intention of giving the manuscript to the Widow Snook, and was determined not to let him have it. While he was in the bookstore that night, he must have tucked most of the Tarlton script into his precious tuppence worth of cat poetry and handed over its cover and another page or two to Slugger, after cramming in a pile of some other papers he'd either found in the bookstore or taken with him.

Had Phineas lied to me then, when I asked him whether Slugger Joe had taken the *Seven Deadly Sins* script? That wasn't like him. He'd said he had given it to Joe, but he hadn't. Most of it he'd kept. Then I remembered Phineas' habit of telling the exact truth — which can lead to problems. It had in this case. He'd told me he'd handed over the *Seven Deadly Sins* folder. He'd said nothing about its contents. This confusion had a happy ending though: Phineas was to be freed and I had the play.

I repacked the bag with its precious contents and clutched it closely to me just in case Flint himself was about to sneak up on me and seize it. After tomorrow Slugger, Flint and Lairy John would all be eager to greet Phineas in their own particular way — and at the moment I was holding the answer to everything they wanted.

Was it everything, though? My part in this story would not be over with Phineas' release. Not only was Mr Harcourt's killer probably still at large, but Mrs Fortescue's also. The dark shadow hanging over me was that somewhere in the smoke and grime of London's fair city was Flint. And I had not taken his advice.

*

Phineas was quiet as Doshie picked his careful way over the granite setts on Saturday morning. He clutched a coarse green bag which held his few possessions. His hair was sprouting again, his beard had grown and he was very pale. Worse, his eyes were dull and he stared at his surroundings with little interest. I decided not to bother him until we reached his lodgings and I'd fetched Ned and Cockalorum.

I need not have made any such plan. When we arrived at his home, there was Ned sitting at the foot of the steps and Cockalorum perched at the top of them.

'Hey nonny, Ned,' Phineas said with delight and already he looked happier. I could see that in time all would be well — at least with Phineas.

A feast awaited us when we walked inside. Phineas must have felt like Bob Cratchit in Mr Dickens' story when he saw the turkey that Scrooge had bought for him. There was no turkey here but I had brought some pies with me, supplied by Clara, and a jug of ale. Mrs Snook must have paid a visit too for there was a cake and a ham and fruit, even a bunch of flowers. Phineas just gazed at it all, Cockalorum sprang into his basket and went to sleep while Ned and I lit the fire.

'It's May Day tomorrow, Phineas,' I said. 'You'll be going to the procession, won't you?'

As I had feared, he shook his head. 'I've changed my mind.'

It's hard for a man to lose his liberty and fear for his life. In Phineas' own world that couldn't happen, but now he knew the real world. Somehow, I had to make sure he lived in both.

'Hetty's to be Queen of the May,' I ventured.

'And I'm Jack-in-the-Green,' Ned piped up.

Phineas said nothing, even when I added, 'She'll be sad if you're not there, Phineas.' But he did raise his head and show interest.

As a master sweep, I should be at the head of the procession with my fellow master sweeps in the Tower area, but I needed to protect Ned, too. As Jack-in-the-Green in his wicker cage he should be safe enough, but I had to reckon on the chance that Flint might be around and he might have other plans. Perhaps this was unlikely given that neither I nor Phineas would have brought the script with us, but who knew, where Flint was concerned?

'I've brought back the cat poem,' I told him, delving into my bag. He hadn't even asked me about it and didn't look at it when I handed it to him, which showed his spirits were still low. 'I saw you'd slipped something inside it,' I ventured.

'The Shakespeare script,' he told me matter of factly.

I blinked. 'Tarlton, not Shakespeare. He was an Elizabethan fool, Phineas. It's true Shakespeare might have added something here and there.'

'I meant Shakespeare looked after it,' he explained. 'For Pip.'

Eh? What was this? 'Who's Pip, Phineas?' I was at a loss.

'I can't quite remember. I think he was my great great great great — 'He counted on his fingers — 'great great great great great great grandfather,' he ended triumphantly. 'The Boy in Panyer Alley.'

I stared at him. Had Newgate turned his brain? Ned gasped at the mention of the Boy. 'What's he to do with it, Phineas?' I asked.

Phineas looked puzzled. 'Pip is the Boy.'

I gulped. Take this carefully, Tom, I warned myself. 'You mean the Boy is your ancestor, Phineas? How do you know that?'

'Yes. My father told me. Pip was the son of Mr Tarlton, and Mr Shakespeare was keeping the manuscript for Pip until he was grown up because he was only six when his father died.'

My head was spinning like a top. Was this going to link up with Zechariah's story? 'Mr Timpson said Pip was murdered by a crooked lawyer.'

'He can't have been, because I'm descended from him. But I don't think he ever knew about the play. Shakespeare's great-nephew knew about it though — Charles Hart was an actor at Drury Lane theatre and lived in the house where Mr Harcourt's home was. He met Pip's son.'

I'd seen a flaw in this. 'How did your family get hold of the *Seven Deadly Sins* if Pip didn't know about the play?'

'It was something to do with the Boy in the Alley. I'm not sure of the details.'

221

Another squeak from Ned. 'I knew it, guvnor. I said that Boy had something to do with that bloke's death.'

There'd be no holding Ned now, I thought despairingly. The Ordinaries were going to be most interested in Phineas' story too — especially if Mr Shakespeare had really played a bigger part in writing it than they thought, or pretended, he did.

'There are a lot of people who want to see the Tarlton manuscript, Phineas,' I warned him.

'I know. I was stupid to take it to Mr Harcourt, even if it did mean I could marry Hetty with the money. Joe swore he'd give the manuscript to my mother when we had it back, but I knew he wouldn't. That's why I tricked him out of it.'

'You hid it well.'

'Thanks to my cat Jeoffry,' said Phineas fondly. I thought of his cat Jeoffry fighting Slugger Joe and now he was looking at us as though butter would not melt in his mouth.

'What will you do now, Phineas?' Flint might not guess that the Tarlton script was back here yet awhile but it wouldn't be long before he did, so it couldn't stay here. My question had been about his plans for the manuscript, but Phineas wasn't bothered about that.

'Ask Hetty to marry me.' He glanced at me and smiled. 'I'll go to the procession tomorrow.'

That was good news — except that the Tarlton manuscript would be here in his room unguarded, save by Cockalorum. I saw Cockalorum's eyes follow Ned as we left Phineas' home, but he made no attempt to follow. Ned took that bravely but I could see he was hurt.

For all my pleasure at Phineas' release, I was filled with foreboding at what might happen tomorrow. The *Seven Deadly Sins* manuscript had been responsible for two murders, and one, probably two, false imprisonments. And tomorrow there might be further mischief. When we reached Hairbrine Court, however, Kwan-yin sang to us so peacefully that I wondered whether she and Cockalorum were the most sensible of us all.

CHAPTER SIXTEEN

The Coming of May Day

'It's May Day, guvnor.'

I didn't need Ned's shouts of joy to tell me that, for all that my eyes were still closed. No chimneys would be swept today, but what awaited us might be far from joyful, unlike my usual pleasure at the sweeps' celebration. Normally we sweeps lead the procession through our respective areas, heralded by a brass band. I've never known why this tradition grew, but it is our day of glory, the one time of the year when sweeps mix with everyone else without complaint.

The sweeps are followed by three very important people: Jack-in-the-Green, the Queen of the May — and the man who walks alongside with the collecting dish. All very cheery, but mindful of the unknown that lay ahead I decided to take the collection bucket myself, so that I could arrange to be near Ned.

Somewhere in the crowds that would be swarming around us could be Slugger Joe and his crew and possibly Lairy John with his Swell Mob. And hovering over us would be the shadow of Flint. Perhaps I was seeing dark clouds where none existed, but I tried not to fear.

Ned would be partly protected at least, but Flint might have his eyes on another target: Phineas himself would be dancing alongside his Queen of the May, and Phineas would be Flint's route to the *Seven Deadly Sins*. Flint knew Phineas had owned it, he knew it hadn't been found in Phineas' lodgings or mine, nor, he would rightly assume, had it been at Newgate.

Raiding Phineas' home again would present difficulties as at Constable Peters' urging, Inspector Wiley had placed a man to guard his room. But at the procession Phineas would have no such close protection, although there would be uniformed peelers present. How many, I did not know — but they would not be able to shield him all the time, and Flint's men could be posted at intervals along the route from the Tower of London to London Bridge waiting for the arrival of Phineas, the dancing fool. There is nothing so scary as merrymaking all around when the devil threatens.

Somewhere in the crowd would be Constable Peters himself, I hoped, and perhaps one or two of Inspector Wiley's men, but what could they do, surrounded by swarms of onlookers and procession followers?

'Hurry up, guvnor,' Ned pleaded, jumping up and down like a jack-in-a-box. He wouldn't be able to do *that* in his May Day wicker outfit.

'Breakfast, Ned.' This sounds grand as though a table were laid before us with nourishing food, but there was not. I had found three-penny piece in the tin, though, which would buy us a cup of coffee and a muffin.

Our first job after a call at the coffee stall was to collect the greenery I had gathered and left in Doshie's stable. He wouldn't be coming out today, and he was beginning to look aggrieved at the tickly firs that surrounded him. Another master sweep was organising the Jack-in-the-Green cage that would, I hoped, protect Ned to some extent. When all that could be seen of him amid the leaves would be his eyes and part of the rest of his face, it would be hard to identify him and the cage would make it no easy task to carry him off. In the midst of such a crowd, though, how easy for one person to disappear, when screams of fear can be taken as fun …

Between us and reinvigorated by breakfast, Ned and I managed to carry the greenery down to Trinity Square behind the Tower of London, where the procession would be forming.

'Look, guvnor, there he is!' Ned cried.

He sounded so anxious that I thought for a moment it was Slugger Joe he could see, but it wasn't. It was young Bert, a sweep from Wapping way, half hidden under the wicker cage he was carrying. I could hear church bells ringing and they sounded all the more glorious because it was May Day and summer was on its way. When we arrived in the Square it looked as though all London was gathered to welcome the coming of the sun, with bright coloured clothing, pipes, whistles and the sound of singing everywhere. I wondered whether Her Majesty Queen Victoria had her own procession to greet the coming of May, but she was still grieving over the sad loss of Prince Albert.

Ned ran off to be fitted into his cage and have the greenery tucked around him, while I went to greet Hetty, who was already on her wagon with her two pretty attendants just behind her. Hetty was by far the prettiest, though. She was sitting demurely on a stool, her full skirts spread decorously around her, and a stick in her hand for a sceptre.

'There's a surprise coming, Mr Wasp,' she giggled. 'You just wait and see.'

226

By a surprise, she would mean her coronation at the start of the procession when our local chief master sweep places a crown on her head. He isn't really our chief, but he's the oldest of us, nearly fifty years old, which is a venerable age hereabouts. I have great respect for him as he taught me my trade the way it should be, after I'd been snatched away from the fate of being a climbing boy.

The band struck up with a merry song … and off we went. I walked at the back of the sweeps' group as near as I could be to Jack-in-the-Green, carrying my collecting bucket and trying to watch everywhere at once without forgetting my role. Behind the band and in front of the sweeps I could see Phineas dancing and wondered why he wasn't beside Hetty, who had now been crowned and was waving at the crowds just like the Queen herself used to, before Prince Albert died.

I realised then why Phineas chose to be where he was. He knew Slugger might be after him and he didn't want to endanger Hetty. Her wagon was some way behind Ned, who had a little procession of his own, as he swaggered along in his cage behind the sweeps, with his own attendants around him and me at his side. My word, he did walk proud.

We set off in fine style down Great Tower Hill towards London Bridge where we would be meeting the Southwark sweeps' procession from the other side of the River Thames. We passed the spot where Phineas had so often played the fool and I could see him now dancing ahead of the sweeps in his fool's costume; the band's music could hardly be heard what with the yelling crowd.

By the time we turned into Great Tower Street the crowds were swarming all around us and I began to panic, although I wasn't sure what I feared. Another kidnap? Another murder? I remembered Jericho's baleful eyes at the warehouse and William's determined pursuit of Hetty. I remembered Mrs Fortescue's vengeful outbursts against Mr Harcourt and most of all I remembered that Flint might be here.

Rubbish, I tried to tell myself, but you don't have to feel the hail and rain on your face to know there's a storm brewing, and I sensed one was coming at any moment. I comforted myself that there was a band protecting Phineas, together with a dozen or so sweeps, and Ned was safe enough behind them with me as well as his four attendants at his side. What's more, my bucket had already attracted a nice pile of farthings and halfpennies, and even a threepenny piece or two.

We were coming to the end of Great Tower Street, near to where it runs into King William IV street where the grand statue of the late king looked down at us benignly. I began to feel easier because the road down to London Bridge is wider and I wouldn't feel so trapped. I even began to enjoy the music and laughter and I could hear Phineas singing *Under the Greenwood Tree* — though it was Ned who looked under that at present with his little face peering out from the cage.

Then everything changed.

At first I couldn't work out what was happening. This must be Hetty's surprise, I thought, as the procession halted at the turn into King William IV street. It could get no further as another procession was coming in from the Cheapside direction; it must have been arranged that we would join their procession after it had passed the junction with our road. Being stationary made me uneasy, though. As we waited, the music of our band was clashing with theirs which added to the general hubbub; there came their band and sweeps, followed by their Jack-in-the-Green and then their wagons, which had banners proclaiming that they were the City Sweeps.

That's where the real surprise lay. I saw Clara waving furiously from a wagon gaily decorated in huge letters with 'Dolly's Chop House'. She was dressed in all her finery making a grand sight, although Jericho and William at her side didn't look grand or happy at all. I wasn't happy, either. Fears began to creep up on me again, especially when I saw another wagon pass bearing a banner proclaiming 'The Tarlton Ordinaries' with a copy of the picture of Richard Tarlton displayed at Dolly's. There were the Ordinaries, with their fool's caps, just as I'd seen them at Dolly's. One was playing a tabor, another a pipe, though no one could possibly be hearing it in this general din. They looked so innocent, so jolly, that it was hard to believe that a murderer could be amongst them.

Even Mrs Harcourt was present, in her widow's black, breaking with convention perhaps in order to assert her rights to Tarlton's play yet again. It could have been this reminder that I hadn't yet fulfilled my pledge to find her husband's murderer that made me feel I was only a drumbeat away from trouble, though there was no sign of it yet. Our procession duly began to move again, and shortly we reached the hubbub around London Bridge where the Southwark sweeps were already merrymaking.

London Bridge is famous all over world and thousands upon thousands of people and vehicles pass over it each day, the slower traffic to the sides and the faster in the middle. But today all such traffic was halted for an hour or two while the three processions met on the bridge. Today, we didn't even have to pay our tolls. As was our May Day custom, we sang our sweeps' songs together and much jollity followed, with Ned and his counterpart from Southwark jigging up and down while the sweeps blew whistles at them and cups of ale miraculously appeared from nowhere. Even I was carried away with the excitement and whisked Clara nearly off her feet while dancing a jig with her. What's more, I was even able to have a dance with Mrs Snook who kindly said she'd let me off my vow to eat my topper if I saw her dancing.

And then it began.

I suddenly realised with dismay that I'd lost sight of Phineas so I hurried back to Hetty's wagon in the hope he'd be there. He wasn't there though, and a pang of fear struck at me just as despite the noise all around me I heard a cry of 'Tom!' I turned, saw Clara running towards me and somewhere I heard Ned.

'Guvnor!' he was screaming.

I couldn't see him, only hear him, but Clara seized my arm and together we tried to fight our way through to him. What had happened? Was he under attack? We found him sobbing with fear, but otherwise safe.

'What's amiss, Ned? Someone hurt you?' I asked anxiously as Clara comforted him as best she could with that cage around him. 'Who? Where?' It was hard to think let alone see for all the racket and singing and dancing around us.

'It's Phineas,' he sobbed. 'They've got him. *Jericho.*'

I left Ned in the sweeps' care and struggled my way through to where Ned was pointing, with Clara in my wake. By now all three processions had massed together and in the chaos I couldn't see Phineas or Jericho and I'd lost Clara. Then I did see William, just as Clara reappeared and clutched at me.

'Jericho's gone mad, Tom,' she cried. '*Stop* him.'

Me? Stop a six-foot giant? Yes, I could — I had to. My old knack of squirrelling up chimneys came back to me as I wriggled my way through the crowd to the side of the bridge where I was just in time to see Jericho landing a punch on William's face. Phineas? Where was he? When I reached them, I saw him lying at their feet by the bridge railings. Still clutching my bucket, I threw myself at Jericho who, taken by surprise, released his hold on William who promptly ran off.

'You fool!' Jericho yelled at me. 'You've let him go, Wasp.' He seized me, trying to pull me along with him, but I managed to shake him off and drop to my knees beside Phineas.

'What have you done to him?' I shouted.

Phineas wasn't moving.

Jericho yanked me up in fury. 'Not me. William — he and some other chap were dragging him away.'

'Rubbish!' I yelled as he let go of me so suddenly I lost balance and fell down almost on top of Phineas, sending my bucket spinning. Jericho had vanished and I anxiously tried to see how badly Phineas was hurt. At least he was alive as I heard him groan. 'I'll find the peelers,' I told him, trying to stand up but failing. 'They'll nab Jericho all right.'

'William.' Another groan from Phineas. 'It was *William.*'

I couldn't make sense of this. Phineas must be mixed up, because he'd been hit so badly. 'That can't be, Phineas.'

'Joe was with him. William works for him. He's his snitch.'

I was busy picking up farthings and pennies and this information brought me to a standstill. I couldn't understand this. William working for Slugger? Right now though something else was more important.

'Where's that Tarlton script?' I asked Phineas. 'That's what everyone's after. Did you tell anyone where it was?' Did the Tarlton Ordinaries have some other mission here than merely celebrating May Day?'

'No,' Phineas said, hauling up first himself and then me. I was aching all over, but there were no bones broken, I'm glad to say, and Phineas too seemed to have escaped that. 'Jericho got there in time,' he added. 'He fought them off.'

I still could not take it in. I'd assumed that it was Jericho who was the one to watch and William was in fear of him, but instead it seemed it was the other way around. William must be one of Slugger's men, and Jericho had been watching *him*. Instead of the help that they'd given us at Billingsgate being just a moment of compassion for a young boy, Jericho must have forced William to take him to where Ned was. Had Jericho perhaps been following William on his way to Lairy John's when I saw him in Spitalfields? But William was Hetty's devoted swain, Clara's prized waiter, who was so eager for money that he wouldn't want to lose his job at Dolly's. Or had Slugger paid him so well it was worth the risk? It was all a puzzle, and no mistake.

All of this flashed through my mind just as I realised the current danger.

'Where's the Tarlton play?' I yelled at Phineas. Although there was a guard at his lodgings, it was possible Flint might send in more than one of his mob.'

'Don't worry,' he reassured me happily. 'Hetty has it.'

I gaped at this. '*Here*?' That would put her in danger. Wherever that manuscript was, there might be Flint or Slugger. Hadn't Phineas realised that?

Hetty and that manuscript needed protection, I insisted, and dragging Phineas with me we both limped back to her wagon. She was sitting there alone, with no sign of her attendants, but looking anxious, until a big smile crossed her face as she saw Phineas and me. Then she must have seen we were limping. 'Oh, are you hurt, Phineas? And you, Mr Wasp?'

'Take care, Hetty,' I urged her. 'Phineas was attacked by William Wright.'

She stared at me in amazement. 'Oh no. You have it wrong. You mean Jericho.'

'Jericho saved me,' Phineas said proudly.

Hetty looked helplessly at us. 'I don't understand.'

'Nor do I,' I replied. 'But is the Tarlton play safe?'

'Of course. Cockalorum sees to that.' She smiled.

'*Cockalorum?*'

'I'll show him to you if you like,' she added blithely.

With that, she lifted her skirts just enough for my amazed eyes to see a wicker cage with its front open and Cockalorum glaring out at me, ready to pounce. My eyes were even more amazed to see that underneath the cage was something that looked suspiciously like a folder — the *Seven Deadly Sins*. Cockalorum saw Phineas and purred.

My head was whirling with the noise around us and my body was still aching so I was glad when the bands struck up and the return journey began. I decided not to tell Clara of these latest developments as the manuscript would be safe enough while we were on the move. As we approached the junction with Great Tower Street, I began to allow myself to relax. The worst would soon be over. I looked across at Ned but he seemed happy enough still bouncing along in his cage, while I continued to rattle the bucket for more farthings.

It seemed quite peaceful now and it was hard to believe that there could well be at least one murderer near at hand, if not two, given that not only Slugger and his men were here but the Ordinaries too. I'd be thankful when we parted company with the City procession, although there had been no sign of Flint's presence yet. I could see Hetty with Phineas who was now dancing at the side of her wagon — a little stiffly, owing to his injuries, but his soft melodious voice was just as sweet as ever.

Never harm nor spell nor charm, Come our lovely lady nigh ...

I felt my eyes full of tears, but they were tears of gratitude that there are such precious moments in life, despite the dangers we face.

But danger came all too quickly. Just as I became aware that the procession had suddenly come to a halt, I heard shouts and police whistles and rattles, and saw peelers running everywhere. I looked back — and terror struck. They were by Hetty's wagon and using their truncheons left, right and centre, trying to drag someone away. Thankfully I could see Hetty herself standing up, with Phineas at her side and his arm round her. I reached the wagon in time to see three or four stalwart peelers pulling Slugger Joe to his feet and cuffing him.

'Bloody cat!' Slugger was yelling in between sneezes. 'I'll hang his guts out to dry when I get to him.'

Cockalorum, I thought thankfully, I'll buy you a big bit of fish straight from the sea. I wished I'd been there to see the fun.

Then I caught sight of Constable Peters who came over to me chuckling. 'There was Slugger, thinking he'd set about Miss Pomfret when she lifts her skirts and Slugger starts sneezing his head off; then the cat leaps out and attacks him good and proper. As a result we've nabbed Slugger at last and two of his mates.'

I didn't bother to ask the constable if they'd nabbed Flint. I knew the answer would be no. I told him about William Wright though, and he said he'd take care of that rotten apple. Cockalorum, peacefully back in his cage, purred at me as I stroked him. 'You,' I told him, 'are truly of the tribe of Tiger.' Which reminded me that I had to break the news to Phineas that the manuscript of the *Jubilate Agno* was very probably stolen property. I wouldn't tell him today though and spoil his happiness.

'These Ordinaries, Mr Wasp,' said the constable. 'Now we've got Slugger, we need the bigger game. It has to be one of them hired Flint — and if it's not Splendour, which of them is it?'

'Let's have a word with them, Mr Wasp,' the constable continued, 'and then I'll deal with Wright.' I followed him to the Ordinaries' wagon, where I had a private word with Mr Chalcot (who looked most engaging in his fool's cap) to assure him that the *Seven Deadly Sins* was safe. I was hoping it would remain safe too.

The wagon was laden with the seven gentlemen dressed up with fool's caps, one still playing his tabor, and with Mrs Harcourt who sat there as a grim black presence amongst them as if to remind them she was still waiting for her missing play — and perhaps her husband's murderer, too. If only she had known that the manuscript was a matter of fifty yards from her — or that she would never own it. And nor would the gentlemen with her, two of whom had done so much to persuade the world outside their small gathering that the manuscript was valueless.

'Pardon me for interrupting, ma'am, gentlemen,' the constable said to them, 'but an attack's been made on a young lady which we've reason to believe is connected to the murder of Mrs Fortescue, and that might cast doubt on Mr Splendour's arrest.'

'I fail to see why,' Mrs Harcourt immediately sniffed. 'I witnessed someone who was undoubtedly Mr Splendour in the shop with her.'

'Could have been an early customer,' the constable said firmly. 'Any of you gentlemen remember being there early that morning and seeing anything amiss?' he asked. I could see a gleam in his eye that suggested he had something in mind.

Mr Timpson, fool's hat nodding vigorously, could not assist us. 'I arrived at my office at eight o'clock precisely, and cannot recall seeing anything unusual. Splendour's door was open and there was no sign of anyone inside when I passed it.'

Mr Manley too had seen nothing unusual. 'I returned to my office about a quarter past seven — I find an early stroll inspires me in my work — and saw no one enter or leave Mr Splendour's store as I passed by.'

The constable turned to Mrs Harcourt. 'You witnessed the gentleman inside the store, whom you believed to be Mr Splendour, and I understand you did not see him leave.'

'You are correct,' she agreed. 'It was surely Mr Splendour who killed that poor woman, having come down from his rooms, ready with his strop. He then opened the door to make it appear that some ruffian had killed her and run away. But it was he who killed her. A case of blackmail, constable.'

'But which of them was the blackmailer?' the constable enquired.

At that interesting moment Inspector Harvey joined us, together with Inspector Wiley, and after some whispering they all began to move towards the sweeps' procession, leaving Constable Peters' question unanswered. Inspector Harvey beckoned me to join them and I felt most honoured to be amongst them, though this was not entirely to Inspector Wiley's pleasure.

'You buzzing round again, Wasp?'

I agreed that I was, and he seemed satisfied with that. Constable Peters' point about blackmail was a most interesting one. Was Mr Splendour the blackmailer of Mrs Fortescue, because he knew she had arranged Mr Harcourt's death with Flint in revenge for his treatment of her, or was Mrs Fortescue the blackmailer of Mr Splendour, because *he* had hired Flint to kill Mr Harcourt for the sake of the Tarlton manuscript? I didn't have time to answer these questions for myself because Inspector Harvey spoke to me.

'I hear you're not happy about Splendour, Mr Wasp.'

'No, sir. If he were guilty he'd have found that missing manuscript. And he hasn't.'

'The Old Bailey won't see it that way.'

'Then the law is an ass,' I said, unwisely.

'Wasp!' thundered Inspector Wiley, delighted to have the opportunity to roar at me.

'It's a quotation from Mr Dickens,' I said meekly, and at that magic name Inspector Wiley was silenced — especially as Inspector Harvey took this up. He even smiled.

'Mr Bumble,' he contributed. 'My own choice of quotation would be, "The tongues of dying men / Enforce attention like deep harmony." Shakespeare's *Richard II*. In other words, Mr Harcourt and Mrs Fortescue are speaking to us, Mr Wasp, but we can't hear them.'

He looked at me meditatively but I decided to leave literature to look after itself for a while, although I thought I remembered seeing a few of those words in the *Seven Deadly Sins* manuscript, which at least showed Mr Shakespeare had read it.

'This Slugger Joe of yours, constable,' the inspector continued. 'Will he squeal?'

'About Flint? It's possible.'

'About who hired him — Splendour or someone else. Or it could have been two of them in it together — or more.'

Here we go again, I thought, depressing even myself. It was like the old chant, 'There's a hole in my bucket, dear Liza, dear Liza'.

Back we came to where we started. And yet … was I sure of that? What were Mr Harcourt and Mrs Fortescue trying to tell us? Were two Ordinaries working together as Inspector Harvey suggested? One Ordinary hires Flint to seize the manuscript by fair means or foul, the other hides at the gateway to Dolly's yard waiting for an opportunity to pounce on Harcourt? Why then should Mrs Fortescue have been murdered?

Because, I reasoned, growing excited by this theory, *she* had been one of the parties concerned. Perhaps she grew too greedy, especially when the Tarlton manuscript failed to appear. Perhaps she threatened to split on her accomplice?

Inspector Harvey's theory must have appealed to Constable Peters as well, because he too jumped at it. 'It's an idea, sir.'

'Mrs Fortescue may have had a finger in the pie,' I pointed out, 'because she insisted on being escorted home.'

'Who asked you to shove your nose in?' Inspector Wiley demanded.

Inspector Harvey ignored this. 'A good point, Wasp. But who *was* her partner or partners?'

Odd the way ideas come to you out of the blue. How do they fly there? How do they decide whether to stay or pass on? This one came to me through one word, 'harmony', a word Inspector Harvey had just used, and which I now remembered Mr Chalcot had also once used. More importantly, I remembered exactly what he'd said. The word wedged itself in my mind, and then another insidiously crept in: voice. There was no time to lose.

'Ask that wagon leaving for the City to stop, sir. There may be a few questions to ask.'

It's surprising that they took any notice of my dramatic order, but they did.

'Of whom?' Inspector Peters threw at me as Inspector Harvey hesitated, then detailed one of his men to halt it and we began to pushing our way back to the City Sweeps' wagons.

I took a deep breath. 'Mrs Harcourt.'

CHAPTER SEVENTEEN

The Brush at the Top of the Chimney

As we pushed through the crowds, it took only a few minutes to persuade Inspector Harvey that I wasn't talking out of my old topper and Constable Peters was quickly thinking it through for himself. Inspector Wiley, panting at our side, chimed in with: 'There's no evidence against Mrs Harcourt. It's just Wasp buzzing around confusing folk like he always does.'

Even he grudgingly listened though, as we reached a less crowded spot, and it didn't take long for me to work out what must have happened. Inspector Harvey's men were already stopping the City procession wagons from moving off.

'It's my belief Mrs Harcourt and Mrs Fortescue weren't enemies, not at first, anyway,' I said, remembering that Mr Chalcot had spoken of earlier harmony between them. 'They both wanted the same thing,' I continued, 'Mr Harcourt's death. Mrs Fortescue out of revenge for his cruelty to her, Mrs Harcourt for much the same reason, plus she wanted that valuable Tarlton play he'd told her was coming, as well as the rest of his property. One of the ladies had the idea of hiring Flint

— and they agreed the Tarlton evening at Dolly's would be a suitable opportunity for their plan to be put into action.'

'Any *evidence* for Flint's involvement?' Inspector Harvey threw at me. We were drawing close to the City wagons now and I tried to think quickly.

'Why else would Slugger and Lairy John be linked into this Tarlton playscript business?' I asked. 'They're unlikely to risk working on their own.'

'Go on,' the inspector said approvingly.

Thus encouraged, I did so. 'Mrs Harcourt had arranged with her husband, probably at her insistence, that she should travel up early on the Thursday morning to look at this great Tarlton find, thus avoiding suspicion herself, and Mrs Fortescue would have arranged for her maid to witness she had no opportunity to kill him either. But then the Tarlton play vanished and so did harmony. Flint would have wasted no time in letting the ladies know it was missing after Slugger's failed visit to the bookstore. Mrs Harcourt thought Mrs Fortescue had it and Mrs Fortescue was quite sure Mrs Harcourt had nabbed it for herself, although they must have agreed that they should both have an earning from it. When Mrs Harcourt denied having it, Mrs Fortescue could have tried a spot of blackmail on her, threatening to reveal her part in the story. Perhaps, also, it was Mrs Harcourt who arranged Flint's services, which would have given Mrs Fortescue another handle for blackmailing her.'

'Are you suggesting Mrs Harcourt arranged to murder Mrs Fortescue, as well as her husband, through Flint?' Inspector Harvey frowned.

'Possibly,' I said, perhaps wisely in the circumstances, as I hadn't thought this through. I quickly tried to do so. 'But more likely Mrs Harcourt strangled Mrs Fortescue herself. Mrs Harcourt's a strong woman, and taken by surprise from behind, Mrs Fortescue couldn't have protected herself in time.'

The inspector wasn't convinced. 'And the razor strop? Splendour had a new one.'

'Quite innocently,' I pointed out. 'But hanging strops are popular and Mrs Harcourt wouldn't yet have cleared out her husband's belongings.'

A nod from the inspector. 'We'll check with the servants. They may recognise it. We'll ask her to come in for questioning.'

It wasn't much for the police to go on — not that Inspector Wiley was eager to go anywhere where I was concerned — and I thought I should go with them all to the wagon, reluctant though I was. There's a difference between working something out in your head and challenging someone face to face, no matter how much they deserve it. And I believed that Mrs Harcourt did.

I stood back with Inspector Wiley and Constable Peters as Inspector Harvey and his men approached the wagon where she and the Ordinaries were sitting, no doubt wondering what the delay was for. There was much screeching and shouting when Mrs Harcourt was told the reason for it, and I was glad Clara wasn't there. She must have gone to speak to Hetty.

'I,' Mrs Harcourt cried, 'come with you to a *police station*? To answer questions about my husband's death?'

She'd made a mistake straight away and the Inspector saw it, too. 'About the murder of Mrs Fortescue, ma'am, first.'

I almost felt sorry for the Ordinaries, they looked so shocked. Mr Chalcot looked so bewildered that I began to wonder if I'd make a mistake. After all, it was he who had put it into my mind by his talk of harmony in connection with the two ladies — and perhaps too with his reference to the voice of the Lord God in the garden. I tried hard to think straight … Had he been thinking of Mrs Harcourt and Mrs Fortescue in the churchyard garden? I must ask him, *now*. But I was forestalled. Mrs Harcourt was on her feet, but with no intention of leaving the wagon.

'That Fortescue woman?' she cried dismissively in answer to Inspector Harvey. 'I thought you meant my husband. Mr Splendour killed *her*. We all know that.'

'If you'll come with us, ma'am,' the inspector said patiently as she showed no signs of moving.

'I shall not. You cannot prove I have any connection with her death *or* my husband's.'

Inspector Harvey nodded to his two constables to let down the wagon board for her to descend. I thought at first she would not move but she rose to her feet looking round at us all. Something must have changed her mind, because instead of climbing down from the wagon she burst out with:

'Look at that wagon back there. Queen of the May indeed! Miss Pomfret is a common slut. I said to Arnold: you and that Tarlton. He was nothing more than a lecher in pantaloons and so are you. Those blasted Tarlton jests. I must have heard them all a hundred times. There he'd sit, chuckling away, when he deigned to come to see me, either ranting about Tarlton's pretty wenches or his own. And then he'd crown it with his favourite dose of spite. "You recall, my dear," he'd say, "the jest about how Tarlton would have drowned his wife. Such a humorous story of a ship's captain who ordered every man aboard to throw into the sea the heaviest thing he had with him to lighten the ship before the storm. And you know what Tarlton did, my dear?" Arnold thought this so amusing. He'd cackle, "He threw his wife overboard and when asked why he did so, he replied that I was the heaviest thing he had and could best be spared." Well, *you're not jesting anymore, are you, Arnold dear?*' Mrs Harcourt screeched.

I thought I glimpsed one or two of the Ordinaries also thinking this a most amusing story, but most looked as shocked as I was. Harcourt had reduced his wife to this: a ranting harpy spitting venom, and one whom I might have pitied if it hadn't been for my belief that she took not only his life, but Mrs Fortescue's.

Mrs Harcourt descended the wagon and departed with the City of London Police without further outburst. Inspector Wiley managed to have the last word.

'What about Flint? You're so clever, Wasp. Who is he?'

I could give no answer to this and Inspector Wiley smirked in triumph. I was intent on having a word with Mr Chalcot though. I had to get to the bottom of what he'd meant by harmony and that reference to the voice of the Lord God. Fortunately, the other Ordinaries were busily discussing Mrs Harcourt's outburst, and I could speak to Mr Chalcot quite privately.

'Mrs Harcourt and Mrs Fortescue in harmony?' he asked, taken aback.

'And you mentioned too the voice of the Lord God in the garden.'

He still looked blank and I waited on tenterhooks. And then at last the familiar beam.

'Ah yes,' he said. 'I did see them talking and walking apparently amicably a few days before the terrible business of Mr Harcourt's murder. I thought nothing of it, given that it seemed of little relevance to the violent death of Mr Harcourt, and where they were.'

I pricked up my ears at this. 'Where was that, sir, if I might ask?'

'They were attending a Biblical meeting.'

'In St Paul's?'

'The Chapter House by the churchyard. They were escorted by a gentleman, of course.'

'Mr Harcourt?' I asked, puzzled.

'Indeed not. It was the gentleman who sells Biblical tracts in the churchyard. A most obliging person.'

I paled. The one who ordered me not to tread the sinner's way?

'One of the pallbearers at the funeral?'

Mr Chalcot beamed. 'Yes indeed. He spoke to me of the dangers of the seven deadly sins.'

The voice. I knew it now. The tract seller was Flint.

*

Still reeling from this revelation, I returned to my own procession to find Phineas and Ned, expecting to see Flint at every turn now that I knew his identity. Not that he would be selling Biblical tracts here; he could look completely different and that didn't cheer me in the least. Nor did finding Inspector Wiley still holding forth to Constable Peters at the front of the procession, which was about to move off on its return journey.

Flint wasn't on his mind, but the Tarlton manuscript was, and he was determined to have his hour of glory by finding it.

'Ah, Wasp. Constable Peters tells me that manuscript's here today and Miss Pomfret has it. Fetch it, Wasp!'

I had to put the kibosh on this straightaway. 'It's not my property. It belongs to —'

'— You're perverting the course of justice!' he roared, turning to Constable Peters. 'You fetch it then.'

'We've no proof that it's evidence,' the constable said bravely.

With us anxiously hurrying in his wake, Inspector Wiley promptly marched off to Hetty's wagon where she was patiently waiting for the procession to move off. Phineas was lolling at the wagon's side.

'Hand over that manuscript if you please, miss.' The inspector's chest was swelling with self-importance.

Hetty looked at Constable Peters uncertainly but when he nodded she rose obediently to her feet, stepping back to reveal Cockalorum guarding the precious script. The inspector's eyes widened but he was not deterred.

'Come on, pussy cat,' he said, patting Cockalorum on the head with one hand and stretching out for the script with the other. I saw Cockalorum's body tense, but he didn't move. Inspector Wiley thereupon put both hands to the task of dragging him out of the wagon.

This time I was there to see the fun. One hiss and Cockalorum was clawing at the inspector's clothes, hands and arms, yowling, wriggling and squirming to avoid the inspector's flailing hands.

'Call him off!' he yelled, trying to grasp the cat while avoiding those claws.

'I'll try, inspector.' Constable Peters bent over Cockalorum in the pretence of trying to help.

While the inspector grappled with him, Cockalorum slithered this way and that, claws in full use, until finally the constable did manage to detach him from an incoherent Inspector Wiley. Cockalorum thereupon jumped off the wagon, cast a disdainful look at the inspector and disappeared into the crowd.

Meanwhile Hetty and Phineas had also slipped quietly away — together with the *Seven Deadly Sins* manuscript. Although the crowds were noisy and the inspector was shouting threats at Constable Peters and myself, I thought I heard Phineas call something out to me. It sounded like 'Zechariah'.

I was on my own — and so was Ned. I realised with a lurch of fright that I had been so preoccupied that I'd forgotten Ned, and promptly rushed to the front of the procession as it turned into Great Tower Hill. And there, to my relief, was Ned, still surrounded by four attendants — he was safe in his cage.

No, *five* sweep attendants. At first that didn't worry me — there were enough sweeps to protect Ned. As I relaxed, though, it struck me that one of those attendants was unknown to me — a tall man. Then a hammer-blow of fear struck my stomach. Panic-stricken, I rushed up to him, tugging at his arm. He turned around and my fear had been justified. Flint, face begrimed with soot, was staring into my face.

'Tom Wasp,' said that voice, as soothing and caressing as a snake wrapping his coils around its prey. Only this time it wasn't asking what plans I had for eternity — Flint would be all too eager to despatch me there. 'Welcome. Good of you to drop by. I thought my little plan to join the sweeps' community would bring you to me.'

'Flint,' I said, though it sounded more of a squeak than a brave facing up to danger.

'Pray don't think I have no further plans for your Ned, Tom. Or for you. I do have both, but as you have deprived me of Slugger's assistance, it would be foolish of me to act immediately. But I shall, in due course.'

Cold eyes stared into mine, as sharp as the nickname he bore.

'And in the meanwhile?' I tried to sound as cool as he did, but failed.

'To be present at the Old Bailey when Mrs Harcourt is on trial is a temptation, but one I shall resist.'

'She and Mrs Fortescue *did* hire your services?'

'For Mr Harcourt's death? My dear Wasp, I never discuss my customers. Let us say that in this guise of a fellow sweep, I listened to the explanation of the events you have just given and saw no reason to leap forward to correct it.'

'But you won't be here to join Mrs Harcourt in Newgate.'

'I shall be taking up residence somewhere other than in London. But Wasp,' he leaned down towards my face as he hissed, 'do not think you are alone. I will always be with you, the breath of wind that stirs a peaceful garden, the shape that slips by in the fog, and the question mark in your mind as you walk through the crowd of strangers. Never alone, Wasp, *never* alone.'

*

There were two last jobs to perform once our procession had arrived back at Trinity Square. Shaken though I was, I had had to break the news to Clara that her prized waiter had been, or would be, arrested. Constable Peters had told me that he'd alerted Inspector Harvey who had promptly detailed his men to track him down. Clara had taken the news bravely.

'Let's hope President Thomas Jefferson doesn't pop into Dolly's again for a steak tonight. He'd have to make do with me as his waiter.'

Now I had my second dose of bad news to impart. I had to tell poor Mrs Snook that Slugger Joe wouldn't be coming home for supper, although my guess was that she wouldn't be too upset.

'You could move in here for a while,' she said thoughtfully to me. 'I'll take the boy too.'

Clara, who had forsaken the City procession for ours, snorted at my side. 'Thank you very much,' she said with great dignity, 'but he can manage.'

I too thanked Mrs Snook very much, explaining that Ned's and my hours of working precluded my acceptance. Clara remained suspicious and she lingered before taking a cab back to Dolly's.

'What's on your mind, Clara?'

'William and Jericho. You wanted to know how they knew you were at that warehouse. They were looking for you round the Tower and asked a patterer where to find you.'

Enoch, I realised.

'He was shouting out, "Sweepie cuffed at Billingsgate warehouse".' Clara paused, pleased to see me laugh. 'And, Tom,' she added. 'That woman's right. Ned needs mothering. *And* you do too.'

She looked hard at me, and I thought wistfully once more of what life with Clara might be like. Then I thought again of how Ned would feel if we left the only home he had ever known and of how I would feel working as a sweep and living at Dolly's. Did I want to leave the world of chimneys behind? Not yet.

'One day,' I said regretfully, and she nodded.

*

On Monday morning I took the familiar route round the Churchyard, past the orange sellers, past the spot where Flint had sold his Bible tracts, and on to Mr Chalcot's bookstore. He had suggested to me yesterday that he would welcome an early visit from me in order to talk of matters more pleasant than Mrs Harcourt and murder.

We spoke briefly about those therefore, as he was able to tell me that Mrs Harcourt and William Wright had now been charged, and gave me the good news that Mr Splendour had been released. Then, while enjoying the delights of Mrs Chalcot's coffee, I listened with pleasure as Mr Chalcot then spoke of the possibility of his holding a special event with copies of Mr Kingsley's *The Water Babies* on sale at a suitably afford-able price, with Ned and myself appearing as real life sweeps and former climbing boys. The true business of the meeting was then broached.

'And now to our muttons, Mr Wasp,' Mr Chalcot said firmly. 'We now know that the *Seven Deadly Sins* manuscript is safely in the hands of its rightful owner, Mr Phineas Snook. I should very much like to speak with him. My fellow Tarlton Ordinaries and I wish to approach him with an offer to value and purchase it. A common valuation can be agreed by us all once we have established how much was written by Shakespeare and how much by Tarlton himself. We would also agree this price with the British Museum which has expressed an interest in acquiring it.'

'And you wouldn't compete with each other?' I enquired seeing problems arising.

'We shall not. Indeed, I feel a new era is opening for the Tarlton Ordinaries. We have been so shocked by recent events that the need for change has become evident. We are to expand our current activities which consist — I admit — mainly of over-indulgent dining; we shall now concentrate more on the re-establishment of the Tarlton name, in the light of this new exciting manuscript.'

'What's your opinion on how much of the play Shakespeare might have written?' I asked him, donning my most literary expression.

He beamed at this opportunity to express his opinions. 'My estimate, based both on what Mr Timpson was told by Mr Harcourt and on our scant knowledge of Shakespeare's early career, his so-called lost years, is that he contributed quite a lot to Tarlton's play. It was said of Tarlton that he was "nobody without his mirths" but it seems to me that Shakespeare did his best to make Tarlton a *somebody* of mirth while writing his own plays, as he is recognisable in several of Shakespeare's fools. We are thus still enjoying Tarlton's work today.'

I nodded my head gravely, feeling that I was rapidly learning how to be a scholar.

There was one more matter I had to raise with Mr Chalcot and an unwelcome one. I explained the likelihood of Phineas' beloved cat poetry being in a manuscript that was likely to have been stolen property. He listened intently and said: 'Then I will speak with Mr Snook on that too.'

*

After leaving Mr Chalcot, I wasted no time before walking round to find Zechariah as Phineas had suggested. There was Zechariah, sitting on the corner of Panyer Alley slowly and carefully mending another ancient chair as if it had come straight from the late French king's palace at Versailles. I was glad that Ned was not with me, for all he had seemed to accept it when I told him that the Panyer Alley Boy could indeed be sitting on a rooftop and meant nobody any harm. I walked along to pay my respects to the Boy, then came back to Zechariah.

'Tell me a story, Zechariah,' I said.

'What story would that be?' he asked, applying his polishing cloth with great care.

'About the Boy whom you guard so carefully, and the verse carved under him.'

'That be Pip's verse.'

'So you know the name Pip.' This was an advance and perhaps I would at last know how the Tarlton manuscript came into Pip's hand and then down to Phineas. 'I believe you know the Panyer Boy was Richard Tarlton's son,' I said to Zechariah carefully. 'He was also Phineas Snook's ancestor.'

And then Zechariah recounted what had happened, looking at me sadly. 'There was a story I heard tell about an old man who strolled along here one day and sees that old inn sign and knows he's come home.'

'Could that have been Pip's son, another Pip?'

He considered this. 'I believe you might be correct, mister, my reasoning being that this old man had been told that his granddad —so that'd be Pip's dad — left him some treasure and he was trying to find it. He was in this alley and found the old sign that his granddad — that'd be Pip's dad like I told you — kept outside the Castle alehouse; that was on the twenty-seventh of August 1688, so that's what they carved underneath the sign of the Boy, and *inside* the house it stood on, the old man was given the treasure he'd been looking for. I don't know what it was, but the old man must have been pleased to find it.'

He explained more too, but this was the gist of it. I knew what the treasure was: the play of the *Seven Deadly Sins*.

'And now, if you please, mister, I'll have a threepenny piece for a glass of ale.' Zechariah didn't even look as I put one in his hand. He was too busy admiring his chair.

*

'Ned,' I said. 'We're going to see Phineas.'

His eyes brightened. 'Now?'

'Soon as we've done a chimney or two and Phineas is up and about.'

I had a feeling in my bones that we might not be seeing much of Phineas in future and the sooner we got to see him — and Cockalorum — the better, although I wasn't going to tell Ned that. I'd spent last night telling him about the Boy, convincing him that the Boy too had a story just as if he'd been a climbing boy. Ned had grasped the idea. 'I *said* that was a roof he was sitting on. And a roof is the highest ground.'

I let him think so and, who knows, he could be right. After I'd heard

Zechariah's story I had returned to Mr Chalcot and talked the story of the Boy over with him to see if he could make head or tail of it. He did, after giving it some thought, and even explained how the Tarlton manuscript probably reached Panyer Alley, a tale that even brought Mr Harcourt's Hart House into the story. I had even added a thought or two of my own.

'My dear sir,' Mr Chalcot had beamed. 'We work well together as a team of literary detectives.'

My head was twice the size it had been by the time I reached home and I vowed that I would try to write it all down so that Pip's story was never forgotten. Meanwhile Ned was bursting to know what had happened.

'It's not the Boy any longer,' I said to Ned after I'd finished telling him the tale. 'You just call him Pip. He's from Phineas' family.'

He looked doubtful at first, but then his face brightened. 'Yes, guvnor.'

And the reference to the 'highest ground' in the verse on the stone? It couldn't be a reference to the Castle tavern itself, but it could be the roof as Ned said — or, as I like to think and Mr Chalcot agreed, the verse was two lines from the *Seven Deadly Sins*.

'I'll look through the script to see — if Mr Snook brings it to me,' Mr Chalcot had said, happily.

*

And so we arrived at Phineas' lodgings on a May morning a day or two later. Cockalorum was purring halfway up the steps, I could see Hetty was here and there were a few flowers in the garden which she must have planted. She was wearing a blue and white dress, no crinoline today, just a country girl's dress, and she looked a delight.

'Isn't it wonderful, Mr Wasp?' she greeted us. 'Phineas and I are leaving today.'

'Where are you going?' I asked in surprise as Ned and I went up the steps, led by Cockalorum. Phineas was standing there in the doorway to greet us.

'Over the hills and far away,' he laughed, taking Hetty's hand.

'Dancing all the way,' Hetty giggled. She kissed me and I felt like a king. She kissed Ned, too. He doesn't care for kisses normally, but this one he seemed to like.

'I sold the My Cat Jeoffry poetry to Mr Chalcot,' Phineas said blithely, 'and so we have enough money to marry now.'

'And what about the Tarlton play?' I asked, thinking of Mr Chalcot's plan for it, but knowing Phineas it would probably never happen. Instead Mr Chalcot had taken the *Jubilate Agno* to return it to the rightful owner and had personally paid Phineas enough to marry, without letting him know that the money came from him, and the poem was not put up for sale. 'The *Seven Deadly Sins* manuscript could be very valuable,' I felt I had to point out.

'It's a play by a fool,' Phineas said serenely, 'and we're a family of fools. We'll take the play with us and keep it. It can come a-roaming with us.'

And that seemed to me a fitting destiny for it. I hardly dared ask Phineas my next question, but seeing Ned's sad face I summoned up my courage. 'What about Cockalorum?'

Phineas looked surprised. 'He'll come with us.' He picked the cat up who seemed to have sensed that something of importance was happening.

'Will he follow you?' I asked, hearing Ned gasp. Phineas looked troubled. He'd heard the gasp too.

'We'll see what he wants to do, Ned,' Phineas said gently, putting Cockalorum down. I watched, my heart wringing for Ned, as Phineas and Hetty went down the steps and waited for Cockalorum, who stretched and got to his feet, looking up at Ned. Ned snatched him, and looked hesitantly at me. I didn't say anything, just nodded my head. Then I watched while Ned carried Cockalorum down the steps and put him into Phineas' arms.

A Literary Journey

by Tom Wasp

Later, I had several more chats with Mr Chalcot over the interesting matters that had arisen through the tragic deaths of Mr Harcourt and Mrs Fortescue and by the time I came to record Pip's story we had reached an explanation regarding the *Seven Deadly Sins* and the Boy in Panyer Alley that satisfied us both. I would have enjoyed meeting Richard Tarlton as he sounded a jolly fellow, well worthy of his memory being preserved hundreds of years later. He died in 1588 and his play, although performed by the Queen's Men in about 1585, was then lost, although a few fragments of his other work still exist.

Mr Chalcot believes that after Mr Tarlton's death, Mr Shakespeare kept the play safely in the hope that his son Pip, who was only six when his father died, would one day come to collect it. Mr Tarlton had been in great distress about the time of his death, fearing that his family would be cheated of its rights by a fraudulent lawyer who had offered to adopt Pip. What happened, Mr Chalcot told me, is not known, but what *might* have happened is that after Mr Shakespeare's death in 1616 his trustee William Johnson kept the manuscript, with the knowledge of Mr Shakespeare's family, in the hope that Pip might turn up. He didn't, and it's my own belief that he went a-wandering, just as his descendant Phineas has all these years later.

As we knew from Zechariah, after Mr Shakespeare's death, many years passed and Pip's son, now an old man, came to look for the old Castle alehouse to see where his father had been born. He knew about the old inn sign that used to be outside it because the boy carved on it was his father, the original Pip. The little boy had once been lost and Tarlton had found him on the roof of the alehouse, so he carved a picture of the scene on the sign for a joke. But the Castle had gone when Pip's son came to look for it, and so had the inn sign.

Knowing that Mr Charles Hart, the famous actor at Drury Lane, who lived in what was now Hart House in the Row, was a great-nephew of Mr Shakespeare, Pip's son might have called on him to ask him if he knew anything about the inn sign. Mr Hart did know about it and about the play — although not where they were now. The first Pip had never been told about the *Seven Deadly Sins*, and after hearing about it his son must have spent some years hunting round London for both the play and the inn sign, until at last he came upon the inn sign in Panyer Alley. It was outside a house that Mr Johnson used to live in and his descendants still had the play ready and waiting for him.

After they met Pip's son, the descendants not only added the inscription to the carving of the Boy sitting on the highest ground, the roof, but Pip and his stone were given a brick surround to make them look more impressive. As for the play, Pip's son took it to bequeath to his family. In time the house would have changed hands, and memories can be short (unless you're Zechariah), so the stone stayed there merely as a curiosity.

My friend Mr Chalcot remains convinced that Tarlton's influence is reflected in many of Mr Shakespeare's masterpieces.

'Take *Hamlet,* my dear Mr Wasp,' he said, 'consider how many of the deadly sins are represented there, take *Twelfth Night* and *When That I Was and a Little Tiny Boy* or —'

'— *As You Like It,* I added, having seen this at the penny gaff. Mr Chalcot sighed with pleasure.

'Ah, Mr Wasp, what a partnership we have.'

Historical Note

by Amy Myers

Tom Wasp lived in Victorian London, a world different to both our own and the one inhabited by Richard Tarlton in the sixteenth century. The docklands area of London's East End in which Tom Wasp lived was largely obliterated in the Second World War, as was Paternoster Row. The Row had suffered similarly in the Great Fire of London, during which St Paul's Cathedral was burned down, but it escaped that fate in World War II, although it came perilously close to destruction. The Dolly's Chop House of this novel no longer exists, but is factual regarding its history and location in Queen's Head Passage. Clara Pomfret, her daughter and staff are fictitious; in the census of 1861 Dolly's was under the aegis of 52-year-old widow Esther Dewhurst and her daughter.

The Boy of Panyer Alley and the verse beneath him are factual and can be seen today, but, apart from the fact that the actor Charles Hart was indeed Shakespeare's great-nephew, the stories I have allotted to them are my own invention — the true origin of the Boy in Panyer Alley is unknown. In Tom Wasp's time the Boy (complete with the verse and date) was situated further along the alley and was at ground level between two houses; he then had a brick surround, which he no longer possesses. Today, as one comes out of St Paul's underground station the Boy is straight ahead on the wall of the Caffè Nero. The alley itself, however, and the area around it including Paternoster Row and Queen's Head Passage are vastly changed.

And now for Richard Tarlton. Tarlton existed and the information about him is factual, although there is considerable academic debate as to whether his now lost play *The Seven Deadly Sins* forms the basis of the plot of *The Seven Deadly Sins* in the papers of Edward Alleyn at Dulwich College. I have chosen to go with the argument that they are two separate plays. Tarlton's link with the Boy is my own invention, as are the adventures of the *Seven Deadly Sins* script after Tarlton's death. Pip's real fate is unknown, and so is that of the play after its performance in Oxford recorded by Gabriel Harvey.

There is also disagreement amongst scholars as to what Shakespeare was doing during his childhood and so-called 'lost years', and I have chosen to follow the argument that he joined the Queen's Men much earlier than 1587. What is not disputed is that Shakespeare was on friendly terms with Tarlton. Shakespeare's great-nephew Charles Hart is factual, but his connections with the fictitious Hart House and with *The Seven Deadly Sins* are not.

Christopher Smart's poem 'My Cat Jeoffry' is now famous, but was only published for the first time as part of the *Jubilate Agno* in 1939, thanks to WG Stead, who acquired the latter from the library of Colonel WG Carwardine Probert. It had descended through the Carwardine family who might have acquired it originally from Smart's friend, the poet William Cowper. The *Jubilate Agno* was written by Smart in the mid eighteenth century while Smart was confined for insanity. The story of its manuscript's theft and restoration in this novel, however, is entirely fictitious. No such adventures disturbed its peaceful existence in the Carwardine library. Today it resides in the Houghton Library, Harvard University and can be read online.

The quoted lines of poetry that Tom reads from *The Seven Deadly Sins* are from surviving works attributed to Tarlton: two are from *Tarleton's Tragical Treatises* and two from *Tarlton's Jests*.

Lastly, sweeps did have an annual procession on May Day, with a Jack-in-the-Green, although I doubt whether it was as dramatic as in this story.

ENDEAVOUR QUILL

ENDEAVOUR MEDIA